THE
SHIP

THE SHIP

DOUG BRODE

Copyright © 2021 Doug Brode

Registration number: TXu-2-235-745

Published 2021

Cover Design: Enchanted Ink Publishing
Formatting: Enchanted Ink Publishing

ISBN: 978-1-7372255-0-8 (paperback)
ISBN: 978-1-7372255-1-5 (hardcover)
ISBN: 978-1-7372255-2-2 (ebook)

Alien Sky Publishing - First edition 2021

DEDICATIONS & LOVE

Dedicated to Leia and Hayden – to remind them that
anything is possible.

And to my **wonderful** (and patient) **wife, Pamela**.
Without her support and encouragement this book
would not exist.

Also dedicated to my **mom** for, well, absolutely
everything.

Finally, in **memory** of **my dad**, George Brode, Jr. He'd
have gotten a kick out of this.

PART 1

BLACKWOOD

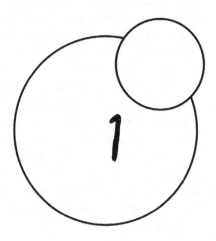

Encased in darkness, Casey Stevens lay trembling. A stink akin to motor oil burned her nostrils. Pressure weighed heavily, as if gravity itself were working against her, pinning Casey within an invisible coffin. The world pitched topsy-turvy, and she tumbled, screaming, into shadow.

This isn't a dream, Casey decided before she landed on an unknown surface.

Waves of pain shot up her spine while electrical sparks rained down, revealing a metallic floor beneath. The material shimmered and pulsed with an energy of its own. Again, the room spun. Casey slid through sparks, collapsing onto another surface with a *thud*. Fighting to inhale, her stomach lurched. The room tossed once more in a final violent spasm.

The dark grew still.

Reeling to her knees, Casey gasped for breath. It seemed to be over. Whatever *it* was.

Her mind whirled, struggling to focus on how she'd

gotten there. A dog had howled outside her cabin. She'd opened the front door. Light blazed from above, neither natural nor phosphorescent. It glowed green, blinding. And then . . . and then . . .?

She was falling.

Casey stood, wobbling. Her muscles ached, and her skin was raw with frost, as if she had been stored in a meat locker overnight. For a moment, she feared this was a freezer of some sort, like the ones in movies with long metal hooks and a killer-stalker. *That's ridiculous*, she assured herself. *There are lots of reasons one might wake in a dark, freezing room, and none of those reasons involve a crazed killer in a hockey mask.*

However, whatever those real-world reasons might be escaped her.

The cold snapped Casey back to the present. Goose-bumps covered her unseen legs, and she realized her lower half was bare. Blinded in the gloom, she assumed she was still wearing the Purple Rain T-shirt and panties from the night before. Was it the night before? How long had she been there? In the cold, the dark.

With outstretched arms, she stumbled forward like Frankenstein's monster until her left foot caught on something. Flailing, her bare knees slammed into the floor, sending shock waves through her body. Stifling a scream, her hand searched for whatever she'd tripped on, stopping at a denim-covered leg.

"Arthur?" Her throat was hoarse. Unable to see an inch in front of her face, she imagined a stream of frosty breath accompanying her voice. "Hon?"

Her fingers moved up the person's leg, finding a belt and a rumpled shirt over a flat stomach. Her fiancé, Arthur, had a "one pack," his name for a flabby gut. This wasn't him. Her arms continued a few more inches before she pulled away, feeling rounded flesh beneath her fingertips. Breasts. A woman lay unmoving on the floor.

"Hello . . ." No answer. "Hey!" she shouted, shaking whoever it was.

Please just be sleeping, she pleaded inwardly. Running her fingers up the feminine form, over cold cheeks and thick lips, she checked for a breath. Through a mess of hair, Casey touched wet ooze.

"Jesus fucking Christ." Without seeing, she knew what the slick sensation on her fingertips was.

Scrambling back up, she bumped into another figure. It toppled with a thick gurgle, like slick meat slapping a table. She didn't need to check to know that person was dead too. Swirling, dazed, the putrid scent of blood reaching her nostrils, Casey's knees buckled, her stomach wrenching.

How many bodies are in here? Is one of them Arthur?

As if on cue, dim illumination flickered to life, revealing her surroundings in fractured chunks. The light emanated from the floor, pulsing in spasms, struggling. The rhythmic light revealed four bodies. Twisted. Broken. Crushed from the same fall she'd survived unscathed.

A crimson smear slid toward her bare feet. Casey stepped away from it and studied the shadows. Above, six tubular metal chambers, apparently sleeping berths, hung empty. The tops of the chambers had broken shards of glass and torn wires—all except one, which seemed to have sprung open without incident. That's why she was alive, Casey assumed, and these poor bastards weren't. At least, she consoled herself, Arthur wasn't among them.

Inhaling sharply, she took in the sheer size of the room. It was oval, roughly fifty yards in diameter, each surface curved with soft metal edges. Except for the corpses and the sparking wires above, the place seemed clean to the point of sterile.

Peering down at the pulsing light at her feet and then toward the chambers above, she realized she was standing on an inverted ceiling. The room was *upside down.*

Her stomach protested as vertigo set in. A tiny, selfish voice in the back of her mind grew louder, desperately hoping Arthur was there somewhere. Waiting for her.

Brilliant and calm, he'd have a clever escape plan. Then she reminded herself that Arthur had jumped five feet the last time there was a spider in the bathroom. *Still,* Casey thought, *I wouldn't be alone.*

Frosty breath escaped her chattering teeth, and her body trembled. Scanning the walls, she couldn't find a single door or exit. Forcing her eyes to what was now the floor, she approached the mangled female corpse she'd tripped over. The woman was in her early twenties, the same as Casey. Casey couldn't help but wonder if they wore the same size clothes. The thought made her stomach tighten. She hunched, trying to keep warm, arms crushed against her chest. Kneeling beside the woman, she avoided the dead eyes staring back.

Focus on the jeans, she reminded herself. *Just the pants. Don't look at anything else. You can do this.* Casey lingered, hovering over the body as if hoping someone would nudge her into action. But there wasn't anyone to help. Another wave of ice crept up her spine, telling her to get on with it.

Rubbing her hands together, she inched closer. With a long, heavy sigh, she unbuttoned the jeans, and her fingers moved down the body. She tugged, but there was no release. The zipper was still closed. *OK, OK, just get this fucking over.*

Teeth grinding, Casey unzipped the jeans and took hold of them on either side of the woman's hips and yanked. They gave way, sliding down blue-tinged legs until they bunched at the ankles. Casey had forgotten about the woman's shoes, which were preventing the pants from coming off. Untying the laces, she grabbed the shoes and the socks too.

By the time she got the dead woman's pants and socks and shoes on, she'd forgotten all about the cold, morbid disgust overruling frozen flesh. Her lower half now clothed, she rubbed her arms, turning toward the other poor souls, searching for a jacket. She found one on a college-aged black man crumpled in the corner, his face half missing. He appeared to have fallen head first through the sleeping berth's glass covering. Casey hoped he hadn't awoken right before the end. Tearing off his red jacket, she completed the makeshift ensemble and rushed to get as far from the bodies as possible.

Trailing the curved wall, she searched again for an exit.

If I got in here, she figured, *I can get out.* But so far, nothing resembled a door.

Fragments of metal machinery had been scattered about from the tumble. What they were or what purpose they served eluded her. Fear rose with each step, like a TV remote switching channels in the back of her mind, escalating from one horror show to another. Visualizing a shadowy figure in a bloody surgical mask, she regretted her late-night movie binges.

Keeping her eyes averted from the scattered bodies, Casey noted a wedged shadow along the far wall. Thick and dark. An arched doorway. Instead of relief, a knot tightened in her stomach. She was *certain* the opening hadn't been there a moment ago, unless she'd walked right by and missed it, which she doubted. Yet, there it stood. An inverted door, open, ominous, and inviting. The gloomy pit seemed to stare back at her.

Bouncing on the balls of her feet, she tried to prepare herself for whatever awaited. Without a backward glance, Casey lurched forward, thrusting herself through the darkened doorway.

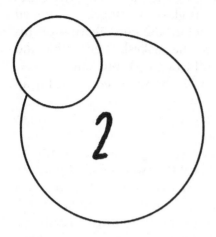

2

General Legault leaned heavily behind a plywood desk, rapping his knuckles against an envelope. Something rattled inside, rhythmically breaking the silence. Major Reese stood at attention opposite the desk, awaiting orders. So far, all he'd gotten was the general's odd glare, sizing him up from head to toe. Reese fought the urge to shift his weight from one leg to the other. He tried not to focus on the trickles of sweat trailing into the creases of his forehead, dribbling to his eyes. Situated on the top floor of Fort Hood's First Army Division building, the small office was bare but clean, with bright fluorescent lights above and a lingering reek of tobacco. The longer the general stared, the smaller the room shrank.

It wasn't until a side door opened, and a civilian woman in her mid-forties entered, that Legault finally put the envelope aside and cleared his throat to speak. He ignored the woman as she sat quietly in the corner, instead focusing on the top sheet of Reese's personnel file.

His eyes hidden behind reflective glasses, he scanned the bullet points. "Major John Murphy Reese. Three tours in Iraq, one in Afghanistan, three commendations, including a Purple Heart."

"Yes, sir. Got hit with a landmine in Iraq, back in oh nine."

"From what I understand, it was another soldier who tripped the mine, but you pushed him aside and took the blast."

"The shrapnel only grazed my side. The report makes it sound more heroic than it was."

"Uh-huh," Legault sighed, as if uninterested in Reese's humility. "And now you're stationed stateside?"

Reese stayed at attention as he spoke, though his eyes drifted toward the woman in the corner. "Yes, sir. Aerial reconnaissance and info gathering."

"Drones—oh, how our president *loves* the drones," Legault said, turning his iron gaze toward the woman.

She works for the White House, Reese assumed.

Legault went back to the open file. "You should be a lieutenant colonel by now, but instead you've been stuck behind a desk for six years. Your choice?"

"I have a daughter, sir."

"That's not what I asked."

Reese's thoughts drifted back toward countless missions, many of which were filled with the corpses of men, women, and even children, all of whom died because Reese had pulled the trigger. His throat turned to gravel as he replied. "Every good soldier has his sins, sir."

"That we do," the general replied, nodding.

"I guess I just had my fair share, sir."

Legault's hands slid to the envelope, fingering its edge. "Please, have a seat, Major."

Reese's body relaxed at the invitation. He sat directly across the desk from the general. Perched in the bare metal chair, he purposefully pointed his knees and chest toward the woman, to keep her in view as well. She met his gaze, brushing a strand of black hair away from her face before forcing a crooked smile. She didn't seem to want to be there anymore than he did.

Legault came around the desk and sat on the edge, leaning over Reese. His smile was more sincere than hers, but if he was trying to appear friendly, it wasn't working. His large mass loomed over the major like a monolith. "Two hours ago an object appeared in the Oregon mountains." He eyed the woman again before continuing. "I *had* assigned a team to investigate, but they've been recalled. It seems *someone* wants you for the job."

As if responding to a prearranged signal, the woman uncrossed her legs, stood, smoothed her skirt, and handed Reese a folder. He flipped through satellite images of the Oregon mountain range. Among the trees and foliage, a round, blurry black spot was in the center of the frame.

"The object is almost a mile wide. Locals don't seem to have noticed it," she said. "Not yet, at least."

Reese did a double take, not believing what he was hearing or seeing. From its sheer size and shape, it was clear that when she said "object" she meant "flying saucer." Little green men. Hollywood stuff. However, the believability wasn't his first concern. "How could residents in the area not see a mile-wide . . . *thing* crash over their heads?"

"It didn't crash," she replied.

"Damn thing simply appeared," Legault finished.

Reese felt rimy fingers creep up his spine, over the base of his neck, and slide up to his scalp. "Appeared?"

The woman grabbed the folder from him, finding the last couple of images. A tree line covered in snow. He eyed the time stamp, and his jaw slackened. "Wait, these times are only thirty seconds apart. That can't be right."

"Stamps are correct, Major. One minute there was nothing, the next, that thing's sitting smack dab in the middle of Oregon. No burn marks. No evidence of a crash site. No damage of any kind. Like I said, it just appeared."

"Jesus . . ." Reese flipped back and forth from one image to the next. Studying them, one thought bubbled above the din of disbelief. "For these time stamps to be accurate, you would have had to have a satellite already in place. That's awfully lucky."

His words hung there for a good long moment before Legault's eyes shot back toward the sealed envelope. The general flopped behind his desk, as if wanting to be close to whatever was inside it. The woman shifted her weight on her high heels and crossed her arms.

There's something they're not telling me. Something worse than a crashed UFO.

"Sometimes you just get lucky," the woman finally replied.

Legault found his voice, though his smile was gone. "We haven't been so lucky with the local weather though. There's a bitch of a snowstorm. Wind's at over ninety miles an hour, so aerial reconnaissance has been a no-go so far. As for ground insertion, there's only one narrow road open this time of year, so nothing bigger than a basic transport vehicle is getting up there. One road—one way in, and one way out." He paused, his eyes dropping to the envelope. "You'll be taking an advance team up there tonight."

"Me?"

"You have extensive reconnaissance experience in the field," the woman replied.

"Yeah . . . me and about a thousand other guys." Reese turned squarely toward Legault. "With all due respect, sir, I don't see why you want me."

Legault ran his fingertips over the bulging envelope. Something shifted inside. "I'm afraid I can't tell you that, son, but I can give you this." He handed the envelope to Reese.

Having observed how nervous this thing seemed to make the general, Reese took it hesitantly. For all the weight Legault's eyes gave the envelope, it was quite light.

Reese ran his palm over the surface and felt something that was perhaps oval-shaped inside.

"What is it?"

"The reason we picked you," the woman said.

A newfound tremble in her voice made him more anxious. Reese's heart pounded, the icy fingers wrapping around behind his eyes now. *Don't open it,* an inner voice blared. Whatever was in the envelope seemed to be as concerning to them as the giant object that had just appeared in Oregon.

Big, scary things in little packages, his mind whispered.

With a fresh gulp of air, Reese sliced the envelope open with a stroke of his index finger. He reached in, wondering what kind of tiny monster could evoke so much horror in the general's eyes as he watched. But no monsters or aliens were lurking inside. Instead, Reese withdrew a simple red string attached to a tiny pink plastic heart. Something made by a child.

He knew the necklace well. His daughter, Noelle, had given it to him the previous year, and he never took it off, not even in the shower. It was one of a kind, or so he'd thought. Holding it with his right hand, his left hand crawled to his collar, withdrawing an identical necklace from beneath his uniform.

"Where'd ya get this, sir?"

Legault and the woman put on their most compassionate faces. "Afraid we can't tell you that either," the general replied.

"I don't understand." Reese's voice cracked as his entrails turned to icicles.

The woman's face lost its kindness. "That's why you're going to Oregon."

1985

The mountainous town of Blackwood, Oregon, was originally built to be a ski resort for tourists heading up from Portland. Sadly, both routes leading into town proved deadly over a series of winters, and by 1968 the resort was shuttered. Still, the town erected around it survived, growing to a thousand citizens by the mid-1980s. As it turned out, they had another viable business—the woods that gave their town its name. Switching to lumber distribution, many people stayed and grew to prefer that few outsiders ventured up that far north. Blackwood was isolated, and that suited its citizens just fine—at least the adults. Most kids couldn't wait to get out, many leaving as soon as their fingers gripped their high school diplomas. Few ever returned.

Arthur Stover was one who had. Not by choice, mind you, but out of necessity. His mother grew ill during a heavy snowstorm in 1983, and he'd come up to take care of her. When she died soon after, he'd planned to return to college by January. Then he began dating Casey. Two years later, Arthur still hadn't left. Not for good, anyway. He'd stay in his dormitory in Portland on the weekdays, then drive up each Friday afternoon to the cabin they'd rented just outside of town.

Some said Blackwood had a way of keeping folks there, as if its ground were a tar pit that sucked at their shoes and didn't let go. Arthur figured that was a fair assessment. Though he had no complaints, not with Casey at his side. She worked at the local diner on Main Street, one of two restaurants in town and the only one that served breakfast. Her tips paid for their cabin and almost everything else while he lived on a scholarship. It was a fact that often ate at his gut, pushing him to succeed. Pride, he found, could be a great motivator. Arthur had promised to give her the world someday, and he planned on keeping his word.

Brow furrowed, he stared at the words in his textbook while loud gunfire erupted from the living room. He wondered if he had a pair of earmuffs in the closet. Gaping over a stack of notes, he watched Sonny Crockett take down a gold-toothed drug dealer on TV. His biology book blurred, and his face reddened. Phil Collins sang above the gunshots. Arthur dug his nails into the textbook's binding, trying to focus. The explosions and pounding musical score grew to a maddening crescendo. Arthur was seconds away from slamming his book down for dramatic effect when the noise abruptly died.

Casey strolled in wearing a Prince T-shirt and black panties. Opening the refrigerator, she bent down, searching for a soda. Arthur's eyes lingered, trailing up her toned legs. When the fridge slammed shut, his attention jumped to her Cheshire grin. "See something you like?"

"Window shopping," he said, returning her smile before burying his nose in his book. "Gotta finish this paper while I'm still young."

She slid behind him, her lips inches from his left ear.

Her warm breath created goosebumps along the back of his neck. "There's other things to do while we're young."

Focusing on his book, he thumbed the thick pages. "I'll be done shortly."

"It's Friday night."

"You think Einstein, Oppenheimer, and Weizmann didn't work weekends?"

"With names like that, maybe skip school and just get a bar mitzvah."

"Clever, clever girl."

"Yeah, right" she said with a heavy sigh, her eyes leaving him.

"Don't do that." Arthur put the book down and stood, finding her averted gaze.

Casey shrugged. "What?" she asked, her voice pitched.

"Doubt yourself." Pulling her close, their bodies swayed, dancing in place. "You're the smartest, shrewdest, most resourceful woman I know."

Ruffling her fingers through his hair, her smile returned. "Outside of your mother, I'm the *only* woman you've known."

"And I wouldn't have it any other way." His lips found hers.

"All right, finish up." She nudged him back to the chair. "Twenty minutes and then off to bed."

"Sure, Mom."

Casey shot him a hard look. Arthur peeked over his papers. "Not—"

"Funny? No." She tossed up the backside of her shirt. "Did your mom have an ass like this?"

"Hey, she was a handsome woman."

Rolling her eyes, Casey slunk away.

Arthur tried to return to his paper regarding bacteria and viruses and the effects they had over generations of bloodlines. It wasn't going well. The kitchen shrank, and his eyes glazed off the page.

Casey wasn't horny. She was trying to get pregnant.

Something neither of them could afford at the moment. Still, Casey seemed to have their whole lives planned. She'd often drop hints about what she imagined: two kids, a house on the East Coast, with Arthur working for some big think tank while she stayed at home raising their children. Though not politically correct, even in 1985, Casey wanted to be a housewife, or at least she wanted to *settle* for being a housewife. If she had any bigger dreams or aspirations, Arthur had yet to discover them. Arthur knew her low self-worth had come from her father, though it was a subject they strictly avoided. Whatever that bastard had done, it had certainly left a scar.

Either way, Arthur's dreams were big enough for them both. As a biophysics major, he was working toward a graduate degree in biology with an undergraduate degree in physics. He hoped to do for biology what Einstein had done for physics, but first he had to get through this chapter.

The words on the page blurred, and his mind wandered. When the TV volume returned, he imagined Casey curled up on the couch in that tiny T-shirt, playing with her hair. He pictured the way her breasts would heave as she drank her soda and—

No, no, stop. Focus. Be an adult. Think: master's degree.

A dog barking outside grabbed his attention, and he wondered if the universe just didn't want him to get his homework done. He heard a metal trash can tumble and roll. The animal's growls turned sinister. It no longer sounded like a dog. *Coyote,* he figured. The animal's pitch grew higher, frantic. He was about to shout at it to shut up when a gust of wind slammed the cabin's roof so hard the kitchen shook. Pots and pans crashed behind him. The walls buckled; plaster cracks formed.

Springing from his chair, he ran his fingertip along the open plaster. The wound widened, and hissing air pushed through, shooting a draft into the kitchen. *Shit.*

Arthur turned to the window. It wobbled weakly in

its frame, as if about to burst. He slid the window open, letting a gust of wind inside. Pages scattered. Gathering his homework, he threw it in a cupboard, then rushed to open as many windows as he could. The wind tossed the cabin's contents about. *A little mess is better than broken glass everywhere.* It sounded like a storm until—

A bright light poured in, turning the cabin pale green. His scalp prickled with fear. Casey was at the other end of the cabin, opening the front door. Grabbing his glasses from the kitchen counter, he followed. *A truck, maybe?*

He glanced up. The wall clock had stopped at 9:57 p.m.

Outside, Casey screamed. Her cry sent Arthur into action. Racing to the door, his feet grew heavier with each step, as if encased in dried cement. Nails sprang from floorboards, pointed ends twirling about. Covering his face with his arm, he felt rivets slice his skin. Overhead, the ceiling drooped, its wooden structure whining from an unseen weight. His body protesting, he propelled himself forward, each step a slow agony, toward the exit. Through the door all he could see was bright light. His stomach turning as if gut-punched, stars blotted Arthur's vision, blinding him.

From outside, Casey's screams grew shrill. "Arthur! ARTHUR!"

Summoning a last reserve of strength, he grabbed the doorframe, pulling himself outside. Clearing the door, Arthur stepped onto the porch and—

The night was dark and silent, and the earth no longer shook, the light and noise extinguished. Arthur stood alone at the porch's edge, studying the mountainous path leading up to the cabin. His truck's windows were blown out. He scanned the gravel road, noting garbage spilled from inverted trash cans. Silhouetted trees danced in a gentle breeze. Peaceful, serene. Unseen forest creatures stirred, snapping twigs in their flight.

Casey was nowhere to be seen.

Above the evening horizon, between silhouetted mountain peaks, an enormous round shape faded from existence. Casey's distant voice, like a ghostly whisper, carried on the breeze, so faint that later he wondered if he had imagined it. Desperate, pleading, the voice screamed.

"Help . . . me! Aaarrrthhhuuur . . ."

4

Present day

"I still hear it sometimes."

"Her calling out to you?" Major John Reese asked, shifting his weight in a creaky wooden rocker, trying to get comfortable. He wondered what it was about old people and vintage furniture. *Couldn't he get something from the current century? At least a cushion.*

Arthur, now sixty years old, nodded. "It never goes away. Oh, a few months, maybe a year can go by, but it always snaps back when I least expect it. The sound of her screams."

Reese glanced around the haphazard living room, hoping to find something to lighten the mood. He would not get what he needed with this guy wallowing in the past. The two-room apartment, filled with photos, clothes tossed about, and with vinyl stacked in the corner, reminded Reese of his college days. Only this guy was over sixty. Above the mantel he noted a weathered family photo: two adolescent boys and a woman. Arthur was divorced, but Reese hadn't had time to dig up info about the kids.

"How old are your sons?"

"Todd's twenty-seven. Mike's thirty." Arthur leaned back and wiped his face. "Mike's in New York, doing God knows what. I hear from him on the holidays. Todd stays with me though. He's head chef at a bar and grill. Saving up for his own restaurant."

"They know about what you saw?"

"Read the book, I suppose. Same as you." Arthur grabbed his vape pen, taking a deep hit. "Your dad writes a book about aliens, you're bound to open it at some point, I'd imagine."

"I thought you didn't believe in aliens." Reese pulled out a paperback copy of Arthur's book, flipping through dog-eared pages filled with passages underlined in red ink. "Says so right here. 'Whatever I saw, I cannot confirm whether it was of alien origin.' You still stand behind those words?"

"Most scientists believe in life throughout the universe," Arthur said, his lips widening to something between a grin and a sneer, "*except biologists*. Do you know why that is?"

"I'm sure you'll tell me."

"Physicists study the vast number of stars, examining equations and mathematical odds, and say there must be something else out there like us. Biologists look down at our own planet, at all the specific things that occurred for evolution to work, and say, 'not likely.' It's not a math equation, but if it were, the sheer odds of other sentient life even remotely like us are *incalculable*—even in the vastness of outer space."

"Then what is it you think you saw?"

"As a scientist, I'm OK with stating, *I don't know*."

Reese paused, thinking it over. "I take it no one believed it back in eighty-five?"

"Not then, not now." Arthur's shoulders sagged as he took another hit of the vape pen. "They thought I killed her. Everyone did. Two years of police investigating until they came to the brilliant conclusion that they had no case." He stood, arching his back, stretching, as if he'd told this story a million and one times, which Reese knew he had. "Even my school thought I did it. Cost me my scholarship."

"You still received a PhD."

"From a third-rate university."

"Is that why you teach high school biology instead of practicing it?"

Arthur glared through a cloud of vapor. "Why are you here, Major?"

Reese shrugged. "Just paperwork. Background stuff for unidentified objects, that sort of thing. You're one of a dozen interviews I'm doing across the country." He huffed dramatically. "Honestly, I pissed my superior off. This is his revenge."

"You really know how to make an old man feel special."

"Sorry, it's been a long night." Reese pulled out a topographic map of Blackwood Mountain, splaying it across a cluttered coffee table, and handed Arthur a red marker. "If you could just mark the place where you saw the ship, I'll get out of your hair."

Arthur hovered over the map, circling a small grid in the lower-left corner. Reese thought back to the surveillance photos, matching the images in his mind. It was the same spot. He had his confirmation. Whatever that thing waiting in the mountains was, it had been there before. Arthur handed the marker back and locked eyes with him. "Why now?"

"I told you, background—"

"Research." Arthur held up the map. "After thirty years?"

Reese put the map and the marker in a leather bag, flipped it closed, and turned toward the door. "I'm just a cog in the machine, sir. If someone tells me to come ask some questions, I ask."

Arthur grabbed his shoulder. "You found something out there, didn't you?"

The old coot was more perceptive than Reese had expected. He averted his gaze, focusing on the door. Spreading his lips wide, he smiled, an "aw shucks" grin. "If they did, it'd be way above my pay grade."

Snaking around the old man, Reese went for the door, but Arthur blocked his path. "I want to join the team."

"What team?"

"The other scientists. You'll need physicists, biologists—"

"There's no team, sir." Reese's voice pitched. "I'm simply doing busywork."

"*Three decades* later?"

Reese reached for the doorknob, but Arthur held the door shut. "I could be helpful."

"You have been. I've got your report."

"Please, that thing—it took everything from me."

"I doubt your sons would agree." Reese's voice dropped to a murmur. "Take it from someone who knows, don't allow yourself to be a prisoner of past trauma. It never ends well."

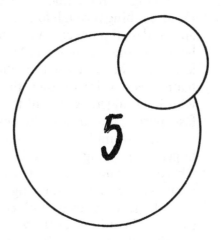

Inverted gray walls stretched hundreds of meters, curving out of sight. Lights at Casey's feet flickered, creating moving pockets of shadow around her. The temperature warmed, and the stench of burning metal and blood from the room she'd escaped receded. Still, the hallway had its own more subtle horrors.

Reflections crawled up the walls, shimmering in an eerie green glow. Her ears pricked at the sound her oversized shoes made against the ground, *flip-flap, flip-flap.* In the dense silence, each footfall echoed. Casey's breath grew ragged. Forcing herself to exhale, she let out a long, quiet hiss, hoping the sound wouldn't reverberate. Watching shadows slither about, she wondered if the echo chamber twisted light as much as it did the sound of her footsteps.

Maybe the icebox filled with corpses hadn't been so bad after all. At least back there, light and sound stayed where they belonged, not bouncing about with a life of their own.

Trying to remember how she got there, her mind raced, pushing through fog. She recalled looming shapes and cold, damp fingers. As soon as the memory entered her mind, she shut it down. Maybe she was better off not knowing. Then a worse thought occurred to her. If that hadn't been a dream, then the looming, wet creatures with long fingers were still there. Somewhere. Perhaps fast approaching around the next corner.

Casey stumbled in her oversized shoes, the thought lingering. Leaning around the next turn, she swallowed a hard gulp and then inhaled sharply, trying to process what her eyes were witnessing.

A huge, thick tree trunk covered in snow and frost stood in the middle of the walkway. Its top and bottom vanished through the floor and ceiling, as if built into the metal structure.

She touched the tree, confirming it wasn't a figment of an overzealous imagination. Her fingers flinched at the frost-covered bark, and the sudden cold sent a shock through her system. Lingering, she gazed at the absurdity of it, half expecting to see a talking rabbit dash past the tree, check his watch, and whimper about being late.

Yep, that's where I am: Wonderland. The creepy-crawly version.

Ahead, the sound of crashing glass made her skin prickle, the echo rolling past her like a wave. Casey jumped, positioning herself behind the tree in case some monster-killer approached. But nothing came.

Her lips whispered, counting to fifty before she stepped out. Inhaling deeply, she crept around the curved corner. The next hall, as gray and dimly lit as the last, awaited, thick chunks of shadow wedged on either wall. Four doors total, two per side, large with wide arches. Wondering who or *what* might need such an enormous entrance, her mind flashed to Jessica Lange curled inside King Kong's enormous paw. The mental image of a giant gorilla stalking the halls made her laugh, and her breath (which she'd been holding without realizing it) erupted in a gasp that echoed down the hall.

Shit. She stopped on the tip of her toes.

Girl killed in strange hallway because she laughed, news at eleven. Good one, Case.

She came to the first door on her left, hesitating at the pitch-black edge.

Nope. Awful idea. Move along.

Casey passed another entrance before stopping at the third. Light pulsed and flickered within. "Hello? Anyone in there?"

I'm here, Honey Bunny, a masculine voice whispered in her head.

Casey spun, half jumping out of her skin. Eyes swiveling in their sockets, she searched the hallway.

I'm always with you, my Bunny, the voice added.

Her body trembling, she turned back toward the doorway. Through inky blackness, the smell of aftershave wafted to her nostrils.

"You're dead," she said, her voice turning to gravel.

Maybe you are too. Ever think of that?

Shaking her head back and forth, she answered with a silent *no.*

Staring into blackness, she felt the thick voice slither around the back of her skull. *Maybe you're dead, and this is hell. I've been waiting for you. Waiting in the dark where we can play.*

"No!" she screamed, lunging through the doorway. Her father was gone, she reminded herself. She'd watched the cancer eat away at him, like invisible bugs gnawing his meat and bones until nothing was left. When he finally died, she'd assumed her fear and anger would die with him, but it hadn't. It had lingered in her gut for the last five years, and now it seemed to have followed her there, wherever she was.

As she crossed the room's threshold, her father's taunting whispers receded. The softer his voice became, the bolder her footsteps grew.

Casey squinted in the dark, glimpsing fractured pieces of odd surroundings. A table hung from the floor above. Encircling it, several inverted machines hummed with quiet energy. They appeared to be encased in thin panes of shattered crystal. A few sparks rained down from unseen circuits, hissing as they fell. Still, she decided with a sigh, the room appeared empty. No dead bodies. No withered, cancer-eaten father lunging from the—

Stop it, she cursed inwardly. Her shoes crunched broken glass while her eyes scanned the inverted fixtures. *Now would be a good time to wake up.*

As if in protest, the world lurched. Casey tumbled to her knees, grabbing a light fixture for support as the room swung upwards, like a hamster wheel. Her stomach danced in her belly, vomit rising with each quake. Attempting to keep her body from sliding, she dug her fingers into the lights beneath her. Glass shards skittered past. Her hands held until the shaking subsided. Gulping four deep breaths before finding the nerve to rise, Casey dug a piece of glass out of her forehead and wiped away blood.

Could have been worse. The thought made her giggle. *Define "worse."*

Laughter turned to crying. Wanting to be angry instead of afraid, Casey's body refused to stop trembling. No longer concerned about a possible killer, she screamed, releasing all her pent-up fear in a single burst. She yelled so loud that the veins on her neck popped, and her legs and arms quivered. Not stopping for breath, Casey continued screaming and screaming until her voice broke in a hoarse cough. Then she curled into a ball, weeping.

From the dark, something answered back with a bellow. Deep and guttural, as if from an animal. It caused the hairs on Casey's body to stand on end. Craning her neck, she spied a hulking shadow peering from behind the inverted table above. It glared, uttering a low growl.

Trembling, Casey stood, unable to move. Her mind raced, but her legs refused to follow as the thing dripped over the table. *Come on, Case, move your ass. One foot in front of the other.* Still, no matter how much she protested, screaming inwardly, her legs wouldn't budge.

The shape drooped into view, reaching from the shadows. A glimpse of sharp talons finally urged her body into action.

Tripping over herself as she spun, Casey bolted for the door.

Her feet skidding into the hallway, Casey continued as far and as fast as her legs could take her. Stopping herself from glancing back, not even for a peek, in case the *thing* was right behind her, she ran until her chest burned and her legs wobbled like rubber bands.

After racing through another tunnel, Casey brushed aside sweat-dampened blond hair and turned back the way she had come. Nothing followed. She finally stopped, her chest heaving.

Leaning beside another open door, Casey decided she wasn't checking any more rooms. *Stick to the lit fucking hallway, Case. Frankenstein's monster is in the lab, and he's looking for a mate.* This time she couldn't even get herself to smile, let alone laugh.

Then something reached out from the doorway and yanked her inside.

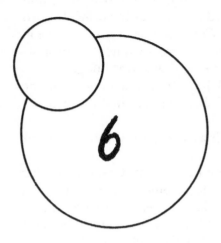

6

Major John Reese had never wanted kids. He'd seen them scuttle about various bases and civilian locations—loud, messy, and altogether obtrusive to one's life. A far shot from the structured order the military had provided since he was eighteen years old. Even if he had ever gained a notion to breed, he assumed he'd have a son. A chip off the old military block.

That all changed the day Staff Sergeant Suzie Chatsworth told him she was pregnant. Worse, it was a girl. They weren't in love, so marriage wasn't discussed. Neither was abortion. The one thing they did decide over the nine months that Suzie grew larger and larger was a name for their daughter: Noelle. Conceived during a drunken fling on Christmas Eve, the name fit nicely.

Noelle Freeman Reese was born over four years ago, in the fall, with blue eyes and brown wavy hair like her daddy. She also stripped off her clothes around the house every chance she got and wore next to nothing, even at almost five years old. John assumed she got that from her mother. Despite her casual use of clothing or her penchant for poking around absolutely everything in his home during the weekends she visited, he couldn't help but admit he loved the little tyke more than anything, including God and country. Funny how kids could do that, even to a soldier.

Having not seen combat in almost ten years, Reese had never planned for what he might do if orders came down to be sent back into a hot zone. When General Legault showed him the satellite images, two thoughts raced to his mind, and neither involved little green men:

1) *Whatever it is, this thing's dangerous.*
2) *I may never see Noelle again.*

Those same two thoughts still tugged at his gut like heavy rocks as Reese rubbed the twin pink necklaces dangling over his gray camo. Peering through a darkened window at cascading snow, he heard the truck's engine groan. *We'll be lucky if we don't get stuck out here.*

Reese's watch read 0530 by the time his team of three military trucks made their way through the winding wooded pass just outside Blackwood, Oregon. He sat in the lead vehicle's passenger seat with a young female lieutenant whose name he'd already forgotten driving beside him. Normally, a motor transport officer would be driving, but with only a limited team at his immediate disposal, the young lieutenant had volunteered, assuring him she could navigate the snowbound pass due to having grown up in the Midwest. He hoped she was right; the last thing they needed was to end up in a ditch. The term "rag-tag operation" came to mind. Reese rubbed his eyes, forcing sleep away with a stifled yawn. *Even God's not up yet*, he thought, searching his pockets for a cigarette before remembering he'd quit last month.

Not finding anything to stop the nicotine fit, he incessantly rubbed his hands along the legs of his pants. He was sure the young officer noticed and probably assumed he was nervous. He wasn't. Reese knew what had to be done, and clarity gave him confidence. In a single night, he'd received his orders in Texas, done background research on the location, assembled and shipped out an advance recon team (which he led), coordinated a second team of science eggheads who were following a couple of hours behind, met upstate with a potential witness, and was now driving through waist-deep snow in the middle of the mountains. And the sun wasn't even up yet. He nodded to himself. *That's clarity.*

Reese had told Arthur that no scientists were involved, but that was a lie. The last thing Reese wanted was some over-the-hill science teacher out there in the freezing dark screaming about his ex-girlfriend being abducted by aliens. Assuming events would probably get weird enough once they got to the crash site, there was no reason to compound the mess with personal drama.

But Arthur had been helpful. Now that Reese knew the ship up in the mountains was the same type as reported back in the early 1980s, he had a potential pattern to follow. Since leaving Arthur's place, Reese had dug around on his laptop and discovered fourteen other confirmed missing persons in Blackwood, spanning several decades. That seemed like a whole lot for a town of less than a thousand. No mention of flying saucers. The folks just went up there, driving the same pitch-black roads Reese and his team were now traveling, only to vanish from the face of the Earth.

Some were local; some weren't. No obvious link except that they had all disappeared within a five-mile radius of the town. Of the many vanishings, Arthur Stover was the one and only witness, and Reese figured the old guy's girl wasn't the only one taken. *The ship's been here before. It must have picked this spot for a reason.*

He tugged at the two necklaces again and turned his mind back to his daughter. He hadn't given her a hug goodbye. *Flying saucers. Fuck me.*

"Sir," the lieutenant said with a voice that seemed lower and stronger than Reese would have expected from someone under five foot six. She pointed to a sign:

WELCOME TO BLACKWOOD. POPULATION 937.

She snorted back a laugh. Reese watched as her stony face turned beautiful in the blink of an eye. "What's so funny?"

"Just can't imagine who'd want to live in a town of less than a thousand, sir," she said with a husky thickness while her back straightened. She hadn't wanted him to see the girl beneath the soldier, he guessed. Uniform or no uniform, her femininity was hard to miss.

"Probably the same kinda folks who'd want to drive through a godforsaken snowstorm halfway up a mountain," he said with a sly grin. "Democrats."

That made her laugh again. This time Reese joined in.

Suddenly, the lieutenant slammed on the brakes. Reese braced himself. His seat belt snapped across his chest as the truck skidded into a pile of snow, clouds of white spilling over their windshield.

"What happened?" he asked, his ribs burning.

"Something's in the road, sir," she said, unbuckling herself and popping her door open. Reese grabbed a flashlight from the back seat and followed.

Behind them, the other two trucks jerked to a halt. Six soldiers peeked out from various windows: Reese's advance recon team. The best of the best—or at least the best available on quick standby.

The second driver waved. "What's the matter, Major?"

"Stay put." Reese continued around the front of the truck. Headlights illuminated a frozen shape crouched in the middle of the road. Icicles had formed on top, snaking down like an inverted crown of thorns. It was a woman, kneeling in the snow-covered road. Her hooded jacket covered most of her face in shadow, only blue lips and a nose peeking out. The stillness of her frozen body spoke volumes.

The lieutenant knelt beside her. "Mid to late thirties, I'd guess."

Reese swung his flashlight off the road, searching the shadows. "No car. No snowmobile."

"A local?"

"If so, she couldn't have walked out here." Reese pointed his beam down the road, which disappeared into a snaking trail of white. "No footprints."

"How long you think she's been out here, sir?"

"There's a lotta ice buildup." He bent down, opening the woman's coat. Inside, frozen blood crackled and broke like fragile glass. "A good ten, twelve hours maybe."

He surveyed her with the flashlight, tilting the light to her face. It stopped at a gnarled, silent scream, locked in place beneath icy pale-blue skin. Her eyes were gone, leaving black pits in their place. Reese laid the woman on her back, revealing more of her stomach wound. Her entrails flopped to the side. "Animal of some kind."

"Get on the sat phone!" Reese barked over the wind, turning to the men in the nearest truck. "Tell 'em we've found a civilian body!"

A soldier, barely old enough to shave, hopped out of the truck's passenger seat, staring down at his satellite phone. His face was blank. "No signal, sir."

The lieutenant huffed, noting the pounding snow and swaying trees above. "Weather must be blocking us."

"Doubtful," Reese replied. His mind spun like a rat on a treadmill. Military satellite links shouldn't have been affected by a simple snowstorm. It was possible but not likely. Before he could consider it further, the young lieutenant stumbled, knocking into him. "Jesus!" With a soft gurgle, a cloud of frost escaped the seemingly dead woman's lips. Stunned, Reese reached through the gore, checking her blue-tinged neck. There was a faint pulse. Somehow, she was alive.

"Get me a stretcher!"

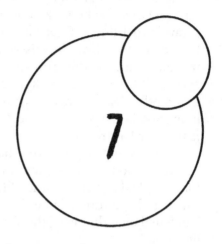

A few hours earlier

Despite having turned the apartment lights off hours ago, Arthur never made it to bed. Pacing in the dark, he used his phone's map to plan a five-hour route to Blackwood. It wouldn't be easy; most roads leading up there would be closed. He figured anyone heading up that way would have to cross Carson's Creek. *If you call that a road,* he thought, *you're using the term liberally.* But Arthur had done it plenty of times before, a lifetime ago. He hoped he could do it again. The key was to keep under five miles an hour on the turns; otherwise, he'd skid off a cliff, never to be seen again, lost in the dark and the woods forever. *Like Casey,* his mind whispered.

Arthur shook himself from his thought loop. This was a moment for action, not brains, or so he hoped.

Pulling the light bulb chain, he ransacked the bedroom closet, dressing himself in three layers. By the time he was finished, Arthur looked a good twenty pounds heavier. *I'll need some blubber up there.*

Scrounging under his twin bed, the only hat he

found was an old, battered Chicago Cubs ball cap. Right after the divorce, he'd taken his two boys for a weekend getaway to Illinois. Deep-dish pizza and baseball. The boys had a great time; he missed his wife. Arthur noticed mustard stains on the brim and felt tears well behind his eyes. He'd thought he was marrying for life. She thought differently. He'd always known she wasn't Casey, not by a long shot. Still, second choice could break a man's heart just as hard as the first.

Casey was his real love. The way he'd lost her and the accusations surrounding it had never left him. Not for a single day. While some of the details—the way she smelled, the hardness of her body, the taste of her lips— had faded over the years, the shrieks of her final screams never had.

Crouched at the foot of his bed, illuminated by his phone's light, memories whirled more vividly in his mind's eye than they had in decades. They came so fast and furious that details of the past seemed to be trip- ping over themselves to remind him of everything he'd shoved into a mental cubbyhole long ago. The way her mouth curled into a crooked smile or how her clothes smelled of spring and flowers, even in the coldest winter. He smiled, remembering how she'd try every Sunday to make a fish dish and yet kept finding new ways to burn it into a dry, black husk. Name a type of fish, and Casey had, at one point or another, burned it to a cinder. Salm- on? Check. Halibut. Check. Cod? Double check. That last one she'd attempted it multiple times, but, shock- ingly, it grew worse with each attempt. Arthur recalled his teeth crunching through a thick layer of burnt skin while trying to act like it was the best thing he'd ever eaten. Looking back now, he thought it was. She was so young. So beautiful. So perfect. Then she was gone.

Arthur snatched the keys from the dresser and head- ed out. After all these years, it was time for some god- damn answers.

Lumbering down the building's steps in what felt like

pillows wrapped about his body, Arthur made his way to his Buick, parked out front. A beep sounded when he opened the driver's door and tried to squeeze inside. Squished between the steering wheel and this seat, his bulk stopped him from actually sitting. Then, stuck in the most ridiculous of poses, a familiar scent wafted to his nostrils, and he sighed. Onion rings and burnt meat.

"Dad." Todd, dressed in a stained flannel jacket, hopped out of a red pickup truck. The stink of the kitchen where he worked was so pervasive that Todd had given it a name, his "evening aftershave."

Arthur spun his head like a child caught with his hand in the cookie jar. "Oh, hey, Todd."

"Going somewhere?"

Arthur paused, peeking about for a quick exit but not finding one. "Just to the store."

As Arthur extricated himself from the driver's seat, Todd's gaze lingered, moving up his legs, toward the rumpled layers covering Arthur's torso.

"It's two in the morning." Todd checked his watch. "What's with the getup?"

"Nothing to worry about." Arthur's face brightened. "Go on in. I'll be back soon."

Arthur turned, again trying to squeeze into the driver's seat, but neither the steering wheel nor his heavy layers were budging; he couldn't fit. Finally, Arthur stood with a huff, unzipping and unbuttoning layer after layer. Conscious of how ridiculous he appeared, he avoided Todd's widening eyes, then squeezed into the seat and placed the extra clothes on the passenger side.

"Whoa, whoa, Dad," Todd said, grabbing the door. "Seriously, where are you going?"

Arthur let out a long stream of breath and stared at Todd. His fake smile faded, and the creases around his mouth drooped into long shadows. "A man from the Army came to see me last night . . ." Arthur began, then told his son what had happened. The words that, a moment earlier, he'd wanted to hide now spilled out in one long, unending sentence, without breaths or gaps. While Todd listened, his face changed from frowning concern to wide-eyed astonishment, then finally sank into sadness. It didn't take a PhD to know his son thought he'd gone around the bend.

When Arthur's story came to an end, Todd patted his father's shoulder, offering a weak smile. "OK, Dad. It's alright. I'll take you."

"No, no, you stay here," Arthur protested. "I don't want you anywhere near that place!"

Todd reached into the car and snatched his father's keys. "You want to get up that mountain? Your Buick *ain't* gonna cut it." He went around to the other side, grabbing his dad's extra clothes, and then headed to the truck. "Come on, I've got tire chains in the back."

Arthur hesitated, torn between what he thought was right and safe for his youngest boy and what would get him back to that mountain the fastest. Then, with a sigh, he climbed out of the Buick and followed Todd.

The mountain had won.

8

Giant hands gripped Casey's mouth and waist, yanking her from the hallway into darkness. She tried to scream, but the heavy fingers muffled her.

"Quiet," someone whispered.

She bit the hand, kicking backwards. Careening off-balance, the figure lurched. Casey spun, shoving a thick fist into the attacker's mouth. He didn't go down, more surprised than hurt. Preparing for the next attack, Casey's heart pounded like a kick drum. "Get the fuck off me!"

"Shut up!" a panicked voice squealed behind her. "Something's out there."

Three masculine figures lurched into view, blocking the exit, surrounding her. The one who had grabbed her was black, about six feet tall, with a bald head and a beard. The other two were pasty white and middle-aged. One wore a tie and rumpled blazer. The second was dressed in plaid, his face obscured behind dark-rimmed glasses. Catching her breath, Casey lowered her voice. "I saw it. He's two doors down, on the right." In the silence, she noted their ashen expressions. "I don't think it followed me."

"Nice hook ya got there." The black man rubbed his lower lip, grinning. "Earl."

"Casey." She nodded, more interested in the surrounding shadows. Satisfied that no monsters lurked inside, she returned her attention to the men. "Anyone wanna tell me where we are?"

The man wearing the tie stepped forward. Disheveled, he smoothed out the creases in his blazer before speaking. "What's the last thing you remember?"

"I was outside. A dog was barking, and there was this light . . . and . . ."

"And a ship," Earl finished for her.

Casey faltered. She remembered the ship. Huge, like a round shadow in the sky. "You're saying we're . . . inside it?"

Tie Guy glanced around the inverted room, gesturing toward the floor above them. "Either that or we're on an upside-down planet. Choose your nightmare." He took her hand from her side and shook it without asking. "I'm Donovan, and," he gestured to the smaller man on his right, "this here is Bill."

Bill nodded absently; his eyes glazed.

"Last thing I remember," Donovan continued, "I was driving home from work, talking on my cell."

Casey caught Earl and Bill's confused look, matching her own. She wondered what the hell a "cell" was. "I woke up a few minutes ago when this ship—or whatever this place is—came apart at the seams. Shook like a mother, flipped upside down, and then it just . . . stopped."

Donovan glanced at Bill and Earl to see if they wanted to add anything. They didn't. Casey looked them over, noting the contrast between the three men, sizing them up. Donovan attempted to project confidence, but with his string tie and greasy hair, he seemed more like the type of middle-management know-it-all that other employees laughed at behind closed doors. Bill, on the other hand, seemed to fade into the background, even standing right before her. Short, stocky, with big round glasses and wet, quivering lips, he lingered beside Donovan, eyes darting from shadow to shadow. Then there was Earl, as big and wide as a truck. Despite his size, his expression was tranquil, with dimpled cheeks and small, soft eyes. White teeth showed beneath his beard, and he seemed like the kind of man women naturally depended upon. *Good,* she thought. *I could use some of that confidence myself.*

"I saw others in the room with me . . ." Casey's tone dwindled to a choked rasp. "They . . . died." Wishing to say more, she felt an urge to confess to stripping a body for clothes, but she closed her mouth, unable to voice it aloud.

Earl nodded sympathetically. "We've all seen shit in here we'd like to forget."

"Tell me about it," Donovan quipped. "I'm trying to forget where I am *right this second*."

"How long have we been in here?"

"Wish we knew." Earl held up his wristwatch; it was dead. The hands were stopped at 3:30. "But I doubt I've been awake more than an hour or so."

"Yeah," Donovan chuckled nervously, "but it's been one hell of a long hour."

Casey met his gaze. "Did you see . . . other bodies?"

He shrugged. "It ain't the dead ones that worry me."

Before she could ask his meaning, a distant shriek startled them. Donovan's back straightened, Earl clenched his fists, and Bill shrank deeper into the shadows. Casey turned to the open door with a compressed shudder. "That thing's still out there."

After a pregnant pause, Earl nudged forward, peering through the entrance. Donovan grabbed his arm. "What are you doing?"

Noting Donovan's hand, which tried in vain to

surround his large bicep, Earl calmly replied, "We can't just sit here."

Bill squirmed, his eyes as wide as saucers. "Whoa, you want to go out there?" He backed away, shaking his head so hard it looked like it might pop off his neck. "No way."

Another shriek echoed, growing closer. "Earl's right. We can't stay in here," Casey said.

Bill shrank another step back. "Fine, you go."

Casey moved closer, offering a weak smile. "We'll stick together, Bill. Take my hand," she said, extending her fingers.

Hesitating, Bill glanced past her toward Donovan, who nodded in consent. "Strength in numbers, right?"

With a strangled sigh, Bill relented as Casey pulled him to the door. Earl led them into the hall, heading away from the approaching growls. Casey was the last one out. As they went around a corner, she glanced over her shoulder, and what she saw made her stumble. Her left foot tripped over her right. Her eyes narrowed, and she opened her mouth to scream, though all she could manage was a feeble gasp. Twenty feet away a twisted silhouette defied gravity, scrambling along the curved wall. It lurched forward, about to pounce.

Casey's throat finally opened, unleashing a scream.

The thing's nails click-clacked against metal, drawing closer and closer. It wore a man's clothing, a flannel jacket and collared shirt, though that's where the human similarities ended. Whatever it had been, it wasn't a man anymore. Even while crouched, the thing was a hulking beast. Its skin was milk white with red veins running along its bald head, its arms stretching past the tattered remains of its dated clothes. But it was the eyes that marked it as alien, or at least not human. They were enormous—black ovals with pinpricks of red lights gleaming within.

The creature seemed to drip from the ceiling like oil, oozing over her. An odorous mixture of burnt flesh and battery acid inflamed her nostrils. Casey tried to turn away, but the oval black eyes seemed to draw her in. The deeper she gazed, the more her revulsion was exchanged for sadness, even sympathy. For a moment Casey wondered if the monster was as afraid as she was. Maybe more so. *How could a man turn into . . . this?*

Suddenly, Bill's hand was at her shoulder, pulling her up. The thing, as if waking from a daze, leapt, baring yellow teeth that extended so long they cut through its own lips in deep red gashes.

As its teeth were about to clamp onto Casey's back, Earl appeared, slamming into the creature, hitting it with his full weight. It stumbled, surprised. Earl struck it with a meaty fist, smashing in two teeth, before kicking it back. The thing cried out, shocked by the attack. Earl was about to hit it again when Casey grabbed him. "Go," she said. They turned and ran.

Ahead, Donovan raced at full speed, never looking back to see if the others were safe. While Casey couldn't blame him for being afraid, she made a mental note that now she knew who she could trust and who she couldn't.

They turned another corner, only to see Donovan skid to a halt. Blocking their path were colossal tree branches, gnarled and twisted.

Behind them, Casey heard the thing scampering along the walls, following close behind. Gaining speed. She ran right past Donovan, snaking her body between the branches. They tore at her jacket and pants. One branch scraped her forehead, drawing a gash of blood that dripped down to her eyes. An eruption of thumping metal announced the creature as it turned the corner, bearing down on them. The men followed Casey through the thicket of branches. The end was almost in sight when her foot caught in a narrow gap between two branches. Behind them, the thing ripped and tore through the branches.

"Go, go!" Earl yelled, right behind her.

Seeing the thing's fiery red eyes through the gaps in

the branches, she yanked her leg, but her shoe was stuck. Bent over, she fumbled with it while the men clawed and pushed their way forward. Finally, her foot popped out of her shoe. She wobbled out of the foliage and fell onto the metallic floor.

The men emerged next, led by Donovan, who ran past and continued down the hall. Bill and Earl snatched Casey's arms, dragging her as they ran. She hobbled along with only one shoe while the thing broke through the wooden barrier behind them. Kicking off her remaining shoe, Casey ran along the cold metal in thin socks. Her heart thundering, she was too terrified to focus on the icicles shooting up through her toes.

Casey knew they needed to find something to put between them and the hulking thing, something stronger than wood, but they'd found no doors or barriers to close in that place. With mere seconds before the creature caught up to them, there didn't seem to be an escape. She imagined what kind of steel barrier might hold such a creature. Probably something like she'd seen in a sci-fi movie, where they swooshed down with lightning speed. Anything less than that wouldn't be able to stop the thing at their heels.

She turned into the next hall, trying to keep up with Donovan. The stink of burnt flesh and the snapping of teeth was right behind her, the creature's breath warm on her neck.

Then, *swoosh*. She felt a gust of wind at her back. The sound that accompanied it was straight out of the movies, as if ripped from her imagination and thrust into reality.

Earl was the first to steal a glance backwards. Then he stumbled to a halt. Casey and Bill followed, stopping in their tracks. An enormous steel slab had slid across the hallway, cutting them off from the creature. They heard it pounding and scratching on the other side.

Earl reeled, clutching his knees, and belted out a laugh. Bill joined in, howling, taunting the now impotent thing behind the door. Casey wanted to join in, but her body shook and spasmed, too terrified to muster anything above a relieved sigh.

"Jesus, that has gotta be the best fucking luck we've had all day," Earl said.

Squatting on the floor, Casey wiped blood from her forehead and warmed her frozen feet with her hands. Her gaze traveled back toward the looming barrier. It was precisely what she'd imagined mere seconds before it appeared. She doubted it was a coincidence. Maybe someone was in there with them, reading her thoughts. If so, she had something to say: *Thanks.*

And fuck you.

9

When the trucks pulled into a gas station midway up the mountain, it was the first glimpse of civilization Reese had seen in a couple of hours. A neon sign painted the cascading snow a dark crimson. *Looks like red rain,* he thought as the truck pulled to a stop.

They'd finally entered Blackwood, Oregon.

Reese climbed out, studying the frost-covered station. Wind howled like a wounded animal. He rushed to the second truck, peering into the back. Two medics had dressed the woman's stomach wound and wrapped her in a blanket. Her eyeless sockets stared upwards. "How is she?"

"Multiple lacerations. Severe trauma to the organs and spine. Third-degree frostbite . . ." Staff Sergeant Lewis Pidgeon listed off her wounds like a grocery list. He was African American and older than most of the other soldiers, all white boys, with some gray peppering his beard. Handpicked for the mission, Reese had known him since Afghanistan. The rest of the recon team was chosen in a rush, Reese having to learn their names as he went. He needed someone he could depend on, and after everything they'd seen together, he counted on the older soldier not dropping his load if a little greenie suddenly appeared. Still, Pidgeon's voice trembled as he added a final detail. "Don't know how this woman is still breathing. Ought to be dead, sir."

"She will be if we don't find a hospital soon."

Reese headed to the station's brightly lit front door. Christmas lights twinkled above. In February. He figured the locals didn't feel the need to rush much in this kind of winter.

Twenty yards to the front door, and he could already feel the cold creeping through his thermal underwear, stinging his arms and legs. Snow chunks blasted about. He forced himself not to cover his face. Better to acclimate to the cold. It wasn't going to get any warmer.

Reese didn't want to admit how relieved he felt as he stepped into the warm room, hovering by the unmanned front counter. He peered behind racks of candy bars and chips, looking around. The sun wouldn't be up for another hour, so he assumed whoever worked there was sleeping in the back.

"Hello?"

No answer. Reese continued past the racks, stopping at two doors. On the left was a bathroom. Fluorescents flickered to life automatically as he entered. The confined space was wall-to-wall flowered yellow tiles, which stank from an overabundance of bleach.

Then a sound: a thump. Reese turned toward the second door. *Thump.*

Reese opened the door to a garage. *Thump. Thump.* Upon entering, a gust of frigid air slapped his face. Thick wedges of shadows crisscrossed over machine parts, stacks of oil cans, and a half-assembled car. At the far end, a sliding garage door banged up and down in the wind. *Thump, thump, thump.* Snowflakes billowed and danced about in the dark as he crept inside. Goose pimples crawled behind his neck, and he knew it wasn't from the cold.

Reese waved his hand along the wall, blindly searching for a light switch. "Anyone here?"

With flailing fingers, he yanked a dangling chain. An overhead light bulb ignited, exposing an empty garage. Shadows receded, offering a plain room filled with haphazard car parts. Nothing of note.

Irritated, he headed back to the front counter. He knew the woman would die if he didn't get an ambulance soon. Grabbing a landline, he dialed 911 and then held the receiver to his ear. The phone was dead.

He was about to head back outside when he noted the cash register. Reese checked to see if it was unlocked. It popped open with a hollow *ding*. After counting a few hundred bucks' worth of singles, fives, tens, and twenties, he slammed it shut. Whoever had been working there had left in such a hurry they hadn't even locked up their cash. Maybe the super-secret alien UFO up the mountain wasn't so secret after all. What if the whole town knew? That would complicate things. The last thing he needed was an entire town running around screaming about aliens.

Gunfire erupted outside. Reese bolted for the door.

Lumbering outside, he searched for the gunshot's origin. Soldiers poured from the first and third trucks, but there was no movement in the second. That answered his question.

He drew his 9 mm and unlocked the safety. Soldiers raised their rifles, circling the truck. Among them, the female lieutenant seemed the coolest headed, issuing orders to the men to keep their distance as the second truck rattled and swayed from some unseen threat. "Check your fire!" she ordered, concerned they might hit the driver or those in the flatbed.

"Hold the perimeter," Reese said, approaching the

truck. It had stopped rocking. Dead silence. Reese heard his feet crunch in the snow with each step, giving away his position. Creeping to the back of the truck, he noted the closed canvas flap. "Pidgeon?" Reese whispered. "You in there?"

With his sidearm raised, he used his left hand to pull back the canvas.

A figure burst forward, tearing through the cover and knocking him to the ground. It was on him at once. Pinpricks of red light for eyes in dark, empty sockets, long, straggly hair waving about. As its teeth lunged for his neck, he realized this seemingly inhuman beast was the woman from the road. Somehow, she was awake and wrestling him to the ground with the strength of four men. He didn't hesitate to fire, pumping three bullets into her chest before her teeth found his shoulder, tearing through his coat and uniform, almost to his skin when—

BANG! BANG! BANG!

A hail of gunfire shredded her, ripping thick pieces of meat from her bones. Blood and brain tissue splattered Reese's face as she collapsed on top of him. A sobbing, feminine gurgle in his ear announced her last breath.

A thick hand grabbed Reese's arm, pulling him from the gory mess. It was Staff Sergeant Pidgeon, his rifle still warm from discharge. When the others hesitated, perhaps afraid they might hit the major, he had taken the shot. Reese nodded a quick thanks, then peered through the torn canvas, seeing a mangled silhouette inside. The other medic. Dead.

He turned to Pidgeon, surprised his friend appeared unharmed. "What happened?"

"She heard you coming. Guess she decided you were the bigger threat."

Pidgeon knelt over the woman's remains. Beneath her pale flesh, red veins crisscrossed her face and body. "These weren't here before." He stood and let out a slow, long-winded huff. "Could be a virus of some sort."

The air grew still. Several men gasped. Reese turned to the remaining members of his team. They were down one medic with two recon teams of four, including a couple of NCOs and six enlisted men, plus Staff Sergeant Pidgeon and the young lieutenant. Reese noticed they all looked older than they had a moment earlier. "We need to check the town before we head up to the crash site," he said, then glanced at his driver. "I'm sorry, I don't remember your name."

"Lieutenant Salvatore."

He filed her name in his head, hoping not to forget it again. "Try the sat phone one more time. The support team should be less than an hour behind us."

"And if I get through?" Salvatore asked. "What should I tell them?"

Reese let out a long, heavy sigh. "We need to prep for possible contagion."

After Salvatore's repeated calls failed, the recon team split up between trucks one and three, abandoning the second truck and its macabre contents in the parking lot. The support team would have to clean it up. Reese had a schedule to keep. His orders had been to secure the crash site within twelve hours, and he was close to an hour behind. He checked his watch. The sun would be up soon, and with it, he hoped, some reprieve from the biting cold.

As they climbed into the vehicles, no one spoke. Seeing a flying saucer had probably sounded fun to most of them, but now, with the threat of a possible contagion, no one looked forward to whatever lay ahead up the winding, snow-covered road.

Pidgeon sat behind Reese in the first truck. He checked his gear in the next seat and then strapped himself in. Sweat dripped down his forehead. He wiped his eyes. His left hand grabbed his right, steadying it, as if trying to shake off whatever adrenaline was still racing through his body.

In the rush to keep moving, Reese never noticed the red veins creeping up Pidgeon's neck.

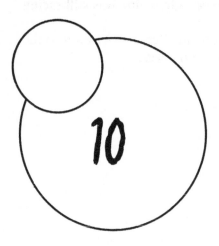

10

Trailing the men, Casey lumbered along on crunchy socks. Her breath was a clouded mist, her feet tingling as she limped, stabbing pain erupting through her toes with each step. No one had spoken in what seemed hours, and she didn't want to be the one to break the silence. The last thing she needed was to be considered the weak link. Or worse, a damsel in distress. The very thought made her want to retch. Funny, she thought, if Arthur were there, she'd know her role: clutching his hand tightly, following his lead. But trapped in this place with real-life monsters and surrounded by strange men, she felt the urge to project strength, whether real or manufactured.

Biting her lip, she kept pace with the others until, thankfully, a patch of darkness along the right wall slowed Earl's lead. The others hesitated around him. Casey leaned against the wall, lifting a tingling foot. The socks crunched from dried ice. She considered stripping them off but worried the metal floor would be even colder. Distracted, she hadn't noticed the grumbling voices growing in pitch until Donovan shouted above the din. "Are you out of your mind?"

Nudging between Bill and Donovan, she found Earl kneeling at an open doorway, leaning over a half-naked woman. Her spine was twisted, contorted in a fashion that left no doubt she was dead. Under any other circumstances Casey would have run to the fallen woman's side, checking for a pulse. Instead, Casey's eyes meandered down the woman's bare legs, finding naked feet with no shoes. Cursing herself for the brief macabre hope of stealing another corpse's shoes, she only half heard the argument playing out between Earl and Donovan.

"No more doorways," Donovan said, his voice shrill. "No more dark rooms, and *no more* bogeymen jumping out! We stick to the fucking hallway."

Earl turned the dead woman over, noting a purple gash along her neck. "She's dead."

"Yeah, and we're not," Donovan replied, gesturing down the hall. "Let's keep moving."

Bill nodded with nervous agreement. Casey remained silent.

Earl's thick hand brushed the woman's eyes, closing them. Bowing his bald head, he whispered a quiet prayer, too faint for Casey to make out. Still, the compassion he showed only reinforced her own guilt. Her first thought had not been one of compassion or even revulsion at what this poor woman had suffered. Instead, it had been one of disappointment at not finding a new pair of shoes. Her cheeks flushed with shame.

When Earl stood, Casey averted her gaze, unable to make eye contact. "You guys do what you want," he said, addressing the others. "There may be more people inside."

Donovan rolled his eyes. "Right, get yourself killed." He turned to Bill. "Come on, let's keep going,"

Bill hesitated, trembling. "B-but, we might n-need

him," Bill stammered. "I mean, Earl's stronger than the rest of us combined."

"I doubt muscles are going to stop whatever's waiting in there."

Casey glanced down at the half-nude figure below, then stepped closer to Earl, the bile in her stomach still twisting and boiling. "I'll go with you," she mumbled.

As if taking stock between strength in numbers or going with Donovan, Bill fidgeted and paced before finally lurching closer to Earl. Donovan still stood apart; three to one.

Earl and Bill went through the doorway. Casey lingered a moment longer, gesturing to Donovan. "You sure you want to miss all the fun?"

With a weighted sigh, Donovan shrugged and offered a plastic grin. "Fine. Let's go see what's inside the dark, scary room."

Casey and Donovan stepped inside, fumbling to find Earl and Bill in the dark.

After a moment's blindness, they saw a shaft of light peeking behind a shadowed corner. Donovan grabbed her arm, pulling her toward it. Bill and Earl stood on the other side of the corner, tilting their heads toward the light's distant source. The plain gray walls curved into themselves like a coiled snake and then shot straight up, vanishing from view into a thick, inky void above. It appeared to be a dead end.

Tilting his head, Earl let out a slow whistle. "How high up do you think it goes?"

"You mean how far down," Donovan replied.

"What are you talking about?" Bill asked. His incessant nervousness still trembled below the surface for all to hear.

Donovan turned to him. "This thing—"

"What thing?"

"This *ship*." Donovan's voice tightened. "All right? Let's just say it. This *space*ship is obviously upside down, so that means this shaft leads down, not up."

Earl shook his head. "Yeah, but it's still *up*. I mean—"

"All I'm saying is that this suggests we're standing at the top of the ship."

"Up, down, left, right, nobody gives a shit!" Bill said, his voice turning shrill. "It's a dead end. What are we going to do?"

As the men bickered, Casey's focus turned to something along the walls. "Look," she said, pointing at the curved wall surrounding them.

The men followed her gaze. Spaced out every couple of feet along the shaft's curved walls were what appeared to be grooves. Like notches in a belt, wrapping around and around, heading up toward the waiting dark. Earl was the first to approach them. As he drew closer, metallic rods slid out from each of the countless gaps, one after the other. They were white, less than an inch thick, each one roughly two feet in length. Sprouting to life, the rods spiraled up along the wall's arc, vanishing out of view.

"A ladder," Casey said in a choked whisper, unsure if this was a good or a bad omen.

Donovan looked at Earl. "Even if we climb it, that ain't gonna hold a big boy like you."

Earl's back straightened. "Call me 'boy' again."

"Calm down. Didn't mean nothin' by it."

Earl arched over him. "That's why you're still standing."

While Donovan and Earl stared each other down, Casey noticed Bill approach the first rod or rung. He climbed nervously onto it. "It's stronger than it looks," he said.

Surprised Bill would be the first to consider climbing, Casey began to reassess the nervous little man. If nothing else, he certainly seemed more focused on getting out of there than arguing like petulant children. Bill stretched his right leg upwards, pressing himself against the wall, struggling to reach the next rung. Panting, his foot reached the second rung. Earl nodded, impressed, but Donovan snorted. "Jesus, he's already out of breath."

"If you're so concerned, you go next," Casey snapped.

"Yeah," Earl said, nodding. "And I'll take up the rear."

Donovan hesitated at the first rung and shot Earl a hard, lingering glare. "You're gonna grab me if I fall?"

Earl smiled. It wasn't a pretty smile.

By the time Bill was on the fifth rung, and Donovan had stepped to the second, Casey had climbed onto the bottom rung. It held her relatively light weight without protest. Bracing her spine along the curved wall, she stretched her sock-covered foot toward the next step—and collapsed onto the floor, panting, dripping with sweat.

Beside her, the three men were curled on the floor, similarly out of breath. However, the floor looked different. Tilting her gaze, Casey noted a long, curved hallway stretched out before them. The dead end and curved walls had somehow vanished, replaced by a new hallway. Lights along the walls glowed brighter, and the shadows receded. Before Casey could ask the others where they were or how they'd arrived, she heard Bill whimpering. He was curled beside her in a fetal position, cradling his left leg. A long gash stretched along his thigh. Blood seeped through his jeans, dripping into a crimson puddle. Casey heard him sobbing into his sleeve, either from pain or fear. She guessed Bill didn't want the others to see him cry.

Earl helped Casey up while Donovan paced at a distance. "Where are we?" he asked. His throat sounded dry as he coughed up the words everyone else was thinking.

Earl shrugged. Casey turned around, stepping away from the lit hallway, and peered into a seemingly bottomless pit behind them. Along the pit's walls, white rods stuck out in a cylindrical spiral. "We're at the top," she said, more fearful than surprised.

Donovan flanked her, peering down. "I don't remember getting up here."

"Me neither," Earl replied, then turned toward Bill, who still lay bleeding on the floor. "But we seem to have made the climb. He musta gotten injured on the way."

Tearing herself away from the new mystery, Casey knelt beside Bill. Recalling her callousness at the corpse in the doorway, this time Casey wanted to show the empathy and care she should have demonstrated before. After a moment's hesitation, she unbuckled his pants and slid them down. Bill yelped, more from surprise than physical discomfort.

"Relax. Nothing I haven't seen before," Casey assured him as she exposed his smiley face underwear and hairy legs, before stopping below the wound. "It's not as deep as it looks."

"There's a lot of blood," he whined.

"That's cos you were walking on it," Earl said. He glanced back toward the hole behind them. "At least I think you did."

Ripping off Bill's right sleeve, Casey wrapped the strip around his thigh, hoping to stop the bleeding. Bill winced. "Ah, not so tight!"

Donovan leaned into view. "Ya heard the woman. You'll live."

Ignoring Donovan's snarky tone, Casey turned to Earl. With a nod, he helped Bill to his feet and pulled his pants back up. As soon as Casey's hand touched Bill's shoulder, she gasped. Like a flash of headlights blazing in her mind's eye, she remembered Bill slipping halfway up the winding ladder. He'd cut his leg during the fall. Tumbled past, screaming. Earl's thick arm had reached out, snatching him from the void.

"Wait." Casey tried to place the fractured pieces into place. "He fell . . ."

"Yeah and almost knocked me off too," Donovan snorted, then stopped. "I remember."

"Me too," Earl said. "It's hazy. Sorta like hitting fast-forward on a VCR."

Bill shook his head. "I missed a rung." He slapped Earl's back. "You saved my butt, man. Thanks."

Earl grinned. "Don't mention it."

"So, if we made the climb," Casey asked, "why can't I remember it all?"

No one seemed to have an answer. "Let's keep moving," Donovan said finally.

"Slow and easy," Casey added as she and Earl helped Bill find his footing.

As they headed down the new hallway, the lights along the walls shone brighter and steadier, no longer pulsing with wicked shadows. Casey's heart slowed in her chest. Wherever they were, she decided it had to be better than where they had come from.

11

The sun was being a straight-up bitch this morning, hanging below the tree line for what seemed to be an exhausting amount of time, unwilling to rise and warm the mountain-shadowed valley. Glancing down, Reese saw that his watch read 0640. Three minutes since he last checked. Either he was growing impatient, or time was moving as reluctantly as the sun. He needed to get up that mountain. *She wasn't human anymore*, he thought, picturing pinpricks of red light from hollow eye sockets.

As they drove over the winding, snowdrift-covered road into town, he could see why they called it Blackwood. Murky pine monoliths spread long shadows over the entire valley. If he'd been making his way leisurely up there, perhaps on vacation or just cutting through for God knew what reason, he might have found the towering trees and blue-stained mountains beautiful. This morning though they filled him with dread. A tickle at the back of his skull told him even before they pulled into town that whatever awaited them would be bad.

Really bad. Worse than Iraq. Worse than Afghanistan. The stuff of nightmares that he might never shake.

From the direction they entered Main Street, the town stretched out like an inverted cross. There were only two roads, one going north and south and a second running east and west. Reese silently named them Street One and Street Two. He liked simplicity. Even though the sun was just rising, he expected to see early morning workers in the street, but no one greeted them as the military trucks rolled into town.

Normally, Reese would have preferred unimpeded travel, but Staff Sergeant Pidgeon had told him a virus had infected the woman, and that changed his mission parameters. He needed to know who else might be infected. *Virus.* The word tumbled about in his head. The support team was bringing a mobile command base and hazmat suits, but they were at least an hour behind.

As the trucks made their way through the seemingly vacant town, Reese was just wondering if he should keep what remained of his unit inside the vehicles until the support team arrived when, on their left, he saw movement. A figure bolted from one building and disappeared behind another.

"There, nine o'clock," Lieutenant Salvatore said, pointing toward a hunting store.

"Yeah, I saw him," Reese replied, though he wasn't sure if it had been a man or woman. The figure had moved too fast for him to make it out. *Morning runner, maybe.* "Keep going. I want to get to the sheriff's station."

Snow crunched beneath their heavy tires. Cars were parked along the side, caked in fresh powder. Last night's blazing wind had died to a soft whistle. There weren't any car tracks or footprints on the street or the sidewalks. The two trucks and the soft breeze were the only things moving. *Still early. They could all just be sleeping,* he thought. He hoped.

At the town's one and only intersection, the sheriff's station came into view on the right. It was smaller than either the sporting goods store or the tour guide office that sandwiched it on either side. Reese doubted the sheriff's station would have more than a single deputy. The theme song to the *Andy Griffith Show* popped into his head, then faded as quickly as it had arrived.

Reese and Pidgeon hopped out while Salvatore and the others waited in the trucks. Under normal procedures, Reese would have had his second in command, Lieutenant Salvatore, join him, but with the possibility of contagion, he chose Pidgeon instead.

The crisp, predawn air stung Reese's cheeks, but this time he welcomed the cold. He'd grown restless in the truck since leaving the gas station. He didn't need to close his eyes to see the dead medic covered in blood. That image was burned, seemingly permanently, on his retinas. *She'd torn his throat out.* Reese had lost men before and knew he might lose more today, but for one to die so horribly before the mission proper had even started, it had eaten at his gut for the rest of the drive.

His eyes swept the town. Across the street, Sally's Home Goods general store had twin windows crowned in a yellow awning, the glass full of sale prices and canned meat. To its right was a barber shop with dusty windows that spoke of a prolonged absence of business. He guessed most folks weren't worrying about a haircut until spring. Beside the barber, a hardware store's windows were shuttered. He counted about twelve shops stretching down Main Street, or, as he thought of it, Street One. With the soft, cascading snow drifting around the mom-and-pop shops, the tall black trees perched above, and swelling blue mountains beyond, the place should have seemed peaceful. *Serene* would be the word, he thought. But it wasn't. Something in his stomach tightened. It was the emptiness of it all. The stillness. His eyes turned toward the trees and mountains. Where were the birds? No chirping. No distant motors or machines. Absolute silence had its own sound, Reese discovered, and it horrified him. He absently chewed the inside of his cheek until he tasted blood.

What if the virus is airborne?

As if hearing his thoughts, Pidgeon handed him a paper surgical mask. Reese turned it over in his fingers. "Will this help?"

"Doubt it," Pidgeon replied. "But it's what we got."

That's reassuring. Reese pushed out a crooked grin before he placed the mask over his mouth and nose. He felt his warm breath clamping to his face and wondered how in the hell doctors wore those things all day. They checked their sidearms, both loaded with a fresh clip, the safety off. Reese led them into the sheriff's station.

Blaring radio static greeted them as soon as they stepped inside. The office was a simple affair with tack boards on three of the four walls, a small reception desk up front, and an office in the back, which Reese assumed was the sheriff's. As he had already guessed before entering, the place was empty. *Unlocked and no one in sight, just like the gas station*, he mused. *Did the entire town just up and leave?*

Pidgeon went around the front desk and killed the radio static. Reese tried another frequency and clicked the radio back on. "Sheriff, you read me? Over. This is Major John Reese, United States Army." More static. He tried another frequency. "Sheriff? Anyone hear me? This is Major John Reese, US Army. Anyone receiving this? Over."

Static spit back. Reese tossed the mic aside. His face turned red, and he rubbed his temples so hard his fingers made marks below the hairline. No phone lines, no satellite signals, not even a fucking radio worked. He cursed inwardly. *And the hits just keep on coming.*

Reese went back outside and glanced at his watch: 0700.

"All right, get out," he said to his waiting unit. Salvatore, a staff sergeant, and the enlisted men jumped out of the trucks, eager to get on with it. "We'll search on foot, breaking into two teams. Each team brings a flare. You find someone, you fire it up. Salvatore and Pidgeon with me. We'll go north." Reese waved the staff sergeant over. "Team Two head south down Main Street. Check shops, cars, and houses."

Noting the soldiers' weapons in the middle of an American town, Reese groaned inwardly. "And *check your fire.*"

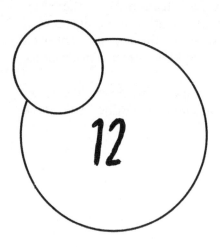

12

Arthur Stover hit the vape pen long and hard, hoping the influx of nicotine would steady the pounding in his chest. Todd's truck cabin seemed too small,
growing smaller with each bump they hit on the narrow
road. Slick turns caused the truck to drift, but it wasn't
the winding, tiny road through the mountains that kept
Arthur's knee shaking or his heart thumping. It was the
sign up ahead: WELCOME TO BLACKWOOD. POPU-
LATION 937.

He was back, after all these years. After all the accusations and nightmares, he was back to where it started.
Where *she* went missing. Where it felt like his life had
ended.

Todd slowed, pumping the brakes so as not to skid.
Arthur's mind returned to the present. Through the
filthy windshield he spied several trucks, metallic and
black. Military, he assumed. The last one was parked
across the road, blocking their path. Todd stopped.

A figure clad in odd-looking armor climbed out of

the truck. The suit was chunky, painted greenish gray, and crowned with a glass visor over the face. Arthur decided it was a hazmat suit, though it was a far cry from the yellow ones he'd seen on television.

Todd shot his father a sideways glance, and for a moment, Arthur thought he saw a speck of belief in his eyes, something that maybe said, *Holy shit, Dad, you were right all along! Your alien stories are real!* Then his features brightened, as if shoving that nonsense aside, and Todd calmly rolled down his window and waved to the approaching figure. "That's some get-up you got on there, buddy. Looks heavy."

"Sorry, road's closed." The armored man's voice crackled through his helmet speaker.

Todd didn't lose his smile. "What's the matter?"

"Chemical spill. A truck flipped a couple miles up the road. I'm afraid you're going to have to take a different route."

"Who'd be driving chemicals all the way up here?" Todd asked, his tone remaining casual.

The man's back straightened, his armor blocking the sun. "I'm afraid I have to insist, sir."

Arthur, who'd been biting his tongue throughout the ridiculous exchange, finally spoke. "I'm looking for Major Jonathan Reese."

The giant figure didn't respond, but they heard his breath catch in the armor's speakers.

"I'm Arthur Stover. Major Reese came to see me. I know about the UFO."

Todd buried his face in his hands and sighed.

The man laughed. "Don't let this get-up fool you. It's a chemical spill, guys. No little green men, I promise. And I'm afraid I don't know anyone named Reese. Seriously, just take another route up to town."

Arthur fumed, his face red. "There is no other way! The other roads are closed in winter."

The armored man's frustration bubbled up, matching Arthur's. "And so's this one, at least for today. You'll have to wait until tomorrow. Again, you *must* turn around. It's for your own safety."

Todd nodded. "We understand, sir. Thanks." Todd put his truck into reverse and began to turn around.

"No, wait!" Arthur roared. "Where are you going?"

"Home," Todd said.

Arthur bounced back and forth in his seat as if ready to jump out the window if need be. "You can't believe him!"

"I don't."

"Then turn back around!"

"No way," Todd said, wiping his brow. "I didn't think there'd be anything here, let alone Darth Vader standing in the middle of the fucking road."

"Then why come?"

"I . . . I guess I figured you had dementia or some such shit, and I was trying to, I don't know, show you it wasn't real. None of it. The aliens, the abducted girl-friend . . ."

"Now you know it's all true."

Todd stopped the truck. "No, Dad, I don't know that it's *all* true. But whatever's going on here, it's beyond us. I flip burgers, and you're a fucking schoolteacher." He turned to his dad, his eyes wet and pleading. "Once and for all, whatever happened before, or is happening now, let it go. Please. For me. For Michael. For yourself. Just. Let. It. Go."

Arthur's throat tightened, making it hard to raise his voice above a whisper. "I can't, son." He grabbed his coat and climbed out of the truck, heading toward the tree line on foot.

Todd jumped out and followed. "Hold on. You can't walk the whole way. You'll freeze to death!"

Arthur glanced at blue-green mountains, silhou-etted by a rising sun. "I was born here," he replied. He arched his back, inhaling the biting air. It filled his lungs and made him feel as if he'd awoken from a dreadful, forty-year dream. His breath spit out in a long misty stream. "I've climbed this area plenty. I can do it again."

"But, Dad, you're . . . ya know . . ."

"I'm not that old, kid. Go on home." Arthur nodded reassuringly, smiled, and then headed up the hill. "I got things to do," he added as he vanished into the foliage.

13

Casey stumbled to a stop at a four-way intersection while her three companions stared down separate shadow-laced tunnels. Sitting cross-legged on the cold floor, she cradled her frozen feet. She needed a pair of shoes before frostbite set in. With a huff, she resigned herself to finding another dead body. Preferably a woman, size eight or nine. The thought made her insides lurch.

Bill turned from his tunnel, sidling up beside Donovan at the left entrance. Earl stood near the center hallway, his thick arms across his chest, eyes burrowing down a third corridor. The men were choosing sides. One by one, they turned to Casey, as if for a deciding vote. *We're trapped in hell,* Casey thought, *and they're having a cockfight.* Unwilling to pick a side, she turned back the way she'd come. "That thing was human. At least it was at some point."

She hoped their common fear of what they'd just been through might dull any coming conflict. After an exchange of sideways glances, it seemed to work. Earl sighed. "You see his outfit? Plaid pants, gold chain. Like, out of the seventies or something."

Donovan shrugged with a jagged grin. "Someone please tell me we won't be trapped here for thirty years like that poor bastard."

"More like five to ten years," Casey replied, returning his smile. She was glad to see Donovan and Earl standing shoulder to shoulder. "Thirty years? He'd be dressed more like Elvis."

The men shared an odd glance. Before she could ask what was wrong, a distant scratching spun their attention to the darkness behind them. Like nails against a chalkboard, the noise put her teeth on edge and shot icicles along her spine. The man-monster was still tracking them.

"It's getting louder," Bill squeaked.

Casey shook her head. "No, *closer*."

"Relax." Donovan mopped his sweat with his dirt-caked tie. "That door was solid steel. No way that thing could have gotten out." He turned to the others, as if expecting them to nod in agreement, but no one did.

"How would you know?" Earl asked. "You never even looked back."

"It *didn't* get out," Donovan shot back. "Don't be such a pussy." Earl glared at him, his back erect.

"M-m-maybe it found a way *around*," Bill stammered, hoping to be a peacemaker. The screech of nails on steel grew piercing. Casey made the choice for everyone, rushing down the center tunnel. Donovan spun, incredulous. "Where you going?"

She continued without reply. Earl and Bill followed, leaving Donovan standing alone.

The scratching continued, growing louder and louder. With a jump, he bolted after them.

Farther and farther into the bowels of the ship they went, through endless frigid tunnels lined with plain gray walls, until finally, the hall opened into a vast chamber. The temperature warmed. For the first time in several hours, Casey's shivers subsided, her breath no longer visible. Specks of color blinked in the dark, like flickering bulbs, which seemed to emphasize the sheer size of the inverted dome. *It's like an upside-down football stadium*, Casey thought.

The men stopped beside her, peering up and down. They were standing on the fourth level, about halfway between the top and bottom levels, each with its own catwalk running along the walls of the large chasm. Lining the surface beside the inverted walkways, bulbous shapes glowed with a spectrum of colored hues, like sunlight dancing through a prism. It was the first beautiful thing Casey had seen in that ugly, death-filled place. Fear subsided to awe and wonder. The chamber's shimmering lights sank through the depths of the bowl's shadows, reminding her of glowing honeycombs in a darkened cave. For all its magnitude though, Casey only mustered a single word: "Whoa."

Earl said it plainer: "Holy shit."

Oblivious to the room's beauty, Donovan instead noted the obvious chasm between them and the other side of the dome. "No straight way across. Figures."

Earl gestured toward the catwalk running along the wall. "Guess we take the long way 'round."

Nodding in silent agreement, Donovan led them along the catwalk, careful to steer clear of the ledge. The others kept pace. It was warm enough for Casey to unzip the winter coat she'd stolen from the dead man. Shaking the memory of it away, her feet quickened. Then, noting the lack of railings, she slowed, hugging the catacomb's surface.

With Donovan in the lead, they made their way along the room's side, passing glowing chambers. Blurred shapes hung suspended inside. Casey hesitated, peering past frosted glass. Earl and Bill paused behind her. Donovan kept going.

Casey leaned closer to one chamber, careful not to touch it. Inside, a silhouette stood, muddy and featureless in the light. Suddenly, the inverted shape became clear—bristled brown beard, red shirt, short hair with dark eyes peering beneath. Casey choked, falling backwards, as her father glared from behind smoky glass. His thin, tobacco-stained lips curled in a wicked grin.

Stumbling, Casey's heel slipped over the ledge, but Earl caught her. "Watch your step."

Casey's eyes reluctantly swiveled back toward the fogged chamber, finding an inverted figure with two arms and legs and a head crowned in dangling feathers. It was human, all right, but it was not her father. Blowing out a deep, heavy breath, Casey wrenched herself from Earl's concerned grasp and studied the figure more closely. Though its features were obscured by the glass, she noted blue and red paint covering a male face. Her focus lifted to tattered tan clothing draping a chest and torso. The familiarity of it knotted in her stomach. "Tell me that's not an Indian."

Earl wet his lips, scratched his head. "Looks like he's got war paint. Like from the movies."

Donovan stopped. "From *history*," he said. "Moron," he added, lowering his voice.

Earl crossed the distance between them with a single step. "What'd you say?"

Donovan ignored him, preoccupied by another chamber. Casey approached, trailing his gaze. She glimpsed a figure through the glass: a white beard, gray uniform, a sheathed sword at his hip. Casey's eyes grew wide, recognizing the outfit.

Donovan huffed. "This one's a Confederate."

Casey shivered. The cold, whether real or imaginary, had returned. As her eyes darted from one chamber to the next, the realization of what they were seeing created a sensation akin to ice water being dumped over her

head, washing through her skull and down her verte-
brae. On the left was a man in a dapper 1950s pinstriped
suit and fedora hat. On the right was a woman in a 1920s
swinging dress with pearls. Within the pressurized
chambers, clothing, hair, and jewels remained in place,
as if the people were insects pinned under glass. Casey
didn't stop, continuing down the line. Each figure was
attired in clothes and hairstyles different from the one
before. It didn't take a historian to figure out that none
of them wore a simple pair of jeans, T-shirt, or anything
like modern 1980s clothing.

"I don't get it," Casey said, more to herself than the
others. "How could so many people go missing with no
one noticing?"

"Maybe someone did notice," Earl said. "Ya know,
Roswell, men in black, all that shit."

"I'm surrounded by morons," Donovan grumbled to
himself.

They kept walking without further comment, the silence broken only by their footfalls against the catwalk's
metal frame. When Casey turned to the fifth and sixth
chambers, her peripheral vision caught her companions
staring fixedly, not at the chambers but at her.

Bill moved closer to Donovan again. Casey noticed
all three men glancing down at her chest, exchanging
sideways glances. She peered down at her unzipped coat
and tight T-shirt.

Stop staring at my tits, guys, she thought. "Problem?"
she asked.

Earl pointed to her Purple Rain T-shirt. "When'd
you get that?"

"I don't know," she stammered. "A few months ago."

Donovan approached. "When, *exactly?*"

Casey shrank from their hardened expressions.

"What *year?*" Earl asked.

"Eighty-five."

The men reacted with deflated groans and sagging

shoulders. Casey craned her neck to make eye contact with Earl. "You?"

He rubbed his sweaty forehead. "Ninety-five."

"Two thousand and five," Donovan said before anyone asked.

When Bill didn't speak up, the others turned, waiting. He shrugged. "Sixty-two."

After a stunned silence, Donovan broke in with a laugh. *He's losing it,* Casey thought.

Donovan looked Bill up and down in his disheveled button-down and jeans. "You don't look like a hippie."

Bill turned blankly from Donovan to the others. "What's a hippie?"

Donovan burst into laughter. Earl knelt, cradling his bald head. "Oh Jesus, Jesus, Jesus."

"Hey, all things considered, he *could* be here," Donovan said. Casey assumed his snide quips were meant to hide his growing anxiety. It wasn't working. Swooning, she thought of Arthur. If it was 2005, would he still be wondering what had happened to her? What if it was the far future, and he was long dead? She clutched her stomach, bile rising to her throat.

"We need to find a way out!" Donovan's cheeks reddened, and his eyes bulged so large, Casey thought they might pop out of his skull. Without a backwards glance, he raced down the catwalk.

"Wait!" Earl shouted. His booming voice snapped Donovan out of his panic attack, at least momentarily. He turned. Earl gestured at the countless chambers running above and below along the curved walls. "What about these guys? There's gotta be *thousands*. I mean, we can't just leave 'em here!"

"Watch me." Donovan moved on again, Bill trudging behind.

Casey's eyes bounced about the vast structure, taking in the enormity of what Earl had suggested. Her head sagged from the weight of it. "He's right, Earl. We can't help them."

"You wanna leave 'em too?" Earl recoiled, avoiding her gaze.

Her cheeks reddened, and her mouth turned to cotton. "We don't have the first idea how to open these chambers," she said, her voice breaking as she spoke, "or what might happen if we did."

"Doesn't mean it ain't worth tryin'," Earl responded. "What if that was you in there?"

"It was."

"But you got out."

"None of us are *out*," she reminded him. "Not by a long shot."

He didn't respond. She put her hand on his thick bicep and felt it flinch at her touch. "If—*when*—we get out of here, we'll return with help."

"And if we never get out?"

"Then better to let them sleep." Her voice flattened, as if putting a final stamp on the conversation. She pulled his arm, as hard and unmovable as granite. Their eyes locked in a silent contest of wills. Finally, he relented, letting her pull him along the catwalk.

At the far end, they found another series of tunnels. When Donovan chose the one on the left, no one protested. Stepping into the darkened exit, Casey and Earl took a last look at the tens of thousands of people they were leaving behind. *We'll come back for you*, she promised inwardly.

A slithering rasp in the back of her mind taunted her in response: *No you won't.*

Legs weakening beneath her, Casey recognized the voice. It was her dead father.

14

After spending a good long while staring at Earl's back as they trailed distantly behind Donovan and Bill, Casey cleared her throat loudly, hoping to grab Earl's attention. Either he didn't hear, or he was ignoring her. She assumed the latter.

Ahead, Casey noticed Bill leaning close to Donovan, whispering. Occasionally, Bill would glance back, as if checking their distance, then continue talking. When Donovan similarly turned, she knew they were talking about her. Or Earl. Or both. Either way, she doubted it was good. Donovan hardly exuded trust, and Bill's allegiances seemed clearly drawn as well. The group was fractured into two teams of two, and now half of her team wasn't even willing to look at her. Casey knew she needed to change this dynamic. Her life might depend on it at some point. She sidled up to Earl.

"You think I was wrong to leave those people back there?"

Earl let the question hang for a moment before

answering. "Probably not," he said, finally turning to her. "But that don't make it any easier."

Casey cursed inwardly. Her conscience seemed to lack what he possessed in spades; namely, empathy. Her shoulders slumped. "How'd you get here?"

"Same as you, I'd imagine. Bright light, big ship."

"No, I mean where were you headed when it happened?"

"What's it matter?"

Casey shrugged. "Just curious."

"I was going to see my sister. She's having a baby soon. A little girl."

"That'll make you an uncle."

"Yeah, if we ever get out of here." Earl squinted, noting the distant whispers coming from Bill and Donovan at the end of the tunnel. "What are they on about, d'you think?"

"Whatever it is, I doubt it's good for us," she said. "I don't trust Donovan."

Earl laughed. "Shit, lady, I doubt Donovan's own mother trusts him."

They continued around another corner. Casey decided to wait before speaking again, hoping Earl might continue the conversation, which he did.

"How about you?" he asked. "Got family?"

"Just my fiancé." Her tone flattened. "I never knew my mom. She died when I was little."

"That's rough." Earl's step faltered, and he made eye contact. Squeezing her shoulder, he offered a comforting nod, then continued to trail the others. Earl didn't seem to want Donovan out of his sight. "What about your dad?"

Casey's eyes found the floor. She shrugged. "Died of cancer. A few years ago."

"I'm sorry."

Her throat turned to ice. "Don't be."

"That bad, huh?"

"Worse," Casey muttered, more to herself than Earl.

"Hey, guys!" Bill shouted. "Get over here!"

Thankful for the change in subject, Casey quickened her pace, catching up to the others who'd stopped at a curved corner. As the next corridor came into view, her jaw slackened. They stared down a rounded tunnel with interlocking mechanisms swirling across the ceiling and walls. Because the hall was inverted, they would have to walk across the turning pieces, which lay before them like a funhouse obstacle course. Or, Casey thought, they could turn back. Neither option seemed ideal.

Earl gasped in her ear, pointing toward the end of the tunnel. Following his gaze, Casey peered past the twisting mechanisms toward the gloomy, shadow-drenched far end. Four figures stood in relief against the moving gray walls. *Human* figures watched from the other side.

"We're not alone," Casey said, her throat pitched with excitement.

Her companions, however, didn't seem as enthusiastic. "Could be good for us," Donavan said. "Could be bad."

Bill nodded in agreement. Casey couldn't fathom their sudden caution. "Are you kidding? This is great!" The distant figures vanished around a corner. "Wait!" she shouted.

Bill grabbed her arm. "What Donovan means is, those people might help us or—"

"They might kill us. And rape you," Donovan finished.

"Jesus, man," Bill said, gulping. "That's not what I was gonna say *at all*. We just don't know their intentions," he added with a meek smile.

"They're trapped, like us," Earl said, agreeing with Casey. "It's worth seeing if we can help each other."

Donovan looked Earl over. "Who'd have pegged *you* for such a softy?"

Before they could continue bickering, Casey bolted down the spinning hall, eager to catch up with the other survivors. Earl ran after her. Bill and Donovan shared a reluctant sigh and then followed. But crossing the moving corridor was easier said than done.

The curved, moving ceiling at her feet reminded Casey of tumblers in a keyhole, rising and falling as they turned in perpetual motion. The hall's purpose was as alien and unknown as everything else she'd seen so far. The moving walkway proved treacherous to navigate. She struggled to know where to step. Her first attempt sent her sprawling. On her second try, Earl caught her before she fell again. Casey paused at the tunnel's entrance, trying to time her steps. When a clear path didn't reveal itself, she decided to take a leap of faith, stepping forward for a third time.

Then she saw the strangest thing so far in that nightmare labyrinth: *herself* crossing the tumblers in a series of duplicate figures, each one identical to her, and each one frozen in place at a different step along the way. The odd vision reminded her of a funhouse mirror with multiple reflections stretching on and on. Only these weren't reflections. Each copy of herself was struck in a different pose, taking a single, solitary step across the twisting tumblers. It seemed to her, for lack of a better word, like an instruction manual on how to cross the tunnel correctly.

Turning to the others, Casey noted their ashen expressions. "You see it too."

Earl nodded. "Yeah, there's, like, a hundred versions of myself crossing this damn thing."

"You see yourself?" Casey glanced back, only to find her own figure multiplied. No one else. "Not me?"

"I see myself too," Donovan said, his face pale and sweaty.

Casey searched the others' faces. "So, what do you think?"

When no one volunteered an answer, Earl huffed. "I guess we follow our own footsteps."

Rolling back and forth on the balls of her feet, Casey lunged forward, stepping into the first reflection, then became that figure, as if animating a frozen image. There was no feeling of physical contact with the apparition; it simply popped out of existence when she took its place. Another step, and she became the next image. And the next. And the next after that.

Her footfalls became more confident. It reminded her of playing hopscotch as a child. Only this time she was bounding across moving gears. Despite the strangeness of it all, Casey couldn't help feeling a fleeting thrill as she leapt from turning mechanism to turning mechanism. It was almost like ballet.

Behind her, the men followed suit. Earl and Donovan lacked grace, lumbering about, but they still made it without falling. Bill, on the other hand, seemed quicker and more agile than any of them. *Maybe because he's so short*, she thought. Then she rebuked herself for the nasty slight.

Suddenly, a series of voices echoed about them. Soft and eerie, it made the hairs on her neck stand erect. Almost at the tunnel's end, Casey stopped in midstride, focusing on the whispered noise. Noticing that none of the men objected, she assumed they heard it too.

A cacophony of murmured whispers swirled about them. Above the din, she heard the echo of children laughing, chanting. "Dipshit Donny! Dipshit, Donny!"

It wasn't until she heard Donovan shriek behind her that she realized the voices were directed at him. Before she could respond, another voice entered the fray: "How am I gonna raise this baby without any man in my life?"

"Shut up!" Earl shouted. "You ain't my sister!"

Another voice grew in the mix. Casey's back straightened and her fists clenched at the sound of it. "You really think you're smart enough to find a way out of here, Honey Bun?"

Her father had found her again. Whether real or imagined, the effect was the same; her skin crawled at the sound of it. No longer concerned with the frozen copies of herself, Casey jumped from one cog to another, leaping across the distance, then crashing at the tunnel's end, cascading along a smooth floor. Her muscles trembling, she lay there and watched as the men followed in quick succession, seemingly as eager to cross as she had been. Forcing herself to stand on shaking legs, Casey noted that the voices had receded, barely audible outside of the turning tumblers.

Having successfully crossed the moving tunnel, the men leaned against the flat gray walls, catching their breath. No one mentioned what they'd heard, though she imagined Earl wouldn't be forgetting *Dipshit Donny* anytime soon. Gulping oxygen, she realized her mirrored selves were now gone. It seemed like someone, or something, was still trying to help them. First the metal door that had saved them from a monster, and now this. She wished whoever it was would simply open a fucking door and let them out. For now though, Casey would take whatever help she could get.

"Holy shit!" Bill cried. "It was us!"

Casey and the others turned back the way they'd come, toward the spinning tunnel. At the far end, beyond the moving tumblers and twisting metal, stood four figures. It was themselves, only minutes prior.

We're chasing our own tails, Casey realized.

15

Texas, five years earlier

Behind shuttered eyelids, Major Reese pictured the grotesqueries of war in horrendous detail. Worse were the sounds that accompanied them, screams drowned beneath thunderous mortar fire. Dropping a whiskey bottle's remnants to the floor of his Ford pickup, he lurched outside, spilling onto the gravel. Still in his uniform, shirt untucked, he wobbled off a dirt embankment onto freshly paved concrete. Someone had spent time and resources to repave a road in the middle of nowhere. Reese groaned. *My tax dollars at work. Christ Almighty.*

His legs wobbled beneath him as he struggled to find the road's double yellow line. Overhead, the moonlight offered little help, half covered in clouds. Stopping in the center, he fixed his gaze down the road. Waiting. It wasn't the most thought-out plan, but better for it to look like an accident than a suicide. He needed the screams to stop, and this seemed the ideal place. Headlights appeared over the horizon, tall and bright. A semi-truck. *That'll do.*

Planting himself firmly in place, he watched the truck grow closer. Considering the vast emptiness surrounding him, with no city lights to give away his position, he figured the driver wouldn't see him until it was too late. The bigger the truck, the longer it would take to stop. The headlight beams grew closer. His phone buzzed in his pocket, the phone's vibration cranking up his leg, then moved to his groin. Shoving his hand into his pocket, fingers fumbling, he blindly hit "ignore." The headlights became blinding.

"Hello?" a feminine voice said from Reese's pant leg. He realized he'd touched the wrong button, hitting "answer" by mistake, Reese couldn't help but chuckle at the ridiculousness of his predicament. His laughter broke the spell. Reese stepped off the pavement, watching the truck whiz by, its blaring horn echoing in its wake. As the truck's taillights vanished, Reese wondered how many more times he'd do something stupid like this before the moment came when he *didn't* step away.

"Major Reese, can you hear me?" The insistent woman calling from his pant leg wasn't going away. Pulling the phone out, the voice became clearer, and he recognized it at once: Staff Sergeant Suzie Chatsworth. They'd spent the last couple of years flirting before a brief fling over Christmas. After that, neither had spoken more than five words to each other; it seemed they both agreed it had been a mistake. Yet now, three months later, she was ringing him up in the middle of the night. Pushing away his drunken stupor, Reese answered. "Hey, Suzie, what's up?"

After a drawn, dull silence, she replied. "I'm pregnant."

That was the last time Reese had considered ending his life.

The first rays of a newborn sun blazed over Black-wood, but it didn't seem any warmer. If anything, Reese thought, the temperature had dropped. Walking along the street in Blackwood, with its white picket fences and pastel-colored homes, he couldn't help considering what might have been if he and Suzie had loved each other. Instead, the best he could offer was a second bedroom in his apartment for his daughter, Noelle, to sleep over on the weekends.

The legal system called it "joint custody." He called it "part-time parenting."

Scanning the seemingly empty homes, he wondered where Noelle was at that moment. Probably getting ready for preschool, he decided. Flanked by Pidgeon and Salvatore as he made his way across town, Pidgeon's incessant cough pulled Reese out of his daydream.

He shot the sergeant a sideways glance. "You alright?"

"No, Major," Pidgeon said with a snicker. "I'm freezing my fucking ass off."

"Aw, shucks," Reese replied, forcing a smile. He was the leader, and that meant he had a role to play, even with an empty town, the birds gone, and a knot the size of a boulder weighing in his stomach. "We'll draw you a hot bath and a cup of cocoa once we get back."

Pidgeon coughed again, hoarse, wheezing. "Can I have marshmallows in it?"

Salvatore joined in. "As many as you want, big boy."

Reese and his team searched the stores first. Most were unlocked, and all were vacant. They headed north of Main Street to the yellow, white, and blue houses sprinkled up the mountain and surrounding the town. They went through each one from top to bottom, calling for anyone who might hear. Dogs barked, and cats meowed, but no voices greeted them. Dishes cluttered tables with half-eaten food. Cups of coffee sat cold. Televisions ran news and sitcoms. In some houses, faucets overflowed from sinks onto tiled or wood floors. While roaming the first few houses, Reese felt he was violating someone's privacy, like a voyeur or something, but by the time he'd strolled through the seventh or eighth home, past charming decorations, glancing at family photos and various-sized Christian crosses, finding food burning on the stove or homework half completed, Reese felt like he knew these people. He knew a girl named Susie was expecting her sixteenth birthday next week, and a widow named Marge was banging her neighbor, Joseph. And most everyone was behind on their tab at the local market. The more he knew about these people, the louder his inner voice screamed. *Where the hell is everyone?*

He met up with Salvatore at a street corner and looked around. "Pidgeon?"

She pointed to a house at the end of the block. "He's checking the green one. I'm sure he'll be out—"

She stopped as a red flare burst over the town. It was Team Two. *They've found something.* Reese started down the street. "Wait here for Pidgeon and then meet up with us."

He heard her say something behind him, but he was already rushing headlong down the slope, as fast as his combat boots would carry him.

Reese's chest burned, and his legs were numb by the time he found the other team outside a white house with yellow trim and matching fence. Two men lingered at the front door, their faces sullen. One of them wiped away tears. Whatever they had to say, it wasn't good.

"Where's the rest of your team?" Reese asked.

"Upstairs, on the left," the man who'd been crying replied.

Reese stepped in, confronting a horror show: furniture tossed about, blood-splattered walls, and a crooked body spread-eagle on the floor. It was a man in his mid-thirties. His chest was a crimson explosion. Shotgun blast, Reese decided. However, as bad as the scene was, it wasn't enough to bring a seasoned soldier to tears. Something else was in the house. Something worse.

He climbed the staircase, finding the rest of his men

outside a closed bedroom door. They seemed as shaken as the two out front. "Report."

One man cleared his throat and gestured to the door behind him. "Two kids inside, sir."

"I see," Reese said, nodding. "Dead?"

"No, sir."

"Then what the hell's the matter?"

"They, uh, um, they're in shock, sir," one of them said.

"The older one, the boy, he has a gun, sir," the other soldier added. "He said he had to . . . to . . ." His voice died in his throat. Reese peered over the railing at the bloody body below and understood. The boy had killed his own father.

Reese tilted his head toward the front. "Wait outside." He took a breath and held it, trying not to think about Noelle. *Five . . . four . . . three . . . two . . .* He exhaled, opened the door—and found himself at the business end of a double-barrel shotgun.

It was a compact pink room with dolls and plush animals strewn about. Under the curtained window, a young girl, maybe five or six, was sobbing hysterically. In front of her, a boy—her brother, Reese presumed—held the shotgun with fidgeting fingers. He looked to be about thirteen, his face wet with tears and his shoes caked in blood. Reese slowly raised his arms and knelt to their level. "My name is John. Can you tell me yours?"

"This is all your fault!" the boy shouted, his finger dancing along the trigger.

"Whoa, what is?" Reese asked. "What happened here?"

"He took them. All of them. Because of you. Because of—"

Reese lunged, snatching the shotgun. It went off with a *BOOM*. Buckshot hit the low ceiling, and plaster rained down. The boy was frantic, punching and kicking. Reese knocked him back with the butt of the shotgun. The madness in his eyes subsided, and his breathing calmed to a rasp.

"Let's try it again. I'm John." Reese tucked the shotgun behind him.

The boy caught his breath, wiped his eyes. "Jacob."

"Where's your mom, Jacob? Your friends? Can you tell me where they went?"

"He took them. All of them." Jacob's tone flattened. "Then he sent Dad to get us. Dad . . . Dad . . . he tried to take my sister . . . I . . . I . . ."

Jacob broke into tears. Reese hugged him. He wanted to tell the boy everything would be alright, but he knew better. "This man you mentioned, who is he?"

"Don't know," Jacob said, wiping his eyes. "Never saw him before."

"Can you tell me what happened?"

Jacob averted his eyes. "You wouldn't believe me."

Reese reached back and grabbed the shotgun. He placed it on the boy's lap.

"Try me."

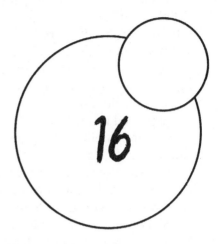

16

The day before

School was long over, and night seemed just out of arm's reach when Jacob noticed a stranger come down the mountain. Halfway across Judith Hill's property, on the eastern edge of town, Jacob rode his fat bike—a mountain bike outfitted with oversized tires to allow for riding on soft, unstable terrain—smashing down powdered embankments like a two-wheeled bulldozer, when a distant sprinkle of color dashed across the white terrain. Bearded, medium height, with a disheveled blue button-down shirt and snow-caked jeans, the man waded through the snow below the tree line. Clutching his handbrakes, Jacob stopped and watched, his eyes narrow slits. "Hey, man, you alright?"

Weird, spiderwebbed red markings lined the man's face as he reeled, coughing. Keeping a wide berth, Jacob shouted again. "You need help?"

The man waved to him from the open field before falling out of view in a powdered puff.

Jacob spun his bike around, pedaling as fast as his

legs would take him. Racing north on Main Street, Jacob had planned to head straight to Doctor Denning's clinic until he saw Sheriff Schreiber's police car parked outside Nancy's Diner. He got off his bike in such a hurry he forgot to flip the kickstand down. The bike tumbled, slicing his shin as he made his way to the front door. Jacob winced, but he didn't slow down, hobbling to the door with a pained grimace.

Sheriff Schreiber sat at the counter, whispering into Nancy's ear. She giggled and covered her mouth. When Jacob rushed over, Nancy's cheeks flushed, and Sheriff Schreiber gave him a glare straight out of a Clint Eastwood movie. "Slow down, son."

Wheezing from the ride, Jacob told the sheriff about the stumbling man in one long, breathless explanation. As the words spilled out, Schreiber listened, stroked his neatly groomed mustache, huffed, and rolled his eyes for dramatic effect. Nancy listened too, her jaw hanging. When Jacob finished, Schreiber's eyes seemed to bore into Jacob's skull, like snakes looking for a hole to burrow in. Finally, the sheriff grabbed his hat and hitched himself out of his seat. It seemed to require a massive effort. "Alright, I'll check it out. You go on home."

"I can show you where he is," Jacob protested, not wanting to lose this first bit of juicy news that had occurred in months. He still needed the "who" and the "why" to complete his "when" and "where" story for the school paper. The way Jacob saw it, Ronan Farrow never left a story half-finished. After all, a good writer knew a solid lead when he found one. Jacob even had a headline: "Mystery Man Falls Down Mountain."

Schreiber wasn't hearing it. "No, no, boy. It's almost six. Run home. That's an order."

Sheriff Schreiber shot Nancy a sideways wink and a smile, then headed to the door. Crestfallen, Jacob trudged behind and climbed onto his bike. He noticed the scratch on his ankle. Blood soaked his pant leg. *Great. Mom's gonna kill me.*

He rode away as the sun fell and shadows grew.

Homes spread out from Main Street, none stretching farther than a couple of miles away, which made things awfully cozy for a town of over nine hundred. On the upside, it made getting around on a bike easy for a thirteen-year-old, even in the dead of winter. Jacob landed on his front porch in less than fifteen minutes, right about the time darkness had settled in for the night.

His family was halfway through dinner when he nonchalantly strolled in. He hoped none of them would notice how late it was. Hanging his coat on the hook, he kicked off his snow-covered boots and rolled up the bloodstained pant leg, concealing it as best as he could.

Upon entering the foyer, he turned toward the dining room and saw his family watching in stony silence. *Crap.* His parents glared from either end of the table. Between them, his sister, Samantha, giggled. "You're sooo late, Jacob!" she said in a singsong voice. "Sooooo laaaaate."

Jacob jumped into his chair and told them what had happened. Like a good reporter, he explained the who, what, where, when, and why. It was an epic tale, filled with lots of big words. When he finished though, his dad still grounded him for being late.

Later that night, Jacob lay in his room thinking about the injured man. He started putting together descriptive sentences in his head, planning the story for the following day's school paper. His English teacher, Mr. Davis, was also the paper's editor, and he was a stickler for details. Details, details, details. Unfortunately, Jacob didn't feel like he had enough.

I bet the injured man's still at the clinic, he thought, then shoved the growing idea aside. It was late, and he couldn't just sneak—

An eerie, high-pitched shriek erupted outside. Jacob felt the hairs on his scalp prickle. His mind raced as he went to the window, drew it open, and leaned into the evening's frost. *Was that a scream? Naw, probably a cat. But who lets their cat out at night in the middle of*

February? He studied the dark for any disturbance but only found his neighbors' serene houses on either side.

Another hour of lying in his room, and the noises persisted: distant, strangled moans. Something was definitely going on outside. For a thirteen-year-old boy constantly on the lookout for a story for his school newspaper, the night held the potential for big, big news. Amidst the flushing in his cheeks and the sweat in his palms, one singular thought rose to the top: *What if the eerie noises and the man on the mountain are connected?*

That was it. He jumped out of bed, threw on two sweatshirts plus tennis shoes (sadly, his coat and boots were downstairs). The bedside clock showed 9:45. Doctor Denning's clinic would be open until 10:00. Quietly, he slipped out the window and climbed onto a tree. He'd done it a couple dozen times but only in summer, and now the branches were covered in frost. He needed to be careful. *Stealthy.* If his parents caught him sneaking out in the middle of the night, he would face a fate worse than death.

Sticking close to the trunk, he slid down the tree and then ran to his bike. With a kick, he raced down the front yard, riding past the picket fence. Knuckles white over his handlebars, his breath rose to a series of quickened gasps. Jacob raced under streetlamps, through his quiet, nothing-much-ever-happens-here neighborhood, to the center of town. The noises, he noted, had stopped.

Jacob continued toward Main Street. Worried someone might see him and call his parents, he went around behind the buildings, riding away from the sparse streetlamps.

About halfway to the clinic, he glanced down the street and realized no one was walking or driving. The town seemed deserted, and it wasn't even ten o'clock. Curious, he rode the last leg of his trip straight down Main Street. The clinic was on the one and only side street, Sutton, so he figured if anyone looked out, he'd just swing back behind the buildings and cut over, if need be. But that was unnecessary. No one was out. Not a single adult was in sight. Not even (thankfully) Sheriff Schreiber.

His cell phone told him he'd arrived at the clinic at three minutes to ten. It had only been a few hours since he'd found the injured man, so he hoped the man might still be inside. A light was on over the door with an "Open" sign dangling in the window. Jacob threw down his bike and then entered.

No one was in the reception area. All the lights were on, but the place looked empty, as if they had already called it a night.

"Hello?"

No one answered. Now was the moment of truth. If he hopped over the desk, he'd be discovered and his parents summarily summoned, at which point, he assumed, life as he knew it would come to a crashing halt. With a sizable gulp, he hopped the desk and made his way down the hall, calling out for Doctor Denning.

No turning back now . . .

Halfway down the hall, his nostrils flared at a strange scent. His feet slowed. It wasn't the normal stench of antiseptic that usually lingered in medical facilities. It smelled like . . . he couldn't place it. Whatever it was, it reeked.

He called for the doctor again, a slight tremble filling his voice. Stepping into the back room, his throat tightened, and his voice died. He suddenly wished he'd stayed out front. Or better yet, at home. Where he belonged. He wished he was anywhere on Earth but there.

The observation room, along with the reclining chair and medical supplies, were splattered with blood. More blood than he'd ever seen.

Stunned, he took a step back and slipped in the crimson mess, falling. It was on his shoes and buttocks. Then he realized the shit was on his hands. He scampered backwards on his elbows before clawing his way back upright. His roast beef and mashed potato dinner rose in his throat, threatening to come out. He reeled, ready to puke, only to dry heave instead. Mouth gaping, he tried to call out, but words wouldn't come. And the blood was still there, right in front of him. It covered the walls in splotches that dripped to the tiled floor. The white walls stressed the horrors worse than a colored wall might. There was nothing to dull the redness.

Jacob bolted for the door.

17

Once safely outside, Jacob spun about, looking for help, but the town was empty and still. He grabbed his phone with dripping fingers. Blood blotched the screen as he tried to swipe it. The screen didn't change. His fingers were too wet. He wiped the blood against his blue jeans, creating purple streaks. He tried the phone again. Still too wet. His breathing was going into rapid-fire mode now. He rubbed his hands over his sweatshirt, fighting to get the wetness off his palms. Holding his breath, he swiped the phone one more time. It clicked open. Dialing his father's number, he put the phone to his face. The screen dripped blood into his ear, but the phone didn't ring. He checked his signal—no bars. *Oh, shit fucking Christ. You gotta be fucking kidding me.*

Climbing onto his bike, fingers trembling over the handlebars, he tilted from side to side until he planted his feet on the ground to steady himself. A distant shriek danced on the breeze and almost sent him tumbling. Tears welled in his eyes. Forcing himself to focus on the street ahead, Jacob pushed his pedals forward. It was six-ty yards to the sheriff's station; it felt like sixty miles.

Arriving at the station, he flung double doors open. "Sheriff! Sheriff Schreiber!" No reply. The police station was as barren as the town. Behind the counter a police radio squawked to life. Racing over, elation building in his chest like a roaring fire, Jacob snatched the mic. "Hello? Sheriff? Can anyone hear me? This is Jacob Anderson."

A burst of static replied, setting his teeth on edge. Then something grabbed his shoulder. Jacob's back went rigid, and his legs refused to move. He dropped the mic, leaving it to dangle off the desk. His eyes twisted in their sockets, landing on the hand at his shoulder, covered in long red veins. Without thinking, Jacob jumped forward and away. The clutching hand tore his sweatshirt with a loud *rip*.

The figure lumbering toward him was Sheriff Schreiber. But then again, it wasn't. The thing inside the sheriff's uniform didn't stand the way a man did. It was slumped, and its legs turned inwards as if he—or it—had never walked before. It shambled forward like a marionette.

Jacob backed away until he bumped into a water cooler beside the reception desk. The inhuman thing gurgled, opening its mouth as a red mist poured out. From behind its eyes, red pinpricks of light shone through the irises. The effect was like a jack o' lantern, a candle glowing through a lifeless husk.

The mist weaved through the air toward Jacob's mouth and nostrils. He rolled around the water cooler and stumbled to the ground. The snaking mist grew closer, surrounding him, about to engulf his legs, his arms, and finally his face. His adolescent mind couldn't fully take in all that was happening, but he knew enough to realize red mist = bad. Really, really bad.

Gathering all his pounding adrenaline into a single burst, Jacob kicked the water cooler, knocking it over with a watery splash. The mist dispersed, spreading like bat wings. The thing that used to be the sheriff paused momentarily. Those precious few seconds were all Jacob needed to force himself up, slipping and sliding and running for the exit.

Outside, he jumped on his bike, pedaling harder and faster than he ever had in his life.

His flight didn't last long before he skidded to a halt. At the southern tip of Main Street, a dozen silhouettes marched along the sidewalk. A few broke off, silently entering houses. Even from a distance, Jacob heard screams echo from the homes. Turning his bike to the snow-covered embankment, he rode up the hill, hard and fast.

When he arrived back home, he burst into the living room, screaming. His parents sprang off the couch as if hit with an electrical current. His dad asked why he wasn't in his room. His mom asked what had happened to his clothes, which were covered in blackish-red stains. Jacob's words spilled out in a tear-filled gush. He trembled as he spoke. His mother hugged him while his father glared. He wasn't listening, more focused on the fact that his boy had snuck out.

Jacob's pleas became desperate. He couldn't understand why they weren't *moving*. Noting the pathetic look in his mother's eyes and the hard stare in his father's, he realized they didn't believe him.

With a sharp tone, his dad ordered Jacob upstairs while his mom peeked outside.

"No!" Jacob shouted, gesticulating wildly.

"That is *enough*," his dad snapped, grabbing Jacob and hauling him upstairs. He tossed him onto his bed. "I've had it with this stupid news reporter thing! It's eleven o'clock!"

"Dad—"

"I don't want to hear it!" he said, slamming the door.

Jacob paced in his room, deciding his next step. He flung open his window. Through darkened tree branches, he saw distant figures approaching. The crowd had grown to thirty or forty people. He couldn't make out their faces, but from the way they shambled along in the street, he already knew what they would look like.

In the front, standing erect and moving with a slight limp, the man from the mountain seemed to be guiding them down the street. Even from half a block away, Jacob could see that his eyes glowed differently than the rest. Brighter. The red pinpricks were more pronounced, filling his eyes with a crimson light. From his mouth and nose, red mist gushed in thick, billowing waves, surrounding the nightmare parade as he led them straight to Jacob's front door.

At the gate, the man stopped, tilting his head upwards. Jacob stepped back from the window, hiding in shadow, those red eyes seeming to bore into his skull. *Please don't see me . . . please don't see me . . .* The eyes turned away. Jacob ran out of his room. He heard the front door open and his mother gasp as he entered Samantha's room. She was sound asleep beneath pink blankets. Without a word, he covered her mouth. Samantha's eyes snapped open.

"Shhh . . ." he said. When she nodded her understanding, he led her out of her room.

As they entered the hall, screams erupted downstairs. It was their mother. Jacob yanked the cord to the attic door and swung it open.

"Mommy!" Samantha shouted.

Clamping his hand over her mouth again, Jacob picked her up, her legs kicking and flailing, and forced her up the stairs into the attic, even as Samantha tried to bite his fingers and scream again. Shoving her to the floor, he grabbed the rope and pulled the attic door shut. Right before the door swung closed, they heard their father scream. Samantha cried out. He put a hand over her mouth and wrapped his other arm around her, cradling her in the pitch darkness.

The house grew quiet. The kids held each other,

trembling. A crunching sound came from below. Then another. Feet climbed the wooden staircase. Jacob slowly released Samantha's mouth, nodding for her to stay silent. He lay on his belly, peeking through a sliver of space between the attic hatch and the wall. Below, his mother loomed in his bedroom doorway. She lingered a moment, scanning the room with her pinprick-red eyes. Then she went to Samantha's room. He could see the red veins crisscrossing her pale, drawn face. But it was how she shambled along, her shoulders twisted and her neck bent to one side, that made him burst into tears. His entire body trembled so fiercely that his knee thumped a railing.

The thing that used to be his mother stopped, peering up at the ceiling with fiery eyes. Jacob wrapped his fingers around his mouth so as not to gasp. He turned to his sister, curled beside him, and prayed.

After a gut-wrenching beat, his mother twitched and limped back downstairs. Jacob wanted to exhale, but he couldn't seem to untie the knots in his chest. He sat there for what seemed an eternity, holding Samantha. Neither said a word. Their breathing slowed, but the tears didn't. He tried to explain what he'd seen and what was happening, but she wasn't listening, instead crying for Mommy and Daddy over and over. Jacob couldn't blame her. He wanted to do the same, only he knew those things were no longer his parents.

After a while, the attic's cold turned freezing. Jacob decided they couldn't stay up there all night. He opened the attic door, quietly helping Samantha down the ladder. His ears pricked for even the softest footsteps, but the house was silent. He put Samantha in her room.

"Wait here," he said.

"I want the light on," she pleaded.

"No, they'll see," Jacob snapped, harsher than he'd meant too. "I'll only be two minutes," he added in a softer tone.

He shut her door and proceeded down the staircase.

His eyes bounced left to right, scanning for any twitching, darkened silhouettes that might be lingering in the living room or kitchen. The front door stood open, snowflakes weaving and bobbing into the foyer, but the house appeared to be empty. When his feet touched the floor, he knelt low, keeping his head away from the window in case anyone might still be outside.

Jacob crawled to the garage and opened the door. Studying the shadows, he searched for the closet. It was a blue metal cabinet with a lock on it. Jacob opened a coffee tin above the laundry machine and dug out a key. Fingers trembling, it took three attempts to get it into the lock. Finally, he snapped the release, and the lock flopped to the side. He swung the cabinet open, revealing his father's shotgun. Reaching for the top shelf, he grabbed a box of shells. It fell, spilling them about his feet. *Shit.* Opening the gun, he slipped two shells inside, one for each barrel. His head swam, and his heart thundered in his chest as he snapped the breech shut. He hoped he wouldn't need it, and, if he were honest with himself, he wasn't even sure he could use it. Still, a loaded gun made him feel safer than he had all night.

Jacob placed a handful of extra shells in his pocket and then headed out of the garage.

He was crawling back along the living room floor when he heard Samantha gasp upstairs. Jacob bolted for the staircase. Three steps up, he saw a man's figure shamble down the hall. Jacob climbed the rest of the way, leveling the gun. It lay heavy in his arms. The lumbering figure reached inside Samantha's doorway.

"No, Daddy!" Samantha screamed. "Please!"

Frozen in place, the figure's red-veined face turned. It was Jacob's dad, alright—or what was left of him. His right arm pulled Samantha into view from the bedroom as a red mist swirled about. Inches from her face. Jacob didn't hesitate; he knew what his father would want him to do.

He unloaded both barrels into his dad's chest. Blood exploded everywhere. His father's long fingers released Samantha before he tumbled over the railing to the first floor. Jacob grabbed his screaming sister, who was covered in gore. Helping her back into her room, he grabbed a blanket and wiped her off from head to toe. Finding a bottle of water on the bedside table, he dumped its contents over her head, the blood dribbled down her skin in a pink mess. He was terrified the blood might be infectious, worried she might turn into one of those things. Mechanically, he popped open the shotgun, pulled out the spent shells, and put two fresh ones in. He'd already decided that if he had to use one of them on his sister, the second would be for himself.

Jacob kept one eye on Samantha and his gun level with the closed door, ready for anyone who might break in. Thankfully, she didn't "turn."

The kids sat awake at the foot of her bed all night, but no one came.

The nightmare parade had moved on.

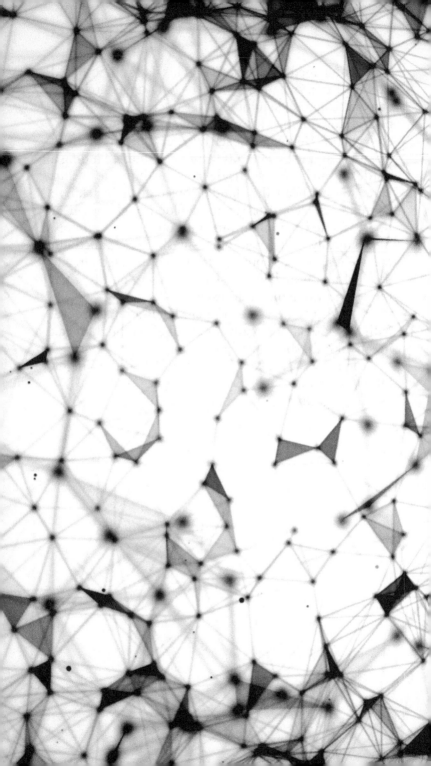

PART II

HYPERSPHERE

18

Plumes of acidic vapor blanketed narrow walls as the four figures waded through emerald mist. Casey's hair hung in icicles, and her breath spit out in frosted gasps. Light grew dimmer down there, or up there, or whichever direction they continued within the upended mess of winding hallways. A putrid reek surrounded them, assaulting Casey's nostrils and causing her eyes to water. Her stomach wound in knots, tighter and tighter with each step.

Approaching an inversely curved entrance, they passed a cluster of tree trunks, stretching from ceiling to floor. Earl paused, running his hand over frozen bark. "Looks like the same kinda trees I saw when I was taken."

"Oregon?" Casey asked.

He nodded. Donovan and Bill did the same.

"Then," Casey said, "we're not far from where we started."

"Unless we're stuck in, like, Roman times or something." Donovan chuckled uneasily.

"Let's find a way out, then worry about it," Casey said, a touch of annoyance layered in her voice. Donovan was grating on her nerves something fierce. Earl's too, she imagined. Bill, meanwhile, seemed to cling to Donovan like he was the next messiah. She couldn't imagine why. As they passed between thick trunks, she examined the trees more closely. Wood sprang up through the metal. "No damage."

"You mean besides the giant tree trunk *tearing through the walls*?" Donovan quipped.

Earl knelt beside her. "She's right," he said. "The metal's not torn or cut." He ran his fingers to the crease where the metal and wood melted together. "It's like this thing somehow grew around the trees."

"Fascinating," Donovan said, rolling his eyes.

On either side, multiple darkened archways opened along the walls. The men didn't seem eager to investigate, instead keeping to the hallway. Casey needed something more than socks to cover her feet, and that, she admitted to herself, meant finding another dead body to pillage. She ducked into the first doorway on her right.

"Whoa, where are you going?" Earl protested.

"I'll be right back," she said, stepping into the darkened entrance.

"That's what *every* lil' white girl says in *every* horror movie, right before the monster pops out and eats her—*every* single time." Earl lost sight of her. He glanced at the other two men. "Hold up."

Bill pulled Donovan's arm, stopping him. "You gotta be kidding," Donovan snapped as he watched Earl enter the archway.

Ahead, Casey followed a short, snaking path into a triangular room. Its slanted structure caused her to duck. *Weirder and weirder*, she thought. At her feet, lamps pulsed with incandescent light, revealing the room in shadowed chunks. With each step, a sense of familiarity tingled at the back of her mind. *I've seen this place before.* She tried to match a memory or image with the sense of familiarity, pushing deeper into her mind for a glimpse of the past that seemed a blank slate to her. A flash of memory hit her like a wave.

"Ah!" she screamed, reeling as phantom pain shot up her spine. Even though it was only a memory, the feeling was so intense that the aftershocks reverberated through her like an amputee aching from a missing limb. She'd been in that room before, and the last time she'd screamed. Casey shook the vision away, not wishing to probe further. *Some things are best left forgotten*, she decided.

"What's the matter?" Earl asked from behind her.

Casey wiped her face, which was wet from either frost or tears, and offered him a weak smile. "Nothing," she replied. Glad he was there but not wishing to discuss it further, Casey continued through the triangular room. Above, a table hung upside down, broken tubes tangled about it like dead snakes. Her eyes followed the serpentine cables down to a crumpled figure in the corner.

Well, she scolded herself inwardly, *you wanted a dead body to pillage. Merry fucking Christmas.*

An Asian man in his mid-thirties lay twisted in shattered repose. Gently, Earl turned him over. The body flopped with a wet *thud*. Lifeless eyes stared back at them. His face and neck were covered in thick red veins, spreading across like haphazard spiderwebs. Moving away from the horrific visage, Earl opened the man's shirt.

Casey choked back rising nausea. "What are you doing?"

Beneath the man's shirt, the veins continued across his chest and arms like scabbed lesions. "That thing that chased us had this same shit all over its body," he said.

Casey shrank back. "You think the—" She stopped herself from saying "aliens." "You think *someone* did this to him on purpose?"

"Fuck if I know," Earl said. "Maybe he caught a Martian cold."

She shook her head. "We're not affected."

Earl held her gaze. "You sure?"

She let that thought hang for a moment. Her eyes traveled to the dead man's tennis shoes. *Crap.* Her fingers hovered. *Stealing a dead man's infected sneakers. You've hit a new low, Case.*

Gritting her teeth, she pulled the shoes off, leveling them next to her sock feet to check their size. A little big but doable, she decided. *Look at you, shoe shopping,* Casey scolded herself.

As she was about to try the left sneaker on, she noted her feet were no longer chilled. Spitting out a frosty breath, she touched her foot curiously. *Too frozen or numb to feel?* She pinched her foot through the sock, and a slight pain shot up her ankle. *Not frozen . . .*

While Earl continued to examine the body, she tore off her socks, checking her feet. They were no longer cold to the touch. Instead, they felt warm, as if she'd just crawled out of bed. *Impossible.*

Casey turned her feet over, checking the soles. Her eyes rounded into saucers, and her chest clenched. She couldn't believe what she saw. The soles of her feet were ashen gray. She tried rubbing it off, but the layer was thick and callused. *Gray skin.*

Her mind swirled, and her heart raced. *Is this hard, gray, callused flesh the first sign before . . . before becoming like this poor bastard? Like that thing in the hallway?* She pictured red veins curling and moving under her skin, imagining the way her eyes might turn to pinpricks of red light—

No!

She swayed, covering her face with trembling fingers. Earl was talking about something, but the heartbeat pounding in her ears drowned him out. When she didn't respond, Earl turned. Casey shoved her socks back on. *Out of sight, out of mind . . .*

I don't think it works like that, Case.

She slipped the dead man's shoes on as Earl snapped his fingers. "Hey, Earth to Casey."

Casey stretched her cheeks, spreading her lips into an awkward grin. "Probably not the best expression when stuck on a flying saucer."

"If that's what this is," Earl replied. His eyes bobbed and weaved around the triangular room. "I mean, if we're in a spaceship, where are all the little green guys?"

It was a fair point, she conceded. But at the moment, a single thought was racing through her mind: *I'm infected.* The pounding, which began in her chest, moved to her temples, growing louder. With a shudder, she turned her back on the vein-covered body, facing Earl. "Get me away from here."

19

Rejoining Bill and Donovan, Casey and Earl passed inverted trees and continued down the cavernous chamber without a word. Eventually, they reached an open entrance on the far side. A glowing, reddish light pulsed from within. Donovan led without hesitation, but something deep inside Casey warned her not to go in there, to shout for the others to *stop—turn back!* Only, turn back to where? The creature was still behind them, she assumed, somewhere. Casey figured it was only a matter of time until it found another route through the maze to get to them . . . eat them . . . crunch them . . . rip and tear and—

A sudden vision of herself with gnarled teeth and razors for fingers made her knees buckle. She imagined her eyes burning with pinprick red lights. Casey reeled, vomiting on the floor.

"Jesus!" Donovan winced.

Earl and Bill helped her up. Casey wiped chunks of

puke from her mouth. "I'm alright," she said, nudging them aside. Her cheeks flushed.

Earl shot her a wink. "I'm one more dead body away from doing the same damn thing."

"I told you not to go in there," Donovan said, reminding Earl with a pointed finger.

Earl scowled at him. "Was I talking to you?"

Donovan turned away, ignoring him. "Let's keep moving."

Casey waved Earl's arms aside. "Thanks. I'm fine."

Images of red veins crawling up her neck still swirled behind her eyes. She shook her head, pushing the thoughts away with a violent jerk.

One foot in front of the other, she told herself. *One gray-skinned foot . . .*

She followed them through the entrance, bracing herself for whatever new nightmare awaited. Except what lay beyond was not another lurking horror. It was, instead, comforting. A light embraced her with a warm glow, melting away her fears as quickly as it did the shivering frost from her hands and face. She gasped, letting the warm air fill her lungs. The awful visions in the back of her mind were swept aside like cobwebs from an attic. With bright illumination, the architecture came more clearly into view. They were standing at the tip of a dome, looking up at the inverted floor far above. On the walls, enormous tubes slithered parallel along the dome, converging toward something in the distance. Casey wiped water droplets from her eyes as she peered beyond the men's shoulders.

She nudged past Earl and Donovan, raising her hand to block the blinding light, which pulsed brighter the closer she stepped. In the center of the dome, a red spherical shape hung, semi-transparent (as if simultaneously there and yet not there), twisting and turning over a tree trunk that seemed to merge with it. The tree stretched from floor to ceiling, as the others had, though this one seemed significantly larger. Casey stared in awe, wondering how the sphere could rotate with a thick tree in its center. *It's like a stabbed heart that's still beating,* she thought. The sphere was over a hundred yards wide and seemed to have a gridded surface, with multiple spheres within; a sphere within a sphere, twisting and turning so that it first appeared to be a sphere, then a different shape altogether, depending on the angle of its ever-changing axis. Despite the enormity and strangeness of the spinning object, something about it was familiar. Somehow, she knew she'd seen it before. But unlike the sensations she'd felt in the triangular room, this place held no horrors or ghostly pain. No, she decided, wherever or whenever she'd seen it, it wasn't in there. It was somewhere else. Somewhere she'd felt loved and safe.

Bill cleared his throat. "What is this place, you think?"

Earl placed his hand against one of the large tubes lining the dome, tilting his ear to the wall.

Donovan shot him a cocked eyebrow. "What?"

"It's humming. Something's running through these pipes," Earl said, closing his eyes and trying to hear the sound more clearly. "Energy or electricity or . . . I don't know, something."

Donovan huffed. "So?"

Earl pointed at the sphere. "Could be the motor."

Curious, Donovan leaned over and put his ear to the tubes. As if feeling ridiculous, he stood and shook his head. Earl's gaze tracked along the inverted dome, following the tubes down toward the sphere. "I know an engine when I see one."

"Right." Donovan snorted. "And I suppose that's the carburetor."

"It's a hypersphere," Casey said, matter-of-factly. The men spun, jaws slackened and eyes wide, as if they'd forgotten she was there. A familiar voice—Arthur's—had whispered the answer to her. A memory from one of his late-night study sessions, she assumed. His whispering continued, and she repeated to the men what he said, word for word. "It's a three-dimensional representation of a four-dimensional sphere."

Their expressions grew ridiculous as they turned to one another, astonished. *Yeah, boys, I know shit too,* Casey thought dryly. After none of the men replied, she smiled and shrugged. "Seriously, guys, it's, like, geometry 101."

Bill shook his head. "No, it's not."

"I think I've heard of it," Earl said, nodding, though he looked as confused as the others.

"What do you mean by 'four-dimensional?'" Donovan asked.

Before Casey could answer, Earl cut her off. "Like, we're in a three-dimensional world, right? But this sphere thing is from the *next* dimension. A *higher plane* of existence."

"Riiiight," Donovan said. "Or, it's just a big red ball. Either way, you know what it isn't?"

"An exit," Bill responded.

"Exactly," Donovan said with a grand sweep of his arms. "So, if we can keep the sci-fi mumbo jumbo to a minimum, I'd like to keep moving."

"Hold on, what if this thing's important?" Earl said.

And they're off, Casey thought. From there, the two men's voices bounced back and forth like tennis balls, growing louder and more ferocious in pitch. Bill, she noticed, stood by the side, content to watch. Casey blocked it all out, focused on the spinning red shape. The hypersphere. It didn't seem so strange and otherworldly to her now that it had a name—and because it reminded her of Arthur. For a moment she'd thought she'd heard his voice as crystal clear as any of the shouts behind her. The sensation had been so strong, she could still smell the lingering scent of his aftershave on the tip of her nose. A cologne that came in a bottle with a ship on it. Fighting back sudden tears, she stole a glance at the bickering idiots. *Where's my genius boyfriend when I need him?*

While the men argued, Casey moved toward the red sphere. Twisting and tumbling, it slowed with each step of her approach. *It knows I'm here,* she thought. Standing below the enormous hypersphere, drenched in its red light, her features turned crimson. Distantly, as if drowned under layers of water, she heard Donovan's shrill voice argue about how this thing was not an exit, but somewhere in the recesses of her mind, a tingle, like an itch she couldn't reach, said, *He's wrong, Casey.*

A way out of here, she thought as she imagined reaching into her skull and scratching the itch with ghostly fingernails.

When? the itch replied.

What do you mean? she asked. No answer bubbled up in her mind. The pulsing light seemed to pour through her eyes, into her skull. Again, she scratched the itch.

Now, a voice whispered.

The light grew brighter, a blinding red flame that seemed to engulf her. She wondered if the others saw it too, but she didn't turn away from Arthur's pulsing hypersphere and its presumed fourth-dimensional power. She reached up, touching it, her fingertips gliding along its slow-moving surface and then—

Her feet crunched virgin snow. A fresh breeze slapped her face, and blinding sunlight made her eyes water. Casey spun around, taking in her surroundings. It took a conscious effort to make herself breathe. Inhaling the crisp air, she choked back tears from the wonderful taste of it. The place was familiar. She noticed white-blue mountains peeking above pine trees. Casey was close to her cabin. *Home.*

In the distance, a figure raced forward. An old man, bulging with multiple layers of clothing. He looked ridiculous, and under any other circumstances, she might have laughed. Casey screamed for help. The old man stumbled with wide eyes, his lips flapping frantically, though she couldn't discern any sound.

Casey waved her arms, shouting. "Help us! We're

trapped in a ship—or something—near here. Please, can you get us some help?"

Suddenly, a firm grip tightened on her shoulder, yanking her from the forest. The red sphere's light flashed in her eyes. Crumbling to the ship's metal floor, Casey shrieked. "No!"

Earl turned her around. "Whoa, whoa, are you alright?"

"Why did you pull me back?"

Earl stepped away, joining the other men who flanked him on either side. Even Donovan seemed speechless for a moment.

"What?" Casey asked, searching their blank expressions.

"Y-you looked like a ghost," Bill stammered.

Earl nodded. "Yeah, we could see right through you."

Donovan's voice went flat. "They mean you were transparent."

Casey glanced at the sphere, which seemed to have sped up again, twisting and turning with its warm red glow. Her feet still tingling from the snow, Casey smiled, a big, warm Cheshire grin. She'd found her exit.

"Hey, boys, you wanna get out of here?"

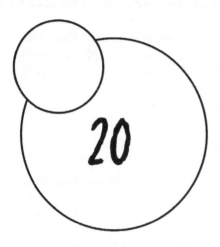

20

Arthur huffed and puffed his way up the tree line, not too far from the road in case he got lost. He followed the sun's western trajectory, which he was relatively sure would take him to the town's border. *Everything looks the same,* he thought, glancing at the giant trees and distant mountains. *Funny. I've aged, but this place hasn't. At least one of us is still what we used to be.*

Then an odd sensation rippled down his spine. Stumbling to a halt, the sensation disappeared as quickly as it had come. Arthur's vision blurred and then realigned, revealing an extraordinary shape floating ahead: a twisting sphere with a transparent, gridded surface and multiple spheres within spheres inside. *A hypersphere,* he thought. It was red and floating in midair before him, like an illusion or a magic trick. A female voice echoed in his mind, as if asking what a hypersphere was, and he replied aloud for all the forest to hear. "It's a three-dimensional representation of a four-dimensional sphere."

The female voice returned, no longer a whisper.

Thanks, babe. He'd know that voice anywhere. *Casey.* The image vanished, and the mountainside turned deathly quiet. Spinning, he glanced about. Nothing moved. No snapping twigs in the distance, no birds chirping, nor deer racing past. He was alone. *And,* he thought, *possibly losing my marbles.*

Feeling pressure in his bladder, Arthur stopped to unzip his pants. If someone were to ask him what the three worst things were about being over sixty, he'd probably put the immediate necessity to piss at every inconvenient moment at the top of the list. *That,* he thought with a snicker, *and kids think you're a crazy invalid.*

Arthur was peeing on a thick slab of fallen tree, trying to make designs in the snow, when something blinked past him. All too quickly, Arthur zipped his fly, staining his pants with urine. Moving around the trunk of a grand tree, he saw a female figure in the woods. Her hair was blond, and her face—*Holy Mother of God.*

"Casey!"

He bolted at the sight of her, running faster than he had in years, afraid to blink or turn away, as if this apparition might vanish like the last one. His feet pounded through the fresh snow, white puffs cascading behind him in a flurry. It was her. He knew it. Those green eyes and that milky white skin had haunted his dreams for over forty years. Every detail precisely as he remembered. Moving with all the speed his weak knees would allow, he drew closer. Yet with each step, she seemed to grow more and more transparent. Brush and foliage swayed clearly behind her, turning greener and lusher the more she faded from view. Her mouth moved, but no sound escaped. With flailing arms, he reached for her as she—

Vanished.

She was gone, again. *No. No. No!* Panting, he crumpled in a puff of snow. "Casey!"

He turned left and right, hoping she might reappear. Long minutes crawled. His wrinkled eyes narrowed, dancing across the surrounding forest. Nothing moved. Head slumped, he recalled Todd's words: *I guess I figured you had dementia . . .*

Dementia. Yes, that would explain everything. *I mean, let's face it—you're running around in the fucking freezing mountains looking for a flying saucer. So, sanity has already gone three sheets to the wind at this point.*

Bracing himself against a tree, he rose and continued through the foliage. His breathing had dropped to shallow gasps. As he walked, an old Robert Frost poem echoed in his mind, "miles to go before I sleep . . ."

I'm not insane. At least not to the point of having visions. Determination built with each step, and his breathing returned to normal. *Casey is out here, somewhere. And I'm going to find her.*

The sun was high by the time Arthur decided he'd only imagined Casey. If, and it was a big *if*, she were alive, she'd be an old fossil like himself by now, not the young bombshell he'd imagined. *Yep, at my age, you go all night without sleep, then cap it off with a morning hike through the Oregon mountains, you're bound to bump into the loony-bin truck at some point.*

Dementia, party of one, your table's ready.

It was right about the time that he was good and convinced it was just his aged mind playing tricks that he glimpsed something that slapped him back to reality—or *un-reality.* The shock of what he saw next didn't hit him as fast or as thunderously as seeing Casey, but what it lacked in familiarity it more than made up for in the creepy category.

Arthur's pace slowed, and he cocked his head to the side, trying to make sense of what he was witnessing. At first it looked like a series of statues lining the mountain ridge, interspersed among the trees. Standing twenty feet apart, the statues stretched as far as his eyes could see, rimming the forest in a single line, forming a barrier halfway up the western mountain. There had to be hundreds of them. Though they weren't statues.

Arthur stopped, and that old familiar un-reality he'd pushed aside in his mind snapped right back into frame. The figures were people. Silhouetted within the trees, he couldn't make out their faces or details, but he was close enough to notice a few of their chests moving in and out beneath T-shirts and sweaters. He opened his mouth to say something, but no words came. Their eyes gleamed in tree-cast shadow. Turning their heads in unison, they spun on him with a red glare. *Demon eyes*, he thought with a choked gasp. Fire erupted in his belly and shot up to his chest. He tried to back away silently, but each footstep on the wet slush seemed like a symphony of squishing noises. Two steps in and his coordination abandoned him. Arthur tumbled backwards, tripping on his own feet. He fell down the mountainside, banging his head and ribs along the way.

The stoic figures observed him without movement, as if an old man wasn't worth the effort. The entire town stood watch, waiting for someone—or something—else to arrive.

21

Reese secured his bulky, metallic hazmat helmet, sealing the armor with a loud *click*. A puff of air pressurized his suit and made his ears pop while holographic displays flickered to life. Reese had never seen anything like this armor before, and he couldn't help wondering where it'd come from or who'd designed it. When he asked the scientists who brought it, Reese was met with shifting gazes and stern silence. It seemed he wasn't supposed to ask too many questions.

On the visor's bottom right, a blinking light reminded him that systems were offline. The suit's internet wasn't the only thing offline though. Behind him the support team had made camp, constructing four tents surrounded by six transport vehicles, and none of their satellite dishes seemed to be working either. Neither did the radios or the phones. So far, there'd been no signals in or out.

The team's makeshift base sat at the northern edge of town. Reese scanned the vast mountains, searching for any sign of a mile-wide spaceship, but so far he'd seen nothing, not even with his visor's enhanced viewing mode. He also hadn't come across any sign of the nine hundred townspeople who seemed to have up and vanished. *Or turned into alien zombies*, he thought.

Studying his lean supplies and his even leaner team size, Reese grimaced. *Makes little sense. A six-man team, now down to five, plus a few support guys who carry PhDs instead of rifles. Must be somebody's idea of a joke.*

Reese strode through camp while doctors unloaded equipment, and the recon team prepared to move out. They were going to be heading up the mountain just after noon, six hours later than scheduled.

In the supply tent's corner, a young girl, Samantha, lay sleeping in a yellow hazmat suit. Her brother, Jacob, wore the same, sitting beside the cot, holding her hand. Behind the visor, the boy's eyes clocked soldiers and scientists with a detached gaze. Breathing too fast, his breath fogged the mask as Reese approached.

Jacob cocked his head. "Any chance you'd let me come with you?"

Reese knelt, watching the little girl sleep. Even through her mask, he could see streaks of dried tears on her cheeks. "Afraid not," Reese said, facing Jacob. The boy's shoulders sagged. "Besides, I need your help down here, at base camp."

"What for?"

Reese gestured toward a team of doctors in yellow suits. "Between you and me, I wouldn't trust these egg-heads to watch my dog, let alone protect your sister, or my camp."

Jacob hesitated. "Do you have kids?"

"A girl," Reese responded, surprised by the question. "She's four."

The boy's gaze drifted, as if he wanted to ask something else, but he stopped himself. Reese leveled his eyes at the boy, his throat tightening. "And if she'd been in your shoes, I'd have wanted her to do the same damn thing."

Jacob's eyes watered. "You'd want her to . . . shoot?"

"Parents die for their kids, not the other way around."

Jacob took that in, finally nodding. "What about Mom?"

Reese glanced through the tent's open doorway, toward the mountains. "We'll find her." He forced himself to smile, pulling Jacob up by his shoulder. "Alright, enough sitting around. Go help the docs bring equipment from the trucks."

Stealing a last look at his sister, Jacob ran over to the support trucks. Watching him go, Reese silently added, *I hope we find her.* The alternative tore at his stomach.

Entering the recon team's tent, Reese found Pidgeon and Salvatore suited up and checking their armor for air leaks. Then they moved to their weapons, loading automatic rifles. Each component checked and rechecked. The other three members of his unit were still fumbling with their new gear.

"Any chance these fancy suits come in extra-large, sir?" one of them joked.

Reese looked the soldier up and down. "Don't you mean extra-small?"

The men laughed. Reese moved to Salvatore and Pidgeon. "Status?"

"We're ready, Major," Salvatore said, turning to the western mountain. "Satellite images showed it to be somewhere north by northwest of here. Unfortunately . . ."

"Our dishes can't pinpoint a location," Reese finished. "Best guess will have to do."

"Maybe the satellites were wrong too," Pidgeon interjected

Reese turned, realizing he had heard little from his friend until then. "What do you mean?"

Pidgeon pointed to the eastern slopes, covered in

mist. "Most of that ridge is obscured. Could be enough to hide a ship."

An odd inflection in his friend's voice caught Reese's attention, but he assumed it must be the helmet's speaker. Reese eyed the eastern mountain. It was miles off from where their satellite indicated. Then again, so far all their equipment had been faulty at best and straight-up broken at worst.

"That's an awfully big detour if we're wrong," Salvatore added.

Pidgeon grumbled. It was an odd sound coming from a medic who Reese had never seen stressed, never mind raise his voice. Reese slapped his back. "Everything alright, Staff Sergeant?"

"Yes, sir," Pidgeon replied, though again, something in his voice seemed off. Even through the metal speakers, Reese could detect irritation. At least Pidgeon had stopped coughing. It wouldn't make the unit comfortable having a medic hocking up a lung when they needed him.

Reese turned from Pidgeon, gazing back at the clouded western summit. He was wondering if Pidgeon might be right about the ship's location when a roar of commotion broke across the camp. Grabbing gear and weapons, Reese led them toward the disturbance.

A familiar voice rang through the valley. "Major Reese! I'm looking for Major Reese!"

Arthur Stover burst through the tree line, stumbling into sight. Reese sighed inwardly. *How in the fuck did he get all the way up here?*

Wearing several layers of clothes, his face caked in blood, and his arms gesticulating wildly, Arthur looked like a madman come down from Mount High.

"Jesus fucking Christ, somebody clean him up, and get him in a hazmat suit," Reese said, storming away. He didn't have time for crazy. Any *more* crazy, he corrected.

Twenty minutes later, the recon team was all set to go. Reese dropped by the medical tent and saw Arthur sitting on a cot near the sleeping girl. The old man bolted up excitedly, his forehead bandaged beneath his hazmat armor. Checking the armor's seals, Reese guessed that the scientists had brought an extra suit for the medic who'd died back at the gas station. *Better pray you have better luck than he did, old man.*

"Come on out here, Arthur," Reese whispered, not wanting to wake Samantha.

Once they were clear of the tent, Reese stopped and turned to face him. "The doctors told me you had something to say. Make it quick. I'm on the clock."

"I'm coming with you," Arthur said matter-of-factly.

Reese chuckled. "Not likely."

"You need me," Arthur said.

"How's that?"

Arthur eyed the deserted town, then spun to face Reese. "Because I know where they are. All of them."

"OK, I'll bite," Reese said, humoring the old man. "Where?"

"Take me, and I'll show you."

Studying Arthur's eyes through the hazmat mask, Reese had to admit he didn't appear crazy or senile. In the distance behind Arthur, Reese glimpsed Jacob carrying supplies. His mind turning to the boy's lost mother, he huffed, a steady stream of mist covering his visor. "If you're lying, I swear to God I'll leave you up there. Without a suit."

Having won, Arthur remained silent. Reese stormed away. "We leave in five."

In actuality, it took another twenty minutes to pack up and leave. As they climbed the mountainside, the trees were alive, patches of green poking through the white of the previous day's snowfall, but nothing moved. Reese's eyes darted from side to side behind his visor, searching for movement. No birds chirped, no distant leaves crackled from unseen deer, not even wind whistled through the trees. The utter stillness gripped Reese's chest and made his head woozy. His heart pounded harder and faster with each slow step. Somewhere ahead they would find the missing people. *And then what?*

Reese didn't have an answer.

22

Arthur trailed the military team, struggling to keep pace. The incline was steep. While the armored suit wasn't as heavy as it was bulky, it still made the climb harder than he'd expected. His breathing dropped to shallow gulps as he kept moving. Still, after decades of doubt, unanswered questions, and innuendos, Arthur would let nothing stop him from finding his long-deserved answers. Certain Casey was somewhere in that forest, Arthur's excited gasps clouded his visor, blocking his vision. He wanted to wipe his face, but the helmet was airtight. His panting breaths echoed in his eardrums.

As they crested a ridge littered with black rocks, Reese threw up a hand signal. The other soldiers crouched, drawing their weapons. Arthur slunk beside the female lieutenant, peering over rocks. *There!* Hundreds of silent silhouettes loomed motionless among the trees, stretching across the summit. *A barrier*, Arthur thought. *And behind that barrier, everything I've ever wanted!*

Reese knelt, knee-deep in snow and foliage, scanning the human perimeter. He saw about fifty shapes dressed in nightgowns and sweatshirts and knew hundreds more were curved around the mountainside. Their eyes watched with red pinpricks of light. *Moment of truth.* He couldn't open fire on an entire town, and he doubted they would let him stroll past. He didn't have a lot of options. Hoping the armor would protect him, Reese began to walk toward the figures.

Salvatore bolted upright from behind a bush. "Sir, what are you doing?"

"Stay back here," Reese said, lowering his weapon. "Don't fire unless they attack you first."

"So, we're just supposed to stand back and watch?" she grumbled.

"Yes, Lieutenant." He kept walking, slow and steady. "Weapons down. Do not fire."

Arthur could feel the soldiers' unease. They watched with bated breath as Reese's booted feet crunched along the snow-packed incline. A chill curled along Arthur's spine. Cold numbness ached in his skull. The things—*people*, he reminded himself—with red veins and nightmarish light for eyes—glared. Their lips curled, baring their teeth. Among them, an old woman with pearls and a boy in pajamas. There was a man in a T-shirt and boxers and a nude woman in her thirties, her flesh blue from the cold. Motionless, Arthur noted how they seemed to await Reese's approach.

Within inches of breaking their barrier, just as he was about to pass through, the T-shirted man and the naked woman spun. Their mouths gaped, and red mist billowed from their lungs, encasing him. Reese kept walking, seemingly unaffected by the mist, and crossed the line. For a moment, Arthur's shoulders relaxed, and he wondered if perhaps the people wouldn't impede the major's progress after all.

Then a dozen figures from the line went rabid, lunging.

The townspeople shoved Reese down, ripping and tearing at his armor. Despite the ferociousness of their attack, the major never fired.

Arthur watched in horror as the group piled on top of Reese. More figures rushed into view, taking the others' place inside the barrier. Again, like statues, they perched, unmoving. Arthur's eyes scanned the barrier of people, searching for an opening.

One soldier raised his weapon, but Salvatore yanked it aside. "Hold."

"We have to help him!" the soldier shouted.

Arthur could practically see the wheels turning behind the young lieutenant's visor. She'd been given a direct order not to fire unless they were attacked, but if she didn't, Major Reese was as good as dead. Eyeing the cluster of forms ravaging Reese's prone body, Salvatore released the soldier's weapon and raised her own. In unison, the line of soldiers aimed at the townspeople, but before they could fire, the figures rushed forward in a blur, swarming the soldiers. Stray bullets flew high. Arthur ducked, groveling in the snow. Fervent, the human shapes emerged through a red cloud, clawing and punching, struggling to make a dent in the military unit's armor. In the close-quarter chaos, some soldiers fired wildly while others were reduced to using their rifles as clubs.

As he watched the assault, a voice whispered in the back of Arthur's mind, like an itch he couldn't reach. Feminine and distant, it buzzed in his head with drumming repetition. *Arthur. ARTHUR!* Casey's voice called to him; her tone frantic.

He *needed* to get past. Nothing else mattered.

As one of the soldiers crumpled under the maddened figures, his rifle tumbled into the snow, right in front of Arthur. He wanted to shrink away from the chaos, hoping to find another, safer, way around, but his gaze bore down on the fallen weapon while his body propelled him toward a grave decision. Seemingly beyond his control, his arms snatched the fallen rifle. His mind protesting, his finger pulled the weapon's trigger, firing blindly into the crowd. *No!* he screamed inwardly. *Stop!* Despite his best attempt to halt the attack, his legs rushed forward with renewed energy, as if someone else were controlling them. He couldn't stop himself from firing. Cursing and screaming, pleading for his body to relinquish the assault, Arthur bolted for the line, firing into the crowd, creating a path. He watched helplessly as his weapon killed an elderly man with a shot to the chest. Next, a woman spun like a bottle top. Fighting against his body's protest, thankfully, he missed more than he struck. His shoulder buffeted by the rifle's recoil, Arthur was unable to stop himself from pushing forward in a mad blaze. He heard a scream thundering in his eardrums and realized it was coming from him.

What the hell is happening to me?

Then, as suddenly as it had begun, Arthur regained control over his body. Instantly, he threw the weapon aside, gasping at the carnage he'd caused. Two seemingly dead, countless others injured. *All by my hand . . .*

Pausing, he leaned over the naked woman until a blur of featureless figures piled on top of him in a wave. A swarm of appendages coiled around his arms, neck, and chest in a frenzied, multi-tentacled embrace. His fingers groped between snow and rocks, trying to escape. He heard nails scratching and felt fists pounding his suit. Their weight pressed the wind out of him. His ribs ached, and his back was on fire. He crawled, pulling himself forward inch by inch. The townspeople tore his shoulder plate asunder. Feminine nails discovered soft flesh. Arthur screamed. Someone dragged him by his feet, across rocks. His visor cracked. Flailing, he placed a gloved hand over the breach while silhouettes clawed at him.

In the distance, one of Reese's soldiers watched, his

helmeted eyes a crimson glow. Arthur couldn't see who it was before his rapid-fire breathing turned the visor to a gray blur, obscuring his view.

We've all gone mad, Arthur decided.

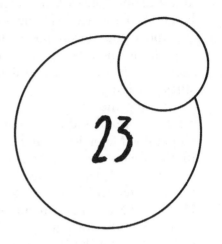

23

Under a gray sky, Jacob stood at the north end of Main Street, staring at closed shops and empty windows. Before him, utter silence, and surreal lifelessness; behind, a flurry of commotion as yellow-clad figures hustled about, doing only God knew what.

Catching their movement through the corner of his hazmat mask, Jacob turned back toward the military encampment with its pitched tents and hulking black trucks. Interspersed throughout, doctors and soldiers never strayed from their camp, as if not wanting to look at or set foot on the town's barren, deserted main road. He wondered if any of them were even aware that they continuously kept their backs to the town or if perhaps it was mere instinct. All these scientists and grown-ups, and yet it was only a thirteen-year-old boy who was brave enough to look at the strange town and its absolute emptiness. It didn't feel like home anymore, he thought with a shudder, more like peering at a corpse of a loved one and realizing they were no longer in there. Like when he had looked down at his father's blood-drenched body.

Above the encampment, dark trees blanketed the monolithic mountains. He knew his mother was up there, lost in the snow and dense foliage while he was stuck down in town.

Passing the medical tent, he found Samantha still asleep. He wondered what to say to her when she awoke. Hopefully, Major Reese and his team would find their mother before then, but he doubted it.

At the end of a row of tents, a large gray truck loomed like a protective shell. On its roof was a satellite dish. He'd heard Major Reese mention that they couldn't get a signal out either by phone or satellite, and his thoughts returned to the sheriff's dead radio at the station. *And the monster in human clothes* . . . Jacob shook the memory away. He had enough nightmares waiting for when he slept. No need to dwell on them now.

The truck's side door opened and several yellow-clad doctors walked out. Within the doorway, he glimpsed blinking lights and computer screens. Then a radio squeaked to life, a garbled voice audible beneath the static. Had they gotten through to the outside world?

Curiosity and hope propelled his feet toward the truck's open door. The static grew louder, but the voice was gone. Through the crack, computers and machines came into view. A printer spit out a constant stream of paper while topographic maps filled several screens. Tilting his head, he glanced at the satellite dish above the vehicle, then back at the monitors. *If the satellite's out, where's the signal coming from?* Taking a quick look about, and finding no one facing in his direction, Jacob snuck inside the truck.

The back of the truck was a makeshift command center, about twenty feet deep and half as wide, filled with machines and screens. The printer's constant churning continued above a dull static emanating through unseen speakers. A monitor's glow lit Jacob's eyes as he leaned over, scanning the maps on the display. Even though he'd never seen a map quite like this, he knew exactly what he was looking at: an overhead projection of the Blackwood Mountains. Not a drawn or computer-simulated image; the various images were photographs taken from far above, either from the atmosphere or outer space. On the bottom screen, he noted the encampment and tiny figures walking about. It was a live feed. *Thank God*, he thought, his mind racing and his heart leaping. *They contacted the outside! More help's coming!*

Turning from the screens, he found a topographic map stretched across a desk. A circle was drawn a couple of miles above town, near the northeastern ridges. *Is that where the people are? Is that where my mom is?*

Feet clanged on the metal steps outside, and the door tilted open. Jacob dove behind the desk as two figures entered. One was a man in military armor, the other a woman doctor in a yellow hazmat suit. The door sealed behind them with a thick crunch, and they took their masks off. Jacob was trapped inside a place where he knew he shouldn't be. He was trying to decide whether to stand up and apologize for being there or not when the soldier typed something at the computer, and the speakers came to life.

"Report," a deep voice boomed.

The soldier leaned over a microphone. "Command, this is Blackwood One. We read you. Major Reese and his team have begun their ascent up the mountain and should reach the site shortly. Over."

"Are quarantine procedures in place?"

"Yes, General," the doctor replied. "Everything's set up for the civilians once they arrive."

A general, Jacob noted. And they expected to find the missing people soon!

"What about the advance unit?" the doctor asked.

"They're not your primary concern."

"If they're going to be exposed to further

contamination—or worse, something we're not expecting—my people could use a heads-up."

"Did you follow protocol?"

"Yes, sir," the soldier replied. "As far as the major and
his team are aware, all communication is down due to
weather conditions."

"I don't understand the point of lying to our own
people," the doctor said.

"You don't need to understand."

"And Major Reese?"

"He won't be coming back."

In stunned silence, Jacob huddled behind the desk,
trying to process what he'd heard. He must have mis-
understood, he told himself. Holding his breath, he
watched the doctor and soldier put their masks back
on and leave. The door shut, drenching him in monitor
light and chunky shadows. Jacob stayed behind the desk,
unsure how long he should linger before making his escape. He waited five minutes, then bolted for the door.

Once safely outside, Jacob raced back to the medical
tent and found Samantha awake. She was trying to peel
away the oversized hazmat suit when he sat down and
stopped her.

"Gotta keep it on," he said.

"Did they find Mom?"

Unsure of what to say or how to explain the confus-
ing conversation he'd just witnessed, Jacob offered up the
warmest smile he could. "Not yet, but they will."

Her lips trembled beneath moist eyelids. "You sure?"

"I promise," he said. "If they don't find her soon, I
will."

Samantha's shoulders shuddered. Jacob gently
pushed her back down on the cot. "Get some rest," he
whispered. "Mom will be back when you wake up."

As his sister drifted into an unsettled sleep, Jacob
stood watch. Peering out the tent's open doorway, toward the monolithic mountains, he wondered how he

expected to keep his promise. Though Samantha hadn't yet blamed him for killing their father, he knew she would eventually. They'd lost one parent already, and Jacob needed to make sure they didn't lose the other.

24

"You wanted an exit," Casey said, gesturing toward the hypersphere. "Here it is."

Donovan choked back a snort. Bill tilted his head. Earl folded his arms. No one spoke.

"What's the matter?" Casey asked, her smile fading. "This is our way out!"

"Maybe she's right," Bill said. The other men shot him a sideways glare. "I mean, it's possible," he stammered, his voice rising. "We saw her disappear."

"No, we saw her turn transparent," Donovan corrected. "Becoming the Ghost of Christmas Yet to Come isn't my idea of a safe exit."

Casey noticed Earl nodding. It was the first time she'd seen them agree. "Dammit, I was outside!" she fumed. "I stood in the snow, I felt that frigid air, and I saw the sun and the trees—"

"But you weren't there," Earl said. "I know cos I pulled you back."

"He's right, for once. Whatever this thing is," Donovan said, approaching the spinning red object, "I doubt it's a way out. At least not the one *I'm* looking for."

Again, Bill came to her defense. For whatever reason, he seemed to have grown a spine. "Hold on. Who says this place uses doorknobs and handles?"

"I'm telling you, this is an engine," Earl replied. "Not a door."

"You're the alien technology expert now?" Bill's face went pale as soon as the words escaped his lips. He took a step back.

"I've been working on engines my entire life, and all machines got one thing in common: the power goes to the engine." Earl pointed a meaty finger toward the enormous tubes running along the walls. "All the power in here is going straight to that sphere."

Casey stepped between them. "Maybe aliens do things differently."

Earl looked into her eyes, and his shoulders slumped. He shook his head. "What's it matter? The damn thing didn't work anyway. You didn't leave."

Casey pointed at the tree that impaled the hypersphere's heart. "Because it's damaged."

Earl groaned. Donovan laughed. Bill hid behind her, out of view. "Hold up," Earl said. "You wanna *fix* this thing?"

"Ladies and gentlemen," Donovan said with a grand gesture, "I present to you the single worst idea in the entire history of bad ideas. Somebody give this lady a round of applause." Donovan offered a fake clap and then headed to a doorway at the other end of the dome. "Knock yourselves out!" he shouted over his shoulder. "I'll try my luck elsewhere."

Casey watched him leave. Earl gave her a hard look. Turning, she held his glare. "This could work, Earl," she said. "Think of it, a way out."

Rubbing his scalp, Earl sighed. "And how do you plan on cutting down the tree?"

"There were sharp objects in the last room," she said, then lowered her voice. "The one with the body."

"I didn't see anything."

"They're there. Trust me. They looked like axes."

Earl huffed, rolling his eyes. "Alright, Bill and I will check it out. You stay here with your new favorite toy." Earl leaned in close. "But if there ain't no axes, we go find Donovan. Agreed?"

She nodded her assent and then Earl led Bill back the way they'd come.

Watching them leave, Casey's heart raced. She let out a long, weighty breath as her hand danced along the hypersphere's transparent surface. Its warmth spread from her fingertips through her nerve endings, calming her heart's rhythm to a slow purr. All the fear and anxiety, the horrors and terror she'd experienced, were nudged aside as a gentle breeze washed through her like a lover's caress. *This was created on another world. Beneath a sun that wasn't ours. By . . . someone not human.* Casey had been so busy running and crying and being terrified that she never stopped and took in what she was standing within: an alien ship. Her thoughts turned to Arthur. *He'd be jealous.* She imagined his eyes growing as big as saucers, staring at this floating red thing from another dimension, another world, or someplace *other*. *Ironic*, she thought with a snort. *The waitress ends up in an alien ship while the scientist chills out in the cabin.* For the first time, Casey decided she might not want to switch places with him.

The quieter it grew inside the hulking dome, the more her mind turned inwards, toward that itch that had whispered promises of wonders she couldn't imagine. *If only I could cut the tree from its heart.* That was the rub. She'd lied to Earl. There weren't any sharp ax-like objects in the other room, or probably anywhere else on the ship.

But Casey had a plan . . .

Closing her eyes, she searched inward for the itch in

the back of her mind. *Come out, come out, wherever you are.* No one responded, no whispered voices or tiny itches to guide her. Still, she remembered the sliding metal door she'd conjured from nothing when the creature chased them. Someone had helped them. Someone had read her thoughts. She pushed herself deeper, focusing on an image of a chopping ax, the sort that Arthur had once bought but never unwrapped. It was still hanging in their closet, for all she knew, with its black rubberized handle at the end of a fiberglass frame. The blade had a red tip, like a warning sign. Casey poured each detail into a singular picture, snapping the jigsaw together until it formed, solid and heavy, in her mind's eye.

Moments later, she feigned surprise when Earl and Bill returned, carrying three axes. Taking one, she smiled with satisfaction. "Looks like our luck's changing."

"Doubt it," Earl said.

Casey clambered to the base of the sphere and began whacking at the thick tree. Chunks of bark and ice flew. Bill joined in. *Whack. Whack. Whack.* Intent on cutting down the branches ensnared throughout the hypersphere, Casey didn't ruminate on the ax's origin, how she'd created it from nothing. If she had, perhaps she might have wondered at the implications of such power. If she could form edged blades out of thin air, what else might she create in that strange place? Instead, her only thought was of escape.

She turned to Earl as he watched from the sidelines. "Coffee break?" she asked.

Earl hefted the ax in his hand, feeling its weight. "These weren't in there before."

Shrugging, Casey ignored the truth of his statement. "You want out of here or not?"

Earl huffed, long and slow, then approached the tree. Creases formed beneath his eyes and around his mouth, creating deep pools of shadow. "You better be right about this."

WHACK. WHACK. The sound of his swings rever-berated through the dome. *WHACK.*

Although Casey didn't have a stopwatch to time it, she figured it took them less than twenty minutes before they'd cut away most of the tree and branches from inside the sphere. Earl had done the majority and hadn't looked happy about it the entire time. With each piece of timber removed, the hypersphere grew warmer, its crimson light brighter, drenching them in red. Casey stopped, letting out a slow, exhausted breath. The men hacked away at the tree under the red glow. *WHACK! WHACK! WHACK!* The image reminded her of a horror movie.

Above the din, a voice shouted. *Casey!*

It was Arthur. She heard him so clearly that she spun about, half expecting to see him standing beside her. He wasn't. *CASEY!* The second time she heard his voice, it rang so loud in her skull that she stumbled backwards. Earl and Bill stopped their work.

"You OK?" Bill asked.

She ignored them. Arthur was there! Somewhere close. He . . . he was outside. Dying. Closing her eyes, Casey felt the itch return in the back of her mind. She tried to scratch it, gently at first. *Arthur!* Then she dug deeper. *Arthur! Can you hear me?*

She didn't hear a voice respond. Instead, it was an emotion. Fear. He was terrified. She tasted acid, her stomach bile rising. Heavy pressure knocked against her chest, discharging the air from her lungs with a violent blow. Invisible arms groped her body. No, she realized, not her body, Arthur's. Someone was beating him, driving his face into cold snow. Her nose and cheeks flushed, but it was his fear that gripped her the most. The fear of not knowing what had happened to her, not knowing how much farther away his answers lay. *A mile? A couple hundred yards? Less? So close.* He didn't want to die without answers.

Casey spasmed on the floor, cradled by Earl and Bill.

For the first time since entering the dome with its warm red sphere, her arms and legs were frozen numb. Ice and snow crunched beneath Arthur's chest while faceless forms piled onto him in a blackened swarm. Shaking Arthur's vision from her eyes, the silhouettes were replaced by Bill and Earl. Spurred more from instinct than conscious thought, Casey scrambled to unsteady feet. Pushing the men aside, she raced toward the hypersphere, her hands outstretched. Her fingers grasped the transparent sphere, and its red lines became solid, clutched in her grasp. Earl started after her. "Wait, Casey, what are—"

Suddenly, an energy wave erupted from the glowing hypersphere, knocking him and Bill across the room like rag dolls. Earl, quicker to recover than Bill, peered up from the floor, watching Casey's inky shape against the red object. He tried to get to her, but his legs went numb.

The hypersphere lost its color as the room pitched with a violent jerk.

Casey collapsed, choking out a single word: "God . . ."

25

Another time, Another place

Casey was sitting at her desk typing one of a thousand reports she needed to finish by the end of the day when a strange tingle rippled her spine and sent her head spinning. Her fingernails stopped over the Corona typewriter, ending the loud *click-clack* of its keys, silencing the room. She swooned. The page's words blurred. Casey shook her head, deciding she needed some air. She couldn't remember the last time she'd slept but doubted it was less than thirty-six hours ago. Maybe forty-eight.

Passing a series of schematics for magnetic armor designs, she glimpsed her reflection in a doctorate diploma hanging on the wall. Checking her face in the frame's glass, something seemed off about the visage peering back. She turned to a mirror for a clearer image. Her blond hair was done up in a bun, a fashion she still hadn't grown accustomed to. Her white lab coat showed an ID badge with her name and black-and-white picture. Forced to wear this abominable thing night and day, Casey hated it because it made her look like her mother. Or worse, her grandmother. Moving to her face, utter shock stared back. It wasn't how she looked—not the first hints at wrinkles around her mouth and eyes or the rumpled clothes that she hadn't changed in a couple days. Rather, it was how separate she felt from the person staring back at her, like a visitor in her own body. As if she were wearing someone else's skin, the way she might wear someone's sweater. The sudden sensation made her stumble. The reflection was her and yet not her. A knock on the door tore her from the mirror. The reprieve was a relief.

"Come," she said, quivering.

A lieutenant, no older than twenty-five, peeked in. Only his head and shoulders entered, the rest of him remaining out in the hall. Her team made the younger staff nervous. A sideways glance at her reflection, and she thought she knew how they felt.

"General's down in the hangar, ma'am," the lieutenant said. "Something wrong with the craft."

"Thank you," she replied. "And it's *doctor*."

"Yes, ma—Doctor." He shut the door before she could say anything else. Women on the base weren't big with the boys, doctors even less so.

Casey headed outside, strolling along the airfield and breathing in the dry Nevada air. She heard planes rocketing off from behind the hangars, lined up in a row like tan-and-green dominos. None of these were her destination though. *That* hangar, the hidden one, required a drive.

Casey hopped in a jeep and drove across the base. Going past barracks and buildings, past rows of trucks and aircraft, she continued toward the farthest end of the base. Toward Groom Lake. Some even called the base Groom Lake, after its location. Officially, it was named Homey Airport. She knew, eventually, it would be called by a much more infamous title: Area 51.

But this was still early days, the United States sitting comfortably between having won World War Two and flirting with the inevitable Korean War. No one knew about Area 51 yet; they still had their anonymity. And she liked it that way. It kept her focused on her work. Besides, she and the scientific development team had another name for the infamous base: Dreamland.

Her jeep followed the lakebed toward the mountains on the south side. At the bottom of a slope, a camo door opened into the tan hillside, like a gash in the earth. She slowed at the gate, showing her badge for what she guessed was the seventh time since lunch. A soldier waved her through, and Casey entered the most incredible location in the world.

The hangar, as they called it, was actually a manmade gorge descending twenty decks into the earth. Each level offered glimpses of futures and worlds undreamed of. The hangar was divided into three categories: 1) Local (things from around there, *à la* the Bermuda Triangle); 2) Research and Development (practical and/or weird shit that wasn't even remotely practical—the stealth bomber would eventually originate from there, but that was still years off); 3) Out of Town (anything not of this Earth—there wasn't a ton of it, just enough to give most people the heebie-jeebies).

Casey parked her jeep and headed for a large steel elevator. A heavy soldier with an aw-shucks grin greeted her. "Hello, Doctor Stevens."

"Hey, Mike," she replied, entering the elevator.

The soldier, whose name wasn't Mike, had been named that by civilian researchers because they weren't told his actual identity. It had become a running joke. Reaching into the elevator, Mike slipped a key into the lock. "Where ya headed?"

"Out of town."

Without further comment, he nodded. Few went down that far. Casey had grown used to the quick swallow and evasive eyes that followed Mike hitting the switch for level 20. He turned away before the doors closed. Casey hummed to herself on the way down, playing Blondie's "Call Me" in her head, a song that wouldn't exist until she was an old woman—or at least in late middle age. Her life had become complicated. Still, she was looking forward to reliving her youth in her fifties. *Eighties, here I come. Slowly but surely, just like this elevator.*

A new thought interrupted. It sounded like her, but it wasn't. *Wait. What year is this?*

The ripple up her spine returned, and once again she felt like she was sharing her skin with someone else. The voice sounded like hers, but it wasn't. Casey braced against a railing as her stomach lurched. By the time the elevator doors opened, vomit covered the floor.

Wiping her mouth, Casey pushed away the inner voice that sounded like hers but wasn't and continued to the heart of Dreamland. She moved through vast inner halls, past glass cases containing technological wonders that no one had yet understood. She paused at a familiar sight, a prototype for magnetic armor. Still years from completion, the armor hung on a rack like a makeshift scarecrow. Based on her design, the suit reverse engineered the ship's magnetic hull in the hopes of protecting the wearer from mental projection—or the "Lil' Red Ghosts," as Casey called them. Using the ship's own protective plating as a basis, these new armored hazmat suits might someday alter the future enough so that her friends would survive this time. Only, she had to invent the suits first.

Casey continued to the center of the vast amphitheater, toward the hulking, broken ship. Its once oval shape was now a hodgepodge of split ends and jagged corners. Suspended by hundreds of steel cables, it drooped over the ground like crumpled paper. Upon her approach, a door formed in its enormous hull, and a ramp descended. Scientists within the hall turned and watched as she strode straight into the heart of the ship. No one else ever went inside. Not anymore. Several had gone in over the years. The lucky ones had mental breakdowns and retired quietly. The not so lucky died.

Now Casey was the only one allowed within the craft. The military had paid for her education and doctorate degree. In return, she gave them all the ship's secrets. Well, almost all. *Us girls*, she'd tell the hypersphere, *must keep a few mysteries to ourselves*. She didn't say it out loud. She didn't have to. It had understood her wishes for years now. Casey approached the hypersphere. The room was pristine, white domed walls reflected pulsing red light from the twirling sphere at its center. *I hear someone's been acting up.*

Striding around the sphere, she waited for that familiar itch in the back of her mind to whisper, but no response came. *Cat got your tongue?*

Curious, she reached out to the sphere, drifting her fingers along its grid-lined design. Energy shot through her fingers, bolting her feet to the ground. Casey's eyes widened, large and white. She gasped for breath, as if all oxygen had left the domed room. Within the hypersphere's pulsing glow, an image between space-time reflected in front of her. Herself. "Oh my—"

"—God!" Casey screamed. The pulse shot out from the sphere, knocking Earl and Bill off their feet, then continued outside of the ship, rippling through the tree-covered mountains. Casey's hand stayed glued to the sphere, unable to budge. She wanted to look away, not from the sphere but rather from what it had shown her. An alternate Casey Stevens with an alternate ship in an alternate timeline. Her mind screamed in protest. As if staring into a bent reflection in a carnival mirror, the two Caseys locked eyes. Abruptly, the sphere darkened.

Casey collapsed, and the ship went black.

26

Major Reese pushed uselessly against the wave of bodies, as if fighting an ocean. The swarm knocked him to the ground with a *crunch*. He wasn't sure if the sound had come from hitting the snow or something breaking in his body. Everything had happened so fast, and his adrenaline was pumping so hard that he didn't have time to register the pain. He knew he'd been standing, and now he was lying in the snow as countless rabid figures thrashed on top of him, crushing him. Then rapid-fire gunshots ripped through the crowd. The noise blasted his eardrums, but he was unable to make out who had fired. The townspeople spun, glaring at someone Reese couldn't see. A few of those on top of him climbed off, racing out of view. Instead of relief, red-hot rage burned through him.

No! Cease fire! I told you not to fire!

He tried to speak, but the pressure of a dozen people on top of him stole his voice. He gasped, struggling to order whoever was firing to stop, when the gunfire died on its own, followed by a high-pitched scream. It was the old man, Arthur. He'd gone in guns blazing, and now they had him. *Shit.* Through the corner of his eye, he glimpsed Salvatore and the other soldiers firing blindly at the swarm.

I shouldn't be here, he thought as one of the figures above him raised a large rock to crush his skull. *They put the wrong man in charge. I should never have even been—*

A giant red wave of energy blasted through the forest, knocking down everything but the tallest trees. Clouds of white powder and brown leaves blew past. Pieces of lumber and rocks ricocheted. The wave slammed into the raging people, tossing them aside. Some tumbled out of view down the mountain. Others slammed into trees. Reese and his people stayed low, seemingly unaffected. Whatever was happening, it wasn't natural. Something or someone had intervened. Something or someone had saved them.

His head thundering, Reese scrambled to his feet. Salvatore and Pidgeon helped the other soldiers. Legs planted firmly so as not to fall, Reese surveyed the team. "Everyone alright?"

Salvatore rushed forward. "No, sir! We are *not* alright." Her finger jutted in front of him. "What were you thinking, telling us not to open fire?"

Taken aback by the forcefulness in her voice, he matched her intensity. "I couldn't have us murder dozens of civilians!"

"They were *enemy combatants!*"

Reese's eyes met hers, and his voice grew to a gravelly growl. "You ever gunned down women and children before? Trust me," he added when Salvatore didn't respond, "terms like 'enemy combatant' don't help you sleep any better."

"Major!" Pidgeon cried.

Salvatore struggled to keep Reese's gaze. "They charged us," she added with a huff.

"*Before* or *after* you raised your weapons?"

She didn't answer.

"MAJOR!" Pidgeon screamed.

Reese and Salvatore turned. Shock stunned them into silence. In the distance, Pidgeon and the other soldiers walked among countless bodies strewn about the mountain. Hundreds of them. Momentarily preoccupied with Salvatore's complaints, Reese hadn't seen the full effects of the red blast, or whatever it was, until then. His stomach tightened. *No . . .*

He raced over to Pidgeon, leaning over a woman's body. "Are they all dead?"

Pidgeon shook his head. "Look." He ran a gloved hand over the woman's face, opening her blue eyes. She seemed asleep, serene, her skin and eyes reverted back to normal. Reese pushed out a lengthy breath. "No more virus."

"It may never have been a virus to begin with." Pidgeon shrugged. "Whatever it was, it's gone."

"I can think of a couple of kids down there who will be glad to hear that," Reese said, feeling a smile cross his face. "Take two men, and start carrying the civilians down to base camp. It'll take a while, but at least they're alive."

"Not all of them," Salvatore interjected.

Reese glanced over, seeing Salvatore kneeling beside a nude woman, her body riddled with bullets. Reese's skin burned, and his eyes flashed. "Arthur."

"He was gone when I got up," Pidgeon said.

Reese's gaze moved up the mountain. "Shit."

"And," Salvatore added, "he snagged a rifle."

Reese turned to his medic. "Pidgeon, take two men, and start carrying the people to base camp. The doctors can help you bring more down once you get there."

Pidgeon's expression hardened, his eyes narrowing to slits. "No, sir. We have a mission to complete."

Reese stumbled back, unprepared for his friend's dissent. *Et tu, Brute?* He'd never heard Pidgeon contradict an order before. "I know the mission, Staff Sergeant, but you are a field medic, and there are hundreds of people *in this field right here*." Reese glared. Regaining his balance, he stepped closer. "You do your job, and I'll do mine, Staff Sergeant."

Pidgeon stared back with iron sights for eyes. Reese ignored him, tilting his head toward the ridge above. "Salvatore, bring two men. The old man's heading for the ship. We need to get to him before he causes any more harm."

He snatched his weapon from the snow and started up the mountain, leading Salvatore and the two men, leaving Pidgeon behind. Through the corner of his eye, Reese noticed his friend reluctantly turn back down the mountain, lumbering out of view.

It didn't take long for Reese and his team to find Arthur. Wheezing and out of breath, he leaned against a tree. Arthur had taken off his helmet and was gulping air when Reese charged forward. Bursting through the foliage, he pinned the old man to the frozen ground.

"You crazy, murdering son of a bitch!" Reese hit him, square in the jaw. "Who told you to grab a weapon and open fire? I saw you, so don't tell me it was self-defense. You ran right through them! How many did you kill?"

Reese would have kept on hitting him if not for Salvatore grabbing his arm. She shouted words he couldn't hear, the thundering in his head drowning her out. He couldn't stop seeing the dead and wondering, was one of them Jacob's mother? Still, Reese knew their deaths were his fault. He'd brought the old man along. The murders were as much on his hands as Arthur's. But that didn't stop Reese from wanting to strangle him. Then another thought occurred to Reese. The sudden swell of anger and rage seemed somehow forced, as if the feelings were only partly his own, intensified by something else. Running his fingers over his armor, he checked for cracks in the suit, wondering if some of the red mist had infected him. But none of the scratches were deep enough to cut through metal plating. That meant either the stress of the mission was getting to him, or something was affecting him even through his armor. Neither idea comforted him.

"I . . . I couldn't help it," Arthur said, rolling onto his knees and coughing up blood. "It was as if I didn't have control over my own body. I wish I could explain what happened."

"You'll get your chance." The boiling rage behind Reese's eyes subsided, and his voice cooled. "My men are taking you back to camp. You're under arrest."

Salvatore gestured to the two soldiers. They approached Arthur as he stood up and stumbled backwards. "You . . . you can't! I'm too close. The ship is just over the ridge. We're almost there!"

The men grabbed his arms, pulling him with an iron grip. He twisted his head to Reese. "She's here! Casey saved us! She saved me!"

"Not from prosecution," Reese replied calmly. Maybe the old man was telling the truth, and maybe he wasn't. Either way, Reese was glad to get him off the mountain.

Suddenly, a burst of green light erupted from the ridge. The thunder of an unseen engine reverberated through the mountain. Wind blew haphazard chunks of snow and ice. The noise was so loud and the flying ice so sharp that everyone covered their heads. Everyone except Arthur. Instead, he ran straight for the light, oblivious to the pain or the deafening of his eardrums.

Momentarily dazed, Reese and his team chased him. As they rounded the ridge's horizon, they pushed past razor whiteness toward an emerald glow.

Then the green engulfed them.

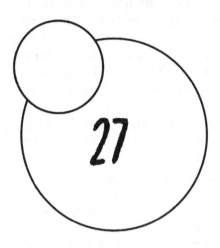

27

Jacob kept watch over Samantha as she slept, fighting off his own fatigue, when soldiers appeared out of the tree line, carrying bodies. He didn't know if they were alive or dead, but he recognized one of them: Mr. Anderson, his social studies teacher. His heart leaping to his throat, Jacob rushed toward them, carrying his cell phone with a picture of his mother on its screen. Doctors poured from the tents, grabbing people and bringing them inside. Jacob tugged on a female doctor's sleeve. "Are they alive?"

The doctor's intercom hissed while she spoke. "Yes, and they seem to be stable. But we know nothing more right now."

Jacob pulled at his plastic hazmat suit. "Does that mean we can take these off?"

"Not yet," she said. "I need to get back to work."

Jacob nodded. In the medical tent, he saw a soldier place a naked woman on a cot, covering her in a sheet. He recognized her immediately: Ms. Broze, his math teacher. Even though she was nearly the same age as his mother, Ms. Broze had a face and a body that no teenager could ignore. A body that Jacob, sitting in the back of class, secretly squirming, had pictured naked a thousand times. But not like this. Clinically eyeing her chest, he noted that the red veins were gone. Had she been cured somehow? After everything Jacob had seen and done, even a blip of light at the end of the horribly gloomy tunnel was the best feeling in the world. Warmth rose in his chest, and his fingers tingled. He had a sliver of hope. His mom might still be alive.

Ahead, a black soldier in armor stood at the tree line. Jacob tried to remember his name. He knew it sounded like a bird of some sort. Hawk? Dove? Pigeon? Pidgeon, that was it.

"Mr. Pidgeon, sir, have you seen my mother?" Jacob showed him his phone.

"No," Sergeant Pidgeon said, moving toward the tree line without the other soldiers.

Jacob followed, still holding up his mom's picture. "Could you look again, please, sir?"

Pidgeon stopped and glared down at the boy with an expression not too different from finding gum on his shoe. "There are many people up there."

"Let me go with you. I can help!"

He kept walking. "Too dangerous."

"I've got a suit on," Jacob persisted. "I'll be safe."

Pidgeon stopped and turned to face him. "There's far more dangerous things out there than a virus," he said, his tone flat, its threat distinct. "You escaped the first time. You may not escape the second."

He left, vanishing into the foliage. Jacob stumbled, suddenly frightened by the soldier. Unsure of what to do, he glanced back at the camp, where Samantha lay sleeping. Doctors and armored soldiers milled about. His young mind swam. Unwilling to lose his chance, Jacob ran back to the tent, finding his father's shotgun tucked away below his sleeping sister's cot. With a final, hesitant kiss to Samantha's forehead, Jacob bolted for the trees.

The sun fell, turning the sky blue-black and dropping the temperature from mildly frigid to deathly freezing. Jacob lumbered in the hazmat suit, fighting through knee-deep snow. He followed Pidgeon's footprints up a winding path, creeping amongst tall pine trees that stabbed at swirling clouds. His eyes scanned the silhouetted peaks, noticing a green light cascading down from higher up the mountain. The eerie glow turned the clouds emerald and blazed through darkened trees, like the morning sun. Only, it wasn't morning, and it wasn't the sun. Whatever the source, he feared Pidgeon's tracks would lead him straight to it.

Jacob had never been up so far, not even hunting with his father. His mind drifting, he still heard the shotgun blast ringing, felt the recoil slam his shoulder, saw his dad's chest explode in a crimson mess. Jacob tried to push the image away, but it was stuck in an endless loop behind his eyelids.

The thick line of trees opened, and he saw something lying crumpled in the distance. Drawing closer, a cluster of intertwining limbs came into view. Countless bodies lay in the snow, stretching east to west as far as he could see. Legs wobbling, his breath slowed to a gurgling wheeze. Jacob scampered to the first body he found. Barney, the barber who all the kids dreaded going to twice a year. His eyesight had gone downhill over the years, and more than one kid had gotten an ear clipped by his scissors. Blind Barney, they called him. He lay in a clump, curled over a woman whose face Jacob couldn't see. It wasn't his mom though.

Jacob leaned over Blind Barney to see if he was breathing, but he couldn't tell with the cumbersome hazmat mask on. Staring at the bodies, lying in disarray, he wondered if they were still infected. Opening Barney's shirt, he noted clear white skin; no red marks or veins.

Jacob pried one of Barney's eyes open and saw nothing out of the ordinary. With a deep breath, Jacob tore off his hazmat mask and leaned down, putting his ear beside Barney's mouth. He was breathing. Jacob rolled the woman onto her side. It was his mom's friend, Ms. Shirley. Her chest heaved rhythmically. She was also alive.

Jacob stood and zipped his yellow mask back on. He wasn't sure how long they could lie sleeping in the snow until they froze to death, but for the moment, his only concern was his mother. He assumed she was there, lying somewhere amongst the hundreds of sprawled bodies. The colder it grew, the more his pace quickened, desperate to find her.

Each shadowed figure revealed a friend or a neighbor. Unwilling to stop his search to help them, he hoped the doctors and soldiers were following close behind.

Traveling westward, he curved up and around the mountain ridge. The farther west he went, the more his trail curled north, bringing him closer to the bright green light blazing above. Adding to the eeriness of it all, the higher his path took him, the more he became aware of a sound building into a thundering roar: *chug, chug, chug, chug, chug . . .*

Sounds like a machine, he thought.

Despite the unease from the glow and the resounding chugging noise, he was grateful for the light because it made inspecting each person faster.

A few moments later, he found his mother, slumped in a shadowed heap. Jacob scrambled over and brushed the snow from her hair and cheeks, revealing blue lips and ashen skin, thankfully, free of red veins. A puff of white vapor escaped through her teeth. Breath.

"Mom! MOM!" He shook her, to no avail. "Hang on! I'll get you out of here."

Pulling her arms, he attempted to hoist her over his shoulder but stumbled and fell under the weight. Glancing around, Jacob searched for something he might use as a makeshift sled. His eyes flew to the hanging pine boughs. His mind racing, he wondered if he might create something with them. As he looked this way and that for anything else that might help, he spotted Pidgeon trudging up a ridge, toward the green glow. Stomping through the snow, the soldier tore his helmet off, tossed it away, and continued up the mountain.

"Mister Pidgeon, sir, please! I need your help!"

Pidgeon's moonlit silhouette stopped, turned. Jacob smiled and waved at him. "Oh, thank God. Thank you, sir," Jacob cradled his mother's head as Pidgeon approached. It took a moment for the soldier's face to come into view. "I need help to get her down the—"

The boy's smile died, along with his voice. His heart skipped, and urine poured down his leg.

Lurching forward, Pidgeon's eyes were blood red.

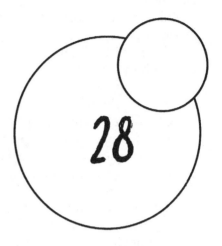

28

"Hey, can you hear me?" Earl whispered in the dark. Casey's eyes fluttered. "I can't see."

"Lights went out," Bill replied distantly.

Casey recalled the military base and a woman that was her and yet not her. "Where am I?"

"Same place, same shit," Earl said, helping her up. She took a few steps on spaghetti legs, pushing the confusion of what she'd seen from her mind for the moment. The sphere sprang to life with a newfound energy. It burst with blinding luminescence, causing them to look away.

"It's powering up!" Bill shouted.

Snapping out of her fog, Casey spun, squinting to see the hypersphere within the crimson glare. "Good. Let's get out of here."

She reached for the turning sphere, then stopped, noticing her left palm covered in gray, callused skin. Casey had almost forgotten about the patches on her feet, or at least pushed them so far back in her mind that she hadn't thought of it. Now, staring at the skin more closely, she noticed tiny ridges along the grey flesh, like reptilian scales. Taken aback, she stumbled into Earl's broad chest.

"Everything alright?" he asked, feeling her shiver against him.

Grinding her teeth, she hid her palm, her throat tightening. "I'm fine."

Using her "normal" hand, Casey ran her fingers over the transparent, twisting sphere, waiting for it to become solid again, but nothing changed. Shuddering, she tried her other, gray, palm. Still no effect. Her shoulders dropped, her head sagging. "It's not working,"

Earl's brow furrowed. "What do you mean?"

"I mean it's not working."

A chugging sound echoed through the dome as the three of them exchanged ashen glances. The engines were starting. Bill shoved past them, reaching for the sphere. His hand floated through the hypersphere, with no effect. The dome quaked and lurched. Earl groaned. "Seriously, we gotta get out of here."

Casey kept her hand within the twirling sphere. "I'm trying!"

"Well, what did you do last time?"

"I don't know. I just touched it."

Above, the dome turned feverish red, reflecting the sphere's light in macabre brilliance. Sweat dripped profusely over Earl's eyes and chest. He wiped his brow, swooning. Casey grabbed him, stopping his collapse. Buckling, his weight brought her to her knees. "Bill, help me."

Bill grabbed one of Earl's arms. "Someone turned the temperature *way* up."

"Earl was right!" Casey shouted over the pounding *chug, chug, chug.* "This is an engine room." Sweaty blond hair stuck to her eyelids, blurring her vision. Her skin was damp, and she felt the room tilt. Casey searched for Bill through the blond blur. "Grab his arm. We need to get out of here."

Hoisting Earl's thick biceps over their shoulders, she and Bill dragged him across the dome and toward the exit through which Donovan had escaped. She hoped he was faring better than they were.

Earl regained his footing soon after Casey and Bill carried him from the engine room and its blistering heat. Back in the frigid tunnels again, his strength returned. His face flushed, Casey thought he seemed embarrassed. Neither she nor Bill had been so easily taken down by the suddenly sweltering temperature. Casey's brow was only slightly damp, and Bill was sweating even less. Still, even though almost unconscious, Earl had been the only one with enough forethought to keep a tight grip on his ax. The others had tossed them aside. His knuckles tightened on the weapon's handle, and Casey wondered if a single blade would offer any protection against ray guns or whatever else might attack. She doubted it.

The lights at their feet bloomed brightly, making travel much easier. The constant *chug, chug, chug* and the thumping and vibrations under their feet made Casey decide she'd rather have the quiet and dark instead. The ship was building in power, its engine humming and unseen motors chugging to life, vibration that could soon lead to movement—or worse, takeoff.

When the ship spasmed, rocking them back and forth along the tunnel, she shared a nervous glance with Earl. Struggling to stay standing as the hallway lurched, Casey wondered if, by fixing the sphere, they had inadvertently sealed their fate. And it was her fault. *Good one, Case.*

Anxiety rising in her chest, Casey absently scratched the gray patch on her hand. She didn't realize what she was doing until Earl spoke. "Did that sphere thing hurt you?"

She shoved her hand under her other arm. "I'm fine," she snapped. The men exchanged glances, obviously not believing her. Thankfully, a light came into view up ahead, turning everyone's attention away from Casey's hidden palm and toward a new doorway.

Her relief vanished as quickly as it had appeared when Bill groaned. "Dear Lord, please, no more rooms." Earl nodded in agreement. Casey kept her pace quick, choosing whatever new danger might await them inside over having to look back down at her discolored hand. Whatever was wrong with her, she'd rather face an outside threat than an internal one. With any luck, this was the aliens' lounge room. *Pool tables, a jacuzzi, wet bar . . .* Glancing back down at her clenched hand, she couldn't bring herself to laugh.

Upon entering the doorway, they were swallowed up in blinding white rays. Before her eyes focused, Casey's ears pricked at the sound of distant whimpering.

"Donovan!" Bill shouted, his vision obviously having adjusted quicker than hers.

The brightness receded from her view, turning to sparkling spots, until at last the room revealed itself. They were surrounded by enormous crystals of every shape and color, jutting toward them from all directions. Earl's arm thrust in front of her chest, stopping her. Casey peered down at a pointed crystal, inches from her breast. With a suppressed shudder, she nodded. "Thanks."

Bill continued toward the shaking figure, huddled in the corner. Donovan's body trembled, snot and tears smeared down his twitching face as his eyes darted about the room. *Something's broken inside him*, Casey thought. *He's gone insane.*

Sighing heavily, Earl helped Donovan to his feet. "What happened?"

"Did you see one of *them*?" Casey asked, not wanting to use the word "alien."

"Whatever happened must not have been good," Bill said when Donovan didn't reply.

"I saw . . . I saw . . ." Donovan stammered, "s-s-school."

Casey wrapped her arm around him. "School?" she asked, keeping her voice even.

"I was back in high school."

"Whatever you *think* you saw was your imagination," Bill said.

"No!" Donovan flung Earl and Casey's arms aside. "I was there! I could smell the bleach on the floor and hear the kids . . . the kids laughing . . ." His voice seemed to die in his throat.

"I saw something," Casey admitted. "My dad. I could hear him," she added off Bill's stunned silence. "In my head."

"I saw my sister, Shanice." Earl grimaced. "She's supposed to be home, having a baby any day now, but instead she was here cradling . . . something that wasn't human."

He stopped with a shudder. Whatever these men had witnessed, it had shaken both of them to the core—just as the vision of her father had done to her. Glancing at her itchy, gray-covered palm, she wondered if perhaps this place, *this ship*, was having more than a psychological effect. Were the others changing physically as well?

And if so, what were they becoming?

29

Reese followed Arthur over the last ridge, into the blazing green light, surprised at how fast the old man could run. It took effort to catch up to him. As the light grew brighter, Reese unlocked his weapon's safety, mentally preparing for whatever might be waiting for them. But nothing could have prepared him for what lay ahead.

His eyes grew wide in the emerald glow, and his mouth slackened to a rubbery hinge. Even though Arthur lingered only a few feet away, Reese never turned from the sprawling craft ahead. He didn't notice Salvatore and the rest of his soldiers stopping beside him either. Nothing stirred him beyond the enormous ship filling his vision, up and down, side to side, as far as he could see. Reese's lungs forgot to breathe. Whatever he'd expected, this went beyond anything he could have imagined. It was stranger, more *inhuman*, than any sci-fi movie. He reeled at the enormity of witnessing something truly alien. The effect weighed on him like a leaden shroud. *Dear God.*

The ship appeared to be a permanent part of the landscape, as if it had always been there. Tree trunks disappeared beneath it, roughly ten feet from the ground, and then sprang up again above the ship, seemingly *growing through* the giant metallic disc. It looked to be over a mile in diameter, though Reese couldn't determine the actual size as it vanished into the wilderness.

No gouges in the earth or black scorch marks, no torn trees, not even a bent twig. The ship sat there, suspended between hundreds, perhaps thousands, of thick tree trunks, as if the Almighty had created the valley one day and then plopped in a flying saucer just for the hell of it.

Despite everything it had taken to get there, Reese felt an emptiness in the pit of his stomach. Staring open-mouthed at the ship and the strangeness of its position, something deep inside told him he'd never make his way back down the mountain.

This is where I die, his mind whispered.

Staring at the huge shape looming above, he recalled a passage from Arthur's book: *I saw the ship drift above the tree-lined ridge until it vanished into the mountainside. It didn't appear to fly away so much as it phased out of existence.*

Yes, Reese concluded, this thing hadn't crashed. Instead, it had somehow phased into the landscape, just like the crazy old man's book had described. Momentarily transfixed, Reese forgot about apprehending Arthur and instead approached the wondrous ship.

Arthur grabbed his arm, trying to stop him. Reese easily tore free. "Get off me."

"Wait," Arthur urged. "Look at the snow."

"Snow?" Reese turned to Arthur, incredulous. "You *do* see the gigantic flying saucer right in front of us, right? The one with *trees growing through it*?"

When Arthur didn't respond, Reese huffed and

turned his attention to the cascading flakes. After a moment, he sucked in his breath, grasping Arthur's meaning. "They're not falling on the ship."

"Yes, they are," Arthur corrected. "The snow is simply moving very, very slowly." He turned to the ground and found a small rock. Bobbing it in his hand, Arthur took a step toward the looming craft.

Salvatore flanked his left. "What are you doing?"

"Testing a hypothesis," Arthur replied.

"Throwing rocks doesn't exactly scream 'we come in peace,'" Reese said, though he didn't move to stop him.

Arthur eyed the soldiers' weapons. "Neither do automatic rifles."

Not waiting for another objection, Arthur threw the stone as far as he could. It soared through the air until suddenly it lurched, suspended six feet from the ship's hull, floating above the ground as if caught in an invisible net. The growing knot in Reese's stomach tightened.

"Jesus," Salvatore gasped. She approached the floating stone, reaching toward it.

"I wouldn't do that," Arthur said.

Reese nodded for her to stay put, then turned to Arthur. "OK, how about you share with the rest of the class."

Arthur traced the path of the rock through the air with his finger. "The rock is still moving, and the snow is still falling, but at a decelerated rate."

Salvatore stepped back. "Slowed by what?"

Arthur shrugged. "Time."

"And the trees?" Reese pointed to the enormous branches disappearing and reappearing throughout the ship's structure. "They're growing through the fucking thing."

"No, they're not," Arthur said, his tone flat and plain. "This ship isn't really here."

"Right," Salvatore responded with a slow drawl, the way one might to a crazy person. She waved to the two soldiers. "Take him back to base camp."

Arthur flinched. "Wait, you don't understand."

Knowing he was out of his depth, Reese nodded for the men to stop. "You're the one here with a PhD, so I'll listen," Reese said to Arthur through gritted teeth. "But talk faster."

"And plainer," Salvatore added.

"I think the ship is both here *and* not here."

"That's not plainer."

His excitement growing, Arthur's words spilled out without a pause for breath. "The trees didn't grow through the ship, just like that rock *isn't* really floating in the air. I think the ship is here, right now, and it's also at some other point in time when the trees don't exist, which is why they seem to be growing through it."

Noticing their blank expressions, he asked them a question. "What happens when you throw a rock into water?"

"It gets wet," Salvatore said.

Reese tilted his head, thinking before answering. "Its descent slows."

Arthur jumped in place. "Exactly! Think of time being wrapped around this ship like a water bubble."

Reese paced. "Say you're right, and this ship is both in the here and now and at another point in time. What happens if we go inside?"

Arthur's face ran the gamut of emotions. "I have no idea," he replied finally, his voice lowered. He turned to the hull. "Or if it's even possible."

Noting the disappointment in Arthur's voice, Reese wasn't sure how to feel. Perhaps it would be better to just turn around and let someone else try to get inside the thing. His mission was to secure the ship. Nothing in his orders told him he had to go inside the fucking thing.

Maybe, he thought with a pang of hope, *I just might see Noelle again.*

30

Casey watched Donovan stalk across the crystalline room, mumbling incoherently. Turning, his eyes wide and maddened, he scanned Earl and Bill until his gaze fell on Casey. "Don't look at me like that!" he shouted, then dropped his voice to a singsong whisper. *"I know what you did."*

"If this is about the hypersphere, I was wrong," Casey admitted. "I'm sorry."

"Hear that, boys? She's sorry. Oh, well, that's fine then." Donovan paused as the room shook and spasmed. When the aftershocks died, he continued. "You didn't listen to me. None of you did. That's why this whole place is rocking and rolling." When no one answered, he leaned into Casey's face. "This thing's taking off, sweetheart."

"We don't know that," Casey said weakly, her voice betraying her concern.

Donovan waved his arms. "Strap in folks, we're going bye-bye."

"That's enough!" Earl barked.

Donovan's expression contorted to an eerie grin. "Mars, here we come!"

Suddenly, a red ball of light appeared between them, floating in the middle of the room. Everyone flinched. It was transparent, with rocky ridges running along its surface. Earl was the first to recognize the form. "Mars."

"See? See? Told ya!"

Casey spun on Donovan, slamming him against crystals. "Just shut up!"

She was prepared for Donovan to counterstrike. Instead, he shrugged, raising open hands. His voice smoothened while his expression kept an eerie sneer. "Whatever you say, sweetheart."

She released him with a final shove. "Don't call me that."

Earl stalked around the translucent ball, then thrust his hand inside. The image shimmered. "A hologram."

"He said Mars, and Mars appeared," Casey said as she watched the turning planet. *Perhaps axes and steel walls aren't the only things that can be conjured up.* Tilting her chin, she spoke with a commanding voice. "Earth."

The red planet was replaced by a blue-and-brown orb. However, it looked strange. Most of the planet was covered in blue water while only a single patch was brown and green, indicating land.

Behind her, Earl sucked in his breath. "That ain't Earth."

Donovan giggled madly in the corner. Ignoring him, Casey remained silent, unsure of what she was looking at. It was Bill, of all people, who finally recognized it. "Yes, it is."

"Sure don't look like any globe I've ever seen," Donovan whispered.

"Bill's right," Earl said. "It's our planet, only the continents aren't separated."

"Earth as it was millions of years ago," Bill replied.

Donovan laughed. "All this technology, and no one thought to update the map."

"Depends on where you're looking from," Bill replied.
Earl nodded. "Outer space."

"If someone watched from far enough away, it could look like this."

Listening to them go back and forth, Casey shook her head. "You've lost me."

"He's talking about *light years*," Donovan offered, as if it were obvious.

Feeling like the dumbest person in the room, Casey fell silent. It was the same way she'd felt whenever Arthur went on and on about whatever he was studying.

It's like I always told ya, a girl can't be pretty and smart, Honey Bun, her father's voice whispered. Suppressing a shiver, Casey grew unsure if the slithering voice was a memory or an effect of the ship. Either way, she was grateful when Bill chimed in.

"When we look at stars, we're looking into the past because of how long it takes light to travel. Someone watching our planet from, say, a hundred million light years away might see something like this."

Noting the rising confidence in Bill's voice and demeanor, Casey didn't want to be the only one without any ideas. She paced around the globe. "Show me where you come from."

Nothing changed; the ancient Earth kept rotating. Bill cleared his throat. "Point of origin."

The orb was replaced by a blue ball, engulfing them. Stepping away from the hologram, Casey noted the white, hazy atmosphere drooping above an endless ocean. No landmass, only crashing waves and wind-whipped spray. "One big sea," she said.

"Show of hands," Donovan said with a chuckle. "Who brought their swim trunks?"

Earl glared. "Another word and I *break something*." Donovan paled in response.

Casey turned her attention back to the floating image. Her palm itched incessantly. She tucked it back in her pocket. "Do you think they live underwater?"

"Who's *they*?" Earl asked, meeting her gaze. "I mean, where *are* the aliens?"

"Maybe they died in the crash," Bill suggested. "Either way, there's oxygen aboard, so whoever built this thing must breathe the same air we do."

"Or maybe this ship never had a crew," Casey suggested. "You know, like an autopilot," she added, noting their odd stares. She thought back to how she'd created walls and axes from nothing. Perhaps it wasn't an alien being that had helped her but the ship itself. Neither idea offered much comfort.

Donovan suppressed a grumbled squeak. "No, no, we're not alone in here. I heard them in my head. Chattering monkeys that whisper . . . terrible things."

Casey's face hardened. "I bet you've got all sorts of voices up there. Now keep quiet."

As she spoke, a faint whisper echoed in her skull. *Arthur?* she wondered. She focused inward, but the voice remained incoherent, like sounds bubbling underwater. Though the words were unclear, the intent was sharp and succinct. It reminded her not of Arthur but of the way a police officer might speak. Or a soldier.

"Casey." Earl snapped his fingers, waking her from a daze. "I said, do you hear that?"

Turning, Casey's body tingled from head to toe, as if her limbs had fallen asleep, the needles stabbing beneath her skin. Without looking, she knew the gray patches were spreading. "Yeah, it sounded like a man," she said, keeping her focus on the whispered voice. "I think."

Bill and Earl exchanged quizzical glances. Bill shuddered. "No, the noise."

Refocusing on the crystal room, Casey followed their gaze toward the entrance they'd come through. Then she heard it. A steady, pounding, *thump*. Fear rose in her chest like an angry fire, burning away all other concerns.

"Could be the engines," Earl said, though the dryness of his voice spoke otherwise.

As if in reply, the metallic crunch was accompanied

by a high-pitched wail. Everyone froze, recognizing the animalistic scream. Casey was the first to say what they all thought: "It got out!"

The pounding drew louder, closer, as a shadow dripped from the entrance ceiling.

Despite Pidgeon's looming approach, Jacob never left his mother's side. Snatching his shotgun, he leveled it at the soldier. A memory flashed of his father's exploding chest, causing him to pause. Closing his eyes, he pulled the trigger—*click!* Of course, the soldiers had emptied it.

Pidgeon knocked the shotgun aside and grabbed Jacob's collar. With a single motion, he tore the plastic suit open. Pidgeon's glowing eyes bore into the boy, his mouth wide, filled with red mist.

"Don't kill me," Jacob choked. He wanted to say more, but the red eyes stole his voice.

"You're already dead," Pidgeon replied, more a statement of fact than a threat.

Jacob noted the calmness behind those glaring red eyes. "Y-you're different than the others," he stammered. "They were wild, like animals. But not you."

Pidgeon smiled, as if impressed by the boy's deduction. "We've met before, Jacob."

"The man from the mountain," Jacob whispered. "Somehow that was you too, wasn't it?"

"And your mother. And your father—before you murdered him," Pidgeon said, glancing at the prone figures strewn about. "I was all of them."

"But not anymore," Jacob spat.

"The townspeople served their purpose by stalling your military, if only for a moment." Pidgeon regarded his own armor. "This vessel had a more subtle mission: reconnaissance."

"Why?" Jacob asked through gritted teeth. "*What the hell do you want*?"

Pidgeon turned toward the glowing green light, shining over the ridge above.

"More time."

Jacob thrashed and kicked as red mist wafted from Pidgeon's mouth toward his own.

Suddenly, a figure bolted from the brush, slamming into Pidgeon. Jacob tumbled aside before the mist could touch him. He rolled over his mother and scampered behind a tree. He didn't recognize the young, bearded man who was punching Pidgeon in the face. The man focused only on the head due to Pidgeon's body armor, but it wasn't enough. Pidgeon took a few blows, then knocked the man twenty feet back with a single swing. Jacob heard the wind go out of the man as he hit a branch, crumpling beneath twigs and pine needles. Jacob's savior had only given him a momentary reprieve.

Yet, it seemed to be enough. Pidgeon turned his attention back toward the green glow and the chugging sound coming from the upper ridge. He shot a last glance at the boy with those pinprick red lights for eyes, then continued back up the mountain, as if bored by the confrontation. Jacob's legs were like overstretched rubber bands, and his arms quivered limply at his sides. He couldn't seem to command himself to move. Gasping for breath, he focused on slowing his breathing, taking air in slow gulps. As the figure vanished in the dark, Jacob heard Pidgeon's words echo in his skull: *You're already dead.*

Pushing the hissing voice from his thoughts, Jacob ran to the man who had saved him. "Hey, mister, you alright?"

The man coughed, reeling in caked snow. "Been better."

Jacob put the man's arm around his shoulder and helped him up. He smelled of grilled onions and beer. "I need help, sir."

"Jus' Todd," he said, cradling his ribs. "I'm not old enough to be a *sir*."

"Todd, sir," Jacob said, catching Todd's odd look. "My mom, she needs help."

Todd moved alongside dozens of prone figures. "What the hell happened?"

"Long story. Please, sir—Todd."

"Sure," Todd said, following the boy over to his mother. He knelt and checked her pulse. "It's slow but steady. We need to get her warm, quick."

Jacob tore off his ripped hazmat suit and wrapped it around her.

"Hold on, I didn't mean—"

"I'll be fine. We need to hurry."

Todd grabbed his arm. "Hold on, I'm looking for my dad. Arthur Stover."

Jacob pointed to the glow above the ridge. ""Maybe he's up there,"

Todd stood, watching the weird light and listening to the constant *chug, chug, chug* as it rumbled through the silent forest, echoing down the valley.

Jacob followed his gaze. "Any idea what it is?"?"

Todd hesitated, as if holding his breath. "Trust me, you don't want to know."

Suddenly, flashlight beams crisscrossed the woods and stopped on their faces. "Who are you?" a man shouted. A moment later, a group of soldiers encircled them, rifles raised.

"Would you put the guns down and get that light out of our eyes?" Todd shouted.

An armored soldier moved forward, pulling Jacob. "Jacob, step away." He kept his weapon trained on Todd.

"I'm looking for my dad, Arthur Stover. I'm his son, Todd."

"How did you get up here?"

Jacob pulled at the soldier's arm. "He's alright. He saved me. Please, my mom needs help!"

Two soldiers grabbed Jacob's mother and put her on a stretcher. Behind them, Jacob saw medics carrying more people down the mountain. The cavalry had finally arrived. Better late than never. The soldier turned to Jacob. "Go down with your mom. We'll—" He stopped, noticing Todd was no longer beside him. "Where'd he go?"

Jacob shrugged. Spinning, the soldier shouted, "Search the area!"

In the distance, Jacob saw a silhouette clambering up the ridge toward the green glow. *Good luck*, he thought.

A doctor wrapped a blanket around his shoulders as he stumbled beside his mom's stretcher. As they descended the rocky slope, her body bumped about, and he steadied her with both hands. Her eyes fluttered open, and a stream of frost escaped her blue lips. "Jacob . . ."

"It's OK, Mom. Everything's alright now." For the first time since this nightmare began, Jacob smiled.

The green glow blazed brighter, encompassing them in blinding light. Wind gathered, blasting shards of ice about in a mad dance. Above, trees swayed so frantically, Jacob feared they might break and fall. Throwing himself over his mother's stretcher, he shut his eyes and gripped her tightly. A distant scream echoed through the valley.

As soldiers rushed past, he knew he'd spoken too soon. The nightmare wasn't over.

His mother's eyes snapped open, suddenly alert. Teeth bared, she croaked dry words into her son's ear: "It . . . must . . . must leave . . . can't stay here . . ."

Startled, Jacob leaned in closer. "What do you mean?"

Her head tilted toward the blazing light as it poured through the black trees. "Don't let them stop it."

Above the ridge, Todd came into view, chased up the mountain by two soldiers, running toward the emerald glow. They disappeared once again behind silhouetted trees.

"It must leave," she reiterated, her voice growing distant. Before Jacob could ask another question, his mother's eyes rolled back in their sockets, and she went unconscious.

Jacob crawled off her prone body as medics pulled the stretcher down the hill. One of them, he noted, was the woman he'd spoken to earlier. She placed a hand on his shoulder. "Come on, let's get back to base camp."

Nodding hesitantly, his feet faltered as he followed them down the slick, icy slope. The pulsing green light illuminated their way.

As they edged into the forest, a series of rapid gunshots stole his attention, and his thoughts flashed back to the sound his shotgun had made before it tore his father's chest to pieces. Blood everywhere. The look in his dad's stunned eyes before he tumbled over the railing. Jacob swiveled, searching for the sound's source, staring up at the eerie, glowing mountain, his mother's words ringing in his mind like a pinball machine. *Don't let them stop it. It must leave.*

What must leave? he wondered.

Another reverberation of gunfire snapped him back to the present. Even before he'd consciously made a choice, his legs were retracing the way he'd come, gaining speed, running full-tilt up the hill, heading toward the sloping ridge above. The doctor's distant shouts, pleading for him to stop, were silenced under the *chug,*

chug, chug noise bursting through trees. Storming after Todd and the soldiers, Jacob raced toward the pale green light.

As he drew closer, the light became blinding.

Moments earlier

The ship's green lights cloaked the forest in emerald shadow. Arthur ignored his body's trembling and the biting cold, staring intently at the behemoth hanging above. All his answers waited inside—if he could find a way in. The ship's lights dancing through tree branches brought back memories of the night he'd lost Casey: blinding lights, high-pitched screams. Wondering if this was the same ship or one just like it, he walked along the western edge of the craft with Reese while Salvatore led the others east. They'd hoped to find an entrance, but after an hour's search, they'd found nothing beyond the intricately machined hull, with its interwoven veins of piping and lights. The ship seemed to be created from a network of metallic mesh conjoined to form a solid whole. The enormous craft reminded Arthur more of a biological body than a manufactured design.

Giving the ship a wide berth, they walked thirty feet from the hull, trailing its seemingly never-ending perimeter. Arthur felt Reese's eyes burrowing into his back, but for the moment, the major seemed content to allow Arthur to stay. *Only for as long as I'm useful,* he reminded himself. Arthur was fully aware of the atrocities of his actions, and on the rare occasions that his eyes drifted away from the ship, memories of his bullets tearing apart the old man and the naked woman sprang vividly back to life. In the moment he'd felt he had no control. Now he wondered if that were true or simply an excuse to hide from how far his obsession had driven him. Guns blazing, he'd raced to find the very thing that his eyes now peered up toward: the ship.

Perhaps Todd was right, he thought, glaring at the looming hull. *I should have walked away.* As quickly as the idea came, it went away. There was nowhere else he'd rather be.

A loud click behind him made him spin around.

He found himself staring down the barrel of an automatic rifle. Reese glared behind the weapon's sight, teeth bared, eyes narrow.

"You murdered those people," Reese said with a growl that bordered on animalistic.

Before Arthur could stammer a reply, a distant scream echoed. "Major!"

Wanting to search for the source but unable to tear his gaze from the rifle, Arthur shouted in shocked reply. "He's over here! Help!"

Again, the shrill, distant voice shouted. "Major!" This time Arthur was able to focus enough to recognize Lieutenant Salvatore's voice calling from the eastern edge of the ship. *Too far to help me,* Arthur realized. Noting Reese's finger on the trigger, Arthur raised his arms and closed his eyes, waiting for the bullets to tear him apart.

After a series of pained heartbeats, he opened his eyes and found Reese staring back at him, a blank expression on his face. As if awakening from a dream, the major lowered his weapon. His face hollow and pale, he seemed as confused as Arthur. Salvatore's echoing scream returned. "MAJOR!"

Avoiding further eye contact, Reese turned and ran from view.

Arthur reeled, clutching his knees and taking deep breaths. *One one thousand, two one thousand . . .* By *ten one thousand*, Arthur's back straightened, and his vision cleared. Slowly, his feet lumbered forward, following Reese's footprints in the snow. With each step Arthur's legs pumped faster.

He wanted to kill me. Arthur's mind whirled as he struggled to keep Reese's running silhouette in view. They raced through darkened foliage, rushing along the ship's circumference. *Out here where no one could see. He wanted to shoot me in the back.*

The ship seemed to have a violent effect on people, Arthur decided, bringing out their basest instincts. He wondered how much worse the effects of prolonged exposure to the craft might be. He also noted that he was surrounded by soldiers, all of whom were armed. Everyone except him.

Ahead, Salvatore's screams grew closer, snapping his attention. "Major Reese!"

Reese led them around another clump of bushes where Arthur saw Salvatore and another soldier yelling at someone else. The ship's emerald glow revealed one of the soldiers, a powerfully built man in his late thirties, who'd seemingly stepped too close to the ship. His left leg was stretched beneath the hull's shadow, as if it had crossed an invisible threshold. Despite not being able to see the cause of the alarm, Arthur could guess—his leg was caught in the time bubble surrounding the ship. His first thought was, *I was right.* His second was to admonish himself for thinking that. The man screamed in agony, trying to balance himself on his right leg while his left leg dangled in midstep. Reese started toward the soldier, but Arthur grabbed him. "No!" Salvatore blocked him as well, as if understanding Arthur's objection.

"Get your hands off me!" Even as Reese cried, Arthur felt him slacken in his arms.

Unable to remain erect, the soldier tumbled off balance, crossing the invisible barrier. Through the soldier's visor they saw his face wither from thirties to fifties to seventies.

He turned toward them, weeping. "Sir . . .?"

The aging continued: eighties, nineties, over a hundred, until his flesh tore away, and all that remained was a gleaming skull, staring back from behind a lifeless visor.

The corpse collapsed under the weight of its armor. It had taken mere seconds to change a burly soldier into a pile of withered skin and bones.

Once released from Arthur's grasp, Reese sagged to the ground. No one approached the shriveled corpse, lying a few feet away. Arthur turned his attention toward the ship, spotting a round hatch ten feet above them. "That's why he approached the ship," Arthur said, his voice barely above a whisper. "It's a door."

Salvatore didn't seem to care or hear him. Reese looked up, eyeing the hatchway. Then Casey's voice returned, closer and louder than before, as if she were standing right behind him, gasping for breath. Terrified.

Run! It's here! Run!

This time, Arthur was certain Casey was alive, still trapped inside the ship. His heart pounded so loudly in his chest that his knees buckled. Sweat stung his eyes. Arthur tilted his head toward the ship, calling out. "Casey? CASEY!" He spun toward Salvatore and Reese. "She's in there! I heard her!"

"Quiet, *please*," Salvatore said with a resigned sigh, staring at her fallen comrade's body.

Turning to Reese, Arthur lowered his voice to a mumble. "We have to get inside."

Stepping away from the others, Reese approached the ship, careful not to cross the invisible threshold, his eyes on the doorway. "We should wait for reinforcements."

"There's no time," Arthur answered. "She needs—"

"Dad!" a familiar voice shouted above the ship's roar.

Before Arthur turned, his heart hammered, and his mind screamed in protest. *No! He can't be here! Not here, not now . . .*

Todd clambered over the tree-lined ridge, stopping, mouth open, as he stared at the enormous craft suspended overhead. Salvatore and the other soldier raised their rifles, halting his approach. Arthur's heart sank, and his knees shook. All his life he'd wanted his boys to believe him, but now, after everything that had happened, the thought of one of his sons being there was a nightmare worse than any he could have imagined.

Two more soldiers appeared behind Todd, breathing heavily. They too stopped, lifting their gaze toward the enormous craft above. If they'd been chasing Todd up the mountain, they seemed to have forgotten their purpose.

"Get this man back!" Salvatore shouted to the newly arrived soldiers.

Arthur bolted between them, shielding Todd. "Wait, he's my son!"

Oblivious to the soldiers or their weapons, Todd never took his eyes off the giant hull. Having seemingly lost his voice, his mouth worked wordlessly. Arthur grabbed him. "Todd?"

Finally, Todd replied with a distant shrill. "Holy . . . shit . . ."

Salvatore turned to Arthur. "What the hell, old man? You bring your whole family?"

Reese waved Salvatore and the other soldier aside, then turned to Arthur. "He can't stay."

Arthur nodded, pulling Todd's attention off the ship. "You have to go back," he said. "It's not safe."

Forcing his wide eyes downward, Todd's expression hardened. "Come with me."

"I have to be here."

"No, Dad," Todd said, wrapping his arm around him. "You don't."

Arthur hesitated, glancing at the looming craft with

its promised answers waiting inside. Though he still heard Casey's distant voice itching incessantly at the back of his mind, he knew what he had to do. It wasn't even a choice. Casey was a lost love, and the ship was his obsession, but Todd was his son. As if waking from a dazed dream, he reluctantly nodded his assent.

"OK," he said. Swallowing, his throat lost its moisture. "We'll go back together."

"Staff Sergeant Pidgeon," Reese said behind him.

Turning, Arthur noticed a blanket of red fog sweep through the trees. In the center stood a silhouetted armored soldier, missing his helmet. The figure's eyes blazed with pinpricks of light.

Todd spoke before Major Reese could approach. "That thing is *not* one of your soldiers."

Ignoring him, Salvatore stepped closer. "Pidgeon? You alright, man?"

The mist thickened, coiling about them with vaporous tentacles. Pidgeon lunged.

33

Jutting shards obscured Casey's view as she hid in the back corner of the crystalline room. Ahead, a silhouette lurched, inching closer, with a heaving breath that stank of blood and excrement. To her left and right, the men huddled behind crystal shards, watching with clenched teeth as the thing lumbered forward. Could the thing smell them as easily as she could smell it? Either way, Casey knew they couldn't remain hidden for long, and their only exit loomed distantly behind the approaching creature. Beside her, Earl held Donovan in place with a firm grip, as if he might bolt no matter the danger to himself or others. Bill huddled on her other side, tight lipped and narrow eyed, as he watched the monster's approach. Casey noted the role reversal, Bill now seeming less fearful than the previously smug Donovan. She couldn't help wondering where his newfound courage originated. Had he been changed by the ship as well?

Pulling her thoughts back to more pressing concerns,

she felt the room lurch with a groan, tossing her to the floor. She thought she heard Donovan's choked gasp, but thankfully, it was silenced, either by Earl's large hands or beneath the quake's thundering assault. From above, tiny pieces of crystal rained down, slicing her scalp and cheek, burning like a dozen paper cuts. Tilting her gaze toward the source, Casey noticed waves of crystals thrusting outward from the high ceiling, dangling directly overhead.

The creature continued, undeterred by the room's violence. It stopped above Bill, lingering just behind the jutting shards that hid them. Though its features were obscured behind colored crystal, crimson light from the thing's eyes danced through fractured glass as it peered this way and that. Unable to move or run, Bill huddled, his body convulsing as he closed his eyes, waiting for imminent death.

As the ship's shudder subsided, Casey kept her focus locked on the crystals overhead. Noting their different shapes and colors, she considered how badly some of the long, pointed crystals might damage the hulking beast. If they struck her or her companions, however, the blows could prove deadly. She would need to focus her attack . . .

Closing her eyes, she reached inwardly to find the familiar itch at the back of her skull. At first dim, it gradually brightened in her mind's eye, growing insistent, while the tiny falling shards slowed their descent about her. Meanwhile, the thing seemed to have discovered Bill. It smashed through obstructions, lunging toward its prey.

Then the attack slowed. Shards stopped in midair as time dawdled within Casey's vision. Keeping her focus on the crystalized daggers hanging overhead, she pulled at them with an invisible tether. As if they were an appendage, Casey felt their weight wrench from the metallic hull, giving way to gravity.

Time snapped back to normal as the crystal daggers

struck the beast. It took the full blow on its hunched back. Crushed beneath a cascade of pointed shards, the monster fell, crashing across the room and sending fractured pieces of crystal skittering across the floor. Without hesitation, Casey yanked Bill from out of his broken hiding place and ran for the distant exit. Earl and Donovan had seen their chance for escape and were already in front, racing toward the door. As usual, Casey noted, Donovan was in the lead, never stealing a backwards glance.

Escaping the room, Casey wondered if anyone would question how or why only that specific section of the roof had caved in. If so, she worried she might be found out. Picturing the scene in her thoughts, she decided Earl, and perhaps Bill, would be grateful she'd saved them. Donovan on the other hand, would consider her a threat—or worse, a monster no different than the one they were fleeing from. She hoped no one would take the time to question their luck. If they did, she decided it might be best to lie. What was the alternative? Admit she could manipulate her surroundings? Create axes from nothing?

Sure, and then I'll tell them about the thick, gray skin growing along my feet and palm.

The more her mind churned, the more she began to question if Donovan would be the only one against her. They might all think she was a monster. *If only Arthur were here*, she thought. He would know what to do. He was close; she knew that. She had felt his presence outside the ship, though whether he could find a way in and save her in time remained in doubt. Even if he did save her, what then? She glanced at the patch on her palm. The gray skin stretched up to her wrist now.

How much longer until it covers my entire body? What will I become?

As if to punctuate the point, Casey heard the creature's thundering footfalls echo behind them. It was still alive. They needed to run faster.

34

Clambering over the ridge, Jacob was assaulted with more information than his young mind could consume. His eyes watered, bewildered at the sights before him, and he flung himself down in the snow. Breaking the confounding scene into smaller chunks, he viewed the images piecemeal.

Overhead, a giant ship, so vast Jacob couldn't find the edges, hung suspended through a network of trees. The craft somehow hadn't destroyed the trees. Instead, it seemed to be fused into the branches, like one of the strange, modern sculptures he'd seen in art class. Below, three bloody soldiers lay sprawled on crimson snow, arms and legs tossed like broken dolls.

Near them, two more soldiers, a man and woman, were still standing. He recognized the man: Major Reese. He was firing a machine gun at Mr. Pidgeon. Jacob saw sparks of metal spurting about Pidgeon's body, as if the bullets were ricocheting off him while he kept his face covered with both arms and lurched forward. It would only be seconds before he reached the major. The woman with Reese wasn't firing. Either her gun was jammed, or she didn't want to shoot Pidgeon. Either way, Jacob knew they didn't have long before Pidgeon tore them both to pieces, like he had done with the soldiers on the ground.

Closer to Jacob, an old man came into focus. He was pulling Todd behind him, stumbling in the snow. Todd's glassy eyes found Jacob where he lay hidden beneath the tree branches. He waved his arms feebly, as if trying to warn Jacob away. Still, Jacob remained on his belly, processing all he saw, unable to will his body to move away from the safety of the ridge's lip.

Above it all, the thunderous *chug, chug, chug* from the ship's engines blasted a snowy haze over the horrific images and muted any screams and gunshots. It was like a vague, silent picture show that Jacob couldn't stop watching.

Unable to break through Pidgeon's armor or fire a killing blow to the head, Major Reese's rifle spit its final rounds and then clicked with hollowed emptiness. He dropped the weapon and drew his sidearm. He doubted it would pack enough punch to stop the quickly approaching *thing*. He no longer thought of the figure before him as Pidgeon. His friend was long gone, and the being that stood in his place had already killed three of Reese's men. Soldiers, he reminded himself, whose names he'd never even taken the time to learn. This was his fault, he acknowledged, remembering how slow he'd been to halt Pidgeon's approach when Arthur's son had warned them. Reese had hesitated, not wanting to fire on his friend, and the three torn-apart bodies lying before him were the result of his indecision. This time he didn't hesitate, unloading every last bullet into the red-eyed armored figure rushing toward him. Still, it wasn't enough.

The bullets tore tiny pieces of the armor away but not enough to break through.

Pidgeon reached Salvatore just as she finally opened fire. She'd been slower to act than Reese, and now that hesitation would cost her. Flinging Salvatore's rifle aside, Pidgeon grabbed her chest armor, hoping to rip the metal apart with his bare hands. Reese leapt onto Pidgeon's back, frantically trying to pull him off her, and the three of them fell in a cascade of blood and snow. Tangled together, Salvatore and Reese hammered Pidgeon's armor with the butts of their handguns, but it proved useless.

With a heavy strike to the abdomen, Salvatore crumpled. Pidgeon spun his attention to Reese, grabbing him by the neck and flipping him over. Breath exploded from Reese's lungs, fogging his helmet. Through the haze, he saw Pidgeon's red eyes glare down at him.

Staring death in the face, Reese thought of Noelle. She would be in bed now, he thought, wishing he could be there to tuck her in. Pidgeon's thick hands descended, clawing at his helmet. Red mist swirled about, blanketing Reese's view.

Noelle, I'm so sorry.

Jacob tried to shout over the ship's roaring engines to draw Pidgeon's attention, but his tiny scream was lost in the din. Grabbing a chunk of icy snow, he hurled it toward Pidgeon. It fell ten feet away. Pidgeon, however, noted the movement. His eyes swiveled off Reese and bore into Jacob, his body twisting around for a better view of his new assailant. Before he could step forward, however, another series of gunshots pumped into his back, exploding through his armored chest. Reese had used the momentary distraction to grab Salvatore's rifle. Pidgeon stumbled but didn't fall. Jacob stood on the ridge's lip, locked in place, as Reese's helmet came into view, peeking from behind Pidgeon's shoulder. Reese fired point blank again and again, each bullet ripping through the same space in Pidgeon's enormous chest, slowly tearing a hole through the near-impenetrable armor. For a moment, Jacob thought Pidgeon might fall from the bullets' rapid impact, but the inhuman thing possessing Pidgeon's body seemed merely weakened, not deterred. It twisted about, fumbling for Reese's weapon. Their bodies became a blurred silhouette within the snow-blasted curtain. Jacob inched closer. One step, then another. At the third step, a hand grasped his leg. An old man pulled at him. Todd's father, he presumed.

"Stay down," the man ordered through gritted teeth.

Jacob tried to tear himself free from the old man's grip. "What about Major Reese?"

Hidden beside the old man, crouched in the snow, Todd struggled to be heard over the ship's engines. "There's nothing you can do."

Unwilling to listen, Jacob twisted free and bolted into the white blur. Pushing through a blanket of howling wind and white blindness, he inched toward Pidgeon's back. Reese knelt on the ground, his weapon now in Pidgeon's possession, leveled at the major's head. Through Reese's visor, Jacob saw the defiance in his eyes, even in his final moment of life. Unsure how to help, his mother's words bubbled to the surface of his mind: *It must leave. It doesn't belong here.*

"LEAVE!" Jacob shouted before Pidgeon could squeeze the trigger.

As if more curious than concerned, Pidgeon's red eyes spun around, finding the boy ten feet behind him. But when he turned, his face was no longer Pidgeon's. Instead, Jacob found himself staring up at a blood-covered mess in a flannel shirt, his chest a gaping, open wound. The jutting ribcage and exposed heart made Jacob lurch, dry heaving from the macabre sight. His father glared at him with burning red holes for eyes.

"Look what you did! My own fucking son!"

Dad?

Jacob's legs gave out, and he sank to his knees. His

mind swirling, he didn't protest as his father raised the rifle. *This is what I deserve. I killed him . . .*

Feeling the snow's biting cold dig into his legs, he awoke with a jolt to the reality of the situation. *This isn't my dad. This isn't my dad.* The weapon's barrel touched his temple. Tears streaked down his cheeks. Finding his voice, Jacob screamed. "You have to leave! Go! No one's left to stop you!"

His father's murderous, blood-drenched form turned back into Pidgeon's blank stare. The gun wavered. Jacob fought to stand on numb feet as he glared at the demon before him. "Now's your chance. Go."

Pidgeon's fiery gaze lost its luminescence as he tilted his head upwards, toward the alien hull hanging ten feet above, almost within reach. Jacob's voice turned to a murmur beneath the craft's roaring engines. "Just *leave*," he pleaded.

Finally, the rifle plopped into the snow.

Riddled with bullet holes, Pidgeon tore his armor off, shedding the shattered metal as he stumbled toward the craft, a trail of carnage in his wake. As he moved closer to the ship, he seemed to cross an invisible boundary. Faster than Jacob's eyes could register, Pidgeon's weakened body shriveled to a dry husk. With each step closer to the ship, skin disintegrated off his bones, revealing the skeleton underneath. By the fourth step, his body crumpled into a heap, and all that remained was a shimmering form made of red smoke. The ghostly apparition floated upwards, disappearing into the craft. At last, Jacob decided, the nightmare was finally over.

Reese's hands wrapped about his shoulders, pulling his attention back to earth. The major tried to smile, but it came out crooked. "You saved us, Jacob."

The boy nodded absently, still dazed by what he'd seen. He noted Todd and his father approaching while Reese turned to help the female soldier to her feet. Above, the ship shuddered and shook violently. Snow cascaded from the trees, falling about them in giant heaps. Todd pulled at Arthur's arm. "We need to leave."

"You go," the old man said before turning back toward the ship.

"No," Todd barked. "You're coming with me!"

"Come on, Arthur," Reese said, growing red in the face. "Right now."

The ship lurched. Jacob and the others ducked as the hull quivered overhead. Everyone except Arthur, who stood rigidly, peering up at the shuddering metal form. Though Jacob couldn't see his face, he knew the old man was staring at the precise point where the vaporous creature had disappeared into the hull. Instead of retreating, Arthur stepped forward.

"Dad!" Todd shouted over the screaming engines.

Reese lunged toward him, grabbing the old man's shoulder, and then—

The two of them vanished.

More snow descended, showering Jacob with chunks of ice. Shielding his face, he heard the woman and Todd shouting. The louder they screamed, the louder the ship's engines seemed to grow in protest. The noise became deafening.

His face covered, Jacob wasn't sure whose hands grabbed him, pulling him out of the chaos. The blanketing white swirl and heavy *chug, chug, chug* lessened as he found himself being guided over the mountain's ridge and down a slope. Unable to process everything that was happening, his thoughts drifted once more to his father, and he realized the nightmare would never truly end. An invisible weight seemed to crush him lower to the ground with each step. Todd and the woman were pulling him on either side, drawing him farther down the slope, taking him away from the blinding, deafening chaos. Behind them the green glow brightened as the ship struggled to pull itself free from the treetops. Jacob didn't look back. He'd seen enough. Instead, he imagined his sister and mother sleeping safely at the base of the mountain, and all he wanted to do was join them. With each step farther down the mountain, farther from the constant *chug, chug, chug* of the engines and the emerald-green glow, the invisible weight crushing his chest seemed to lift a little. His feet grew lighter.

Jacob went home.

35

A pulsating sound drummed in Reese's ears, pounding so loudly he covered his helmet with his hands. When the drumming diminished to a quiet din, his eyes peeled open, though he saw only blurred shadows. Glancing about, he didn't find the others or trees or snow-covered mountains. Reese's vision gradually shifted into focus, and he discovered curved steel walls on either side. No, not steel, he quickly decided, noting how the light shifted along their smooth gray surface. Shadowy shapes crawled about with a life of their own.

He was standing in a dark hallway that pulsed with dim light from an unseen source, as if the walls themselves were generating the glow. A feeling of dread snaked up Reese's spine, pricking the base of his neck. The surrounding hall shook with a violent spasm, and his body shook with it. By the time the spasm had ceased, Reese realized where he was standing—inside the ship.

Curious if Arthur and Salvatore might be trapped somewhere inside as well, Reese spun about. Silent, empty halls greeted him in either direction. Taking a step forward, his booted foot grazed a throbbing, incandescent light fixture. Tilting his head, he noted a curved walkway dangling high above. *I'm standing on the ceiling,* he realized with a nervous, inward chuckle. *Good, because this wasn't weird enough already.*

Switching his visor to reveal thermal heat signatures, colors morphed into blobs of dark blue and fiery orange. Below, tiny, bright footprints trailed along the corridor. The marks were from bare feet, too small to be an adult's. *A child's footprints.* He cursed. He had hoped to pick up Arthur's trail, but the sudden fear that a child was trapped in there made his skin crawl.

With his rifle at the ready, he followed the tracks. Turning one corner and then another, each new hallway Reese discovered appeared to be a carbon copy of the last, seemingly lifeless beyond the thermal footprints. He began to wonder where everyone was. As if in reply, a soft giggle wafted past him, like a ghost brushing by. It sounded like a little girl's laughter, though whether the sound originated from behind or in front of him was impossible to tell. Pausing, Reese turned in circles, searching for the source.

Another giggle seemed to come from inches behind him, but when he turned around, nothing was there. Given the circumstances, he became concerned the faint, childlike laugh might be a creation of his own heightened imagination. Turning his wrist over, he highlighted the armor's controls, replaying audio feedback from the last thirty seconds. The laughter played back, louder and shriller than before, growing into a high-frequency static-filled scream.

Clutching his head from the shocking noise, Reese quickly turned the playback off, reeling against the curved wall. Then his heart stopped. At the end of the tunnel a familiar little girl stared back at him. She was four years old with pigtails and bare feet, wearing a red dress with white lace. Giggling again, the child's laughter tore at Reese's heart. *No. This isn't real. It can't be . . .*

Noelle.

Or at least she appeared to be. Her red lips twisted in a crooked grin beneath dark eyes. The thing staring back made his blood run cold. Not because he feared it was really his daughter but because someone or something had been able to reach inside his mind and make her appear to be flesh and blood. Before Reese had time to call out, the child vanished around a corner, her echoing laughter trailing like a lingering scent. Reese followed at a run.

As he came around the corner, a blast of pebbles swept by his feet. A mixture of browns and ochres, it took a moment for Reese to register what was pelting his armor: sand. More confused than concerned, he raced down the winding tunnel, searching for the "Not Noelle," who'd seemingly vanished. Weapon raised and ready, he turned left, then right, until he stopped dead in the middle of a heat-drenched desert.

Feet stumbling to a halt, he glanced about, finding hovels for homes on either side. A loud thumping sound from a helicopter overhead blew sand about, obscuring his view. Reese didn't need to see clearly to know where he now stood. He'd been there before, in that exact spot, fifteen years earlier. Fallujah, Iraq, December 22, 2004. Twisting about, Reese silently prepared himself for what he knew would come next.

His younger self and three other soldiers were hunched behind a Humvee, taking fire from a small house on the other side of the battle-torn street. Reese didn't move, frozen in place, as he watched his teen-age self roll around the Humvee, firing blindly into the house. His mates joined in. Bullets tore at clay walls until the structure half-crumbled under its fractured wooden roof, just as it had happened before.

Enough, Reese spat inwardly.

The image changed. Reese found himself inside the

wreckage of the Iraqi home. On the floor a woman in her mid-thirties lay spread-eagle, showered in bullets, her weapon dangling limply at her side. Across from her, the three bullet-riddled boys, the oldest no more than thirteen, lay dead in twisted positions of agony. The soldiers lingered in the shattered doorway, eyeing their work. Teenage Reese bolted outside, vomiting. Older Reese, having seen this image in his mind's eye for fifteen years, still tasted the lingering vomit on his tongue. Even so, this was an old nightmare, one he'd lived with for years.

"Enough," Reese repeated, this time saying it aloud. He closed his eyes, counted to ten, and then opened them. A darkened tunnel extended before him. The midnight show was over.

Something clutched his left hand, interlacing around his fingers. Looking down, he found Noelle's bright eyes peering back at him, her tiny hand wrapped around his. *I shouldn't be able to feel an illusion*, he thought.

"What's an illusion, Daddy?"

Hearing Noelle's familiar singsong voice, Reese finally gave in to the full extent of the horror he was seeing and feeling. Ice closed around his skull, and his back buckled. Still, he struggled to keep his tone even. "You're not my daughter." When the little girl didn't reply, he continued. "Who, or what, are you?"

With a giggle that sent his legs trembling, the girl let go, stepping away. Conscious of the emptiness in his hand as her fingers left his, Reese blinked back burgeoning tears. When his vision cleared, she was gone.

Finding his footing, Reese continued, turning the next corner. In the distance, another familiar figure came into view, though this time he doubted it was an illusion.

Arthur ran toward him with a noticeable spring in his step. Behind his visor, his wrinkled face was drawn in a huge grin. "Incredible! Simply *incredible*, isn't it?"

Recalling the last time they were alone together, Reese lowered his rifle and forced a half-baked smile across his face. Having seen what this ship could do to one's mental state, Reese doubted that his earlier instinct to shoot the old man had been his own. Perhaps this ship somehow amplified people's anger and fear. If so, then Arthur's murderous actions may not have been completely his fault, either. At least that was what Reese decided to believe for the moment.

"Any idea how we got in here?" he asked.

The old man rubbed the chin of his visor. Reese thought he was milking it a bit. "Maybe we *thought* our way in," Arthur said.

"Come again?"

"I was desperate to get inside, and now here we are."

"Yeah, here we are," Reese repeated dryly.

Stepping forward, he raised his rifle and led them into the unknown.

36

Fire cranked up the side of Casey's legs, and her chest was a thundering kick drum. Barreling down the hallway at full tilt, she struggled to keep pace with Earl, who was several feet ahead. In the distance, at least twenty yards beyond him, she glimpsed Donovan rounding the next corner. Even Bill, who lacked any muscle mass, ran faster than her gray-patched feet would carry her.

She could hear the creature scrambling, its *click-clacking* talons inching closer, clinging to the inverted floor above. Bringing up the rear, Casey knew she'd be the first to feel those talons when they finally descended, tearing flesh, meat, and bone. Gasping through gritted teeth, she pictured her body torn to pieces—a leg here, an arm there, walls covered in a gory mess. Something stirred in the back of her mind, hinting that what she saw was not her imagination but rather a glimpse of the near future, seconds from now. The horrific image made her legs pump harder, struggling to push through the dull, gray-patched bottoms of her feet. Earl rounded the corner next, blinking from view.

Now it was just her and Bill. And the man-monster breathing down her neck.

No, no, don't worry about me, Casey cursed. *You just keep going. I'll be fine.*

Bill was next to approach the tunnel's end. Rounding the corner, he stole a backwards glance toward Casey. His eyes tilted upwards, and his face drained of color. As he disappeared from view, Bill's terrified expression burned in Casey's mind. *The thing is right above me.*

A stench of burnt flesh invaded her nostrils. A raspy gurgle tickled her ear. The corner drew closer, less than ten feet away, though it might as well have been a mile for how close the thing was to her now. Casey knew she wouldn't make it.

Suddenly, a panicked shout rose above the monster's rapid breathing, and a series of groans emanated from behind the fast-approaching corner. Stumbling on numb feet, Casey wondered if whatever waited ahead might be worse than what stalked inches behind her. A cold, sharp talon sliced the back of her shirt, sending stabbing pain along her spine and pushing away any other concerns. Nothing could be worse than being torn apart by this thing, she decided. Leaning forward, arching her back downward, she burst around the corner at breakneck speed.

Only to crash into a heap of coiled bodies.

Somehow the men had gotten themselves twisted together, and now they lay in a pile, sprawled across the narrow tunnel floor. Stuck within a mass of flailing limbs, Casey's own fear drowned out her companions' cacophony of shrill, panicked screams. She assumed the garbled words were something along the lines of "Get the fuck up!" or "Move!", but her own thundering heartbeat was all she could discern. Bill's feet kicked her face. Earl's biceps crushed her ribcage. Donovan, meanwhile, was nowhere to be found. The blazer-wearing weasel had escaped.

As Bill scrambled to his feet, Casey tried to pull Earl up from the floor. His face contorted and he screamed, his voice high-pitched and shrill. "My back!"

Looking down, Casey noted Earl's body was a twisted pretzel bent into an impossible pose. *Dear Lord, his spine is broken.* Before she could untangle herself further from the mess of flailing limbs, her focus shifted beyond Earl and Bill to the looming shadow clamoring above. She tried to scream, to shout for the others to run, but the fear gripping her chest was so intense that all she managed was a muffled moan. The thing dropped between them, tossing Casey and Bill into either wall. It went for the injured first: Earl.

Black eyes and yellow teeth were the last thing he saw.

The thing lunged, tearing into his chest with knives for claws.

Blinking away the growing darkness of unconsciousness, Casey heard Earl's distant cries, as if from underwater. Her eyes fluttered, searching for him, only to find the monster instead. The thing with a misshapen human body, 1970s-era clothing, and large black eyes knelt over her. It reeked of blood and urine. Maybe, she thought, the smells were clues to the last thing the poor man felt before he turned into whatever he was now.

Then her eyes darted past it, and she lost all sympathy.

Earl lay in pieces. Chunks of bloody meat splattered about like a grotesque jigsaw. It was as she'd seen in her vision moments earlier, only it wasn't her own body that had been shredded. Within a single heartbeat, Casey's mind whirled with a mixture of emotion: a split-second of relief replaced by guilt, only to be replaced again by the horror at what would undoubtedly come next. Her last thought was of Arthur. Just before the thing lunged, she heard his voice in her mind: *I'm coming! Hang on!*

As the yellow teeth descended over her face, she

smiled at the crazy trick of the mind that made her think her lover was there, about to come to the rescue. She knew it was a fantasy. Still, better to die smiling than screaming. Casey closed her eyes as the teeth cut into her cheek.

Then, as quickly as the sharp pain came, it was gone.

There are other survivors was the first thing Casey thought as an old man tumbled into the creature, shoving it aside. Her second thought was that she wished it was someone younger, stronger, and carrying a bazooka. Still, she was alive, a momentary reprieve.

She turned to Bill in the corner, hoping he'd snap out of his daze. He quivered and shook, drenched in Earl's blood, watching with wide eyes. He wasn't going to be any help. She had to do something. Pushing herself up, Casey kicked out at the thing's back. It ignored her. The creature's stench caused her to pause, then she flung herself on top of it, wrapping her arm around its throat and beating its distorted skull with her right fist. Surprisingly, the creature stumbled. By chance she'd found a sensitive area. It was a brief victory. Stomping backwards, it slammed her into a wall. The impact took her breath away. She grabbed its waist, and its mouth widened, reeking of blood.

Suddenly, Casey's earlier prayers were answered. It wasn't a stronger, younger man with a bazooka, but it was the next best thing: a soldier with an automatic rifle. He seemed to have appeared from nowhere. A godsend if ever there was one, or so she hoped.

He fired. The noise was shatteringly loud, amplified through the echoing hallway. Casey curled into a ball, covering her ears. Bursts of light and fire accompanied the deafening sound as round after round pumped into the creature's wide chest. Black blood sprayed everywhere, drenching Casey's hair and eyes, momentarily blinding her with gore. The thing's tortured screams stormed her eardrums, sounding sickly human and high-pitched, like a child.

Instead of falling, the monster dove forward, knocking the soldier's rifle aside and going for his throat. Somehow, Casey knew what was happening, even though black blood caked her vision. Though blinded, she saw everything through her mind's eye. Time slowed as she watched the creature's talons about to dig into the soldier's neck. No, not a creature, it was a man. Walter Davison, age thirty-two, from Florida. He'd been vacationing in Blackwood in 1965 when the ship came and took him. Something had happened when it crashed that changed Walter into this thing. She knew all of this and more, including the soldier's name. And the old man on the floor was—

She gasped. *Arthur!*

Somehow, the old man lying on the ground, seemingly frozen in time now, was the man she loved, a man who had been young and vibrant only last night. Casey was in the future. All of this came to her in a heartbeat. She also understood what she needed to do to save the soldier. The ship told her, communicating not through words or images but through flashes of understanding. As if the answers had been in her mind all along, the ship brought them to the surface, showing her how to survive. The craft, with its seemingly endless hallways and strange rooms, could be reconfigured just as it had been earlier with the whooshing steel door. Though slowed, time wasn't stopped. Walter's elongated nails were still moving toward Reese's neck, about to puncture his skin.

She had to act. Now.

37

A rthur watched helplessly from the floor as Reese's rifle shattered in a hail of hot metal and sparks. The thing grabbed Reese. Its enormous black eyes were filled with hatred, its body riddled with bullet holes, pieces of its shoulders and face blown apart, yet still it stood on wobbly legs. Too strong and too fast for Reese to fight, its clawed fingers tore at his armor. Arthur heard Reese scream, struggling to tear free from its grasp. Until—

The creature vanished.

No, not vanished, *dropped*. A hole had formed in the floor, swallowed the thing up and then resealed in a blink of the eye. Reese now stood alone, wobbling on unsure feet, peering at the gray-paneled floor beneath him. The sudden silence was as disquieting as the chaos before it. Stumbling to his feet, Arthur cleared his throat. "Where'd it go?"

Reese gazed around, shrugging. His face was blank, as if still processing all he'd seen in the last few seconds. Casey approached with a slight limp, her voice thick and distant. "Trapped in a room below us." She nodded absently toward the blood-soaked floor.

Not wishing to view her through a glass visor, Arthur removed his helmet with an audible *click*. Yet, while his eyes swept over her, his lips refused to work. After so many years, he couldn't seem to find the words. Worse, he feared what she might say to him. As if sensing his concern, Casey approached, delicately touching his wrinkled face with polished, white-tipped nails. He shied away, realizing how old he was compared to how young she had remained.

Then her voice was in his ear, as soft and as loving as his best dreams. "Arthur," she said.

He forced his eyes to swivel, meeting her soft expression, devoid of surprise. After so many years, she still recognized him. He opened his mouth to say something, anything, but the words wouldn't come. Tears welled, dripping down his wrinkled face. Instead of finding happiness or relief after all these years, he felt nothing but *shame*. Deep and unbearable, like being engulfed in a vast pit. He couldn't save her, not then and not now.

"I'm alright," Casey replied, reading his sorrowful expression. Pulling him close, she embraced him, limply, more like a friend than an intimate lover. Or, he imagined, more like a distant relative one meets at a family gathering—warm but with distinct boundaries. Arthur wrapped his hands around her, feeling her firm body. He wanted to kiss her, to throw her down on the floor and make love right there. She was so utterly unchanged, like a photograph had come to life right before him. Taking in the aroma of her hair and the feel of her solid muscles, he noted his own slouched back and weathered wrinkles in stark comparison. Arthur knew then that he would never make love to her again. *I should never have come*, he thought, sobbing.

"You haven't changed," Arthur said. His voice sounded hollow to his own ears.

"You have," she replied. It was a simple statement,

though Arthur felt the sting of her words. "But still as handsome as ever," she added, as if reading his thoughts.

Smiling for the first time, Arthur chuckled uneasily. "Liar."

"You came for me?" she asked.

"I wish I could have found you sooner."

She embraced him again, closer this time, warmer. "You found me. That's all that matters."

Wanting desperately to stay in her arms forever, but understanding the reality of their situation, he forced himself to wrench free. Replacing his helmet, he felt fresh tears wet his face. He hoped the visor might hide his reaction. He doubted it did. His throat became a desert. "I . . . I'm an old man, and look at you. You haven't changed at all."

Stealing a glance at the blood-drenched body at the other end of the hall, her eyes grew heavy, and her voice thickened. "Yeah, I have."

"Who was he?" Arthur asked, hearing the pain in her voice.

"A friend."

Casey's back straightened as she stepped over to him, peering down at the corpse. Wanting to give her space, Arthur didn't follow. After a moment, she turned to Reese. "Thank you, Major."

Reese offered a quizzical look as he loaded a fresh clip in his rifle. "How'd you know my rank?"

Casey nodded toward an insignia just visible through his torn hazmat suit. "My dad was in the army."

Arthur noted the flatness in her voice when she mentioned her father. It wasn't a subject she had often brought up, if ever. It was then that Arthur noted the differences in her demeanor. There was nothing coy or simple about the woman standing across from him. The unsure waitress from Blackwood who dreamed of being a housewife had been replaced by someone stronger, more confident. He couldn't help wondering what had happened to her on the ship. He stepped closer, wanting to never leave her side again. Before he could speak, however, a short, fidgety little man in a button-down and glasses pulled at his arm.

"I'm Bill," he offered.

Trying to hide the annoyance he felt at being torn away from Casey for even a second, Arthur forced a faint smile and nodded. "How long have you been trapped in here?"

The little man scratched his head. "Since sixty-two, I guess."

"*Nineteen* sixty-two?" Arthur stammered.

Reese approached. "Just how many people are on this thing?"

Bill shrugged. "Lots."

"We found a room," Casey interjected, "a chamber of some sort. Inside there were thousands." Eyes narrowing, she corrected herself. "Hundreds of thousands."

Suddenly, the tunnel shook, knocking Arthur off his feet. The others grasped walls for support until the spasms subsided. Feeling a distant *chug, chug, chug* reverberate beneath his feet, Arthur knew exactly what was happening. "The ship's moving!" he shouted.

38

We were supposed to grow old together, Casey thought, stealing a glance toward the side of Arthur's helmet. Guiltily, she found herself relieved she couldn't see his aged, wrinkled face. *We were going to have kids, a house. Now, we're strangers.*

The numbness in her feet crawled up her legs, threatening her spine. Absently glancing downward, she wondered how far up the gray patches had crawled beneath her clothes. At least the pain had subsided. Glancing back at Arthur, she couldn't help thinking that one pain had simply been replaced by another.

Another tremor rippled down the tunnel. Casey cursed inwardly. *This ship took everything from me.* She searched for the ever-present itch at the back of her mind and made a vow to whoever might be listening. *I'm going to take everything from you too. You're not lifting off. You're staying right here. That's a promise.*

Following Reese along the narrow tunnel, Casey and the others remained silent. Arthur's visor occasionally turned in her direction, then quickly spun away. He was as crushed as she was, Casey knew. While it had been a matter of a single, nightmarish day for her, Arthur had waited decades for this moment. A reunion both had eagerly anticipated, yet now they avoided each other's gaze.

The silence was deafening. In the oppressive quiet, with only the sound of their breathing and footfalls for company, Casey's thoughts trailed back toward Earl's torn body. What remained hadn't even resembled a person anymore. An arm here, a leg there, his head no-where to be found. Perhaps, she thought, the creature had eaten it.

Suppressing a shiver, she noticed Bill keeping pace with Reese, shoulder to shoulder. Bill seemed to have found a new leader to latch onto, which raised anoth-er question, *Where's Donovan?* Not that she missed his snide remarks or his glaring eyes, but still, he'd gone missing, and now Earl was dead. Two down and two new members in their group to replace them. Eyeing Reese's rifle, she hoped this new team might fare better than the last.

Casey doubted it.

"What happened back there?" Reese asked, glanc-ing over his shoulder. When Casey didn't respond, he clarified his question. "With that thing, the creature, you seemed to know where it had gone."

"His name was Walter, I think." Holding her breath and counting to five, Casey exhaled. "I trapped him in another room below us."

Everyone stopped cold. Arthur's face lit up, obvi-ously fascinated. Bill stared nervously downward, as if something was stuck to his shoe. Reese approached, eye-ing her suspiciously.

Arthur spoke first, his voice rising an octave with ex-citement. "How, precisely?"

She shrugged. "It's hard to explain."

"Try," Reese said with a sharpness in his tone that hadn't been there before.

When she remained silent, Arthur pressed. "Did you *imagine* what would happen before it did?"

"I . . . I guess," Casey stammered, struggling to find the words.

Arthur turned to Reese. "It's as I suggested. This place hears our thoughts."

Reese nodded. "If that's how we got in here, can we get out the same way?"

"I can hear them," Casey whispered before Arthur could answer.

Reese's head spun back to her. "Who?"

"Whoever's controlling the ship." Noting the paleness of the men's faces, she added, "And they can hear me."

Reese's features softened, and his tone followed. "Can you get us out of here?"

Casey raged inwardly, icy fingers slithering up the back of her neck. "We're not going anywhere. Not yet."

Reese looked as if he'd been slapped. "Come again?"

Noting the resolve in her voice, Arthur concurred. "She's right. There's too much to learn here."

"I don't care about *learning* anything," Casey said, her voice growing even colder. "Thousands of people are trapped in here, and I promised Earl we would get them out."

Reese blew a stream of mist across his visor. "We'll need a team for that."

"We have a team," Casey urged.

"A *military* team," Reese snapped. Detecting the urgency in his voice, Casey realized he was as frightened as everyone else; he simply hid it better. "If you can get us out of here—"

"I can't," Casey insisted. "Don't you think I'd have gotten off this thing if I could?"

"You opened the floor up like Houdini."

"Because someone or something on this ship helped me. This isn't the same."

"Why the hell not?"

Arthur stepped between them. "Please, both of you, calm down."

"They don't want us to leave!" Casey shouted over Arthur's quiet protest.

Reese's eyes burrowed into her. "Do you?"

Suddenly, the floor spasmed and gave out beneath their feet. The hallway went topsy-turvy. Falling head-first toward the floor above, Casey wrapped her arms about her head, preparing herself for a hard landing. Crashing into cold metal, wind blew from her lungs. The ship had righted itself, and now the four of them lay crumpled on an octangular-patterned floor.

Struggling to rise, Casey cradled her aching feet. Pulling back a pant leg, she found the gray patch had crawled up to her knee and beyond. As the ship's spasms subsided, she couldn't help thinking that the outward volatility matched what she felt inside. Wondering if there was a connection, she felt a hand touch her shoulder. She yanked her pant leg back down to conceal the enlarged gray patch and groaned. "I'm fine."

"Sure you are," Arthur said through the visor's metallic speaker. She wondered if he'd seen her exposed skin, but if he had, there was no evidence of it from the way his soft eyes watched her.

Pushing away the rage burning her gut, Casey allowed him to help her stand. His arms wrapped about her shoulders. Feeling his gentle, concerned touch, she leaned into him and felt a wave of relief. She slid her fingers over his armored chest, up toward his helmet, and probed for a latch at the base of his neck.

"What are you doing?" he asked.

"You don't need this," she said, taking off his helmet. His gaze swiveled, searching for escape, but no matter where he looked, he found her green eyes staring back.

Below, her lips offered a crooked grin. "After all these years of trying to find me, I'm not letting you hide now."

His face creased into a sad smile. "This wasn't how I imagined it."

"Me neither." Pulling him closer, her lips touched his. A gentle kiss.

"I hate to break in," Reese said, helping Bill to his feet. "But, as I was saying, we need a way out."

Casey hesitated. Perhaps the major was right. Part of her *didn't* want to simply slither out the back door and escape. Not after everything she'd been through. Not after what happened to Earl. She deserved answers. With a final nod to Arthur, Casey spun about, staring past Reese down the twisted hallway. She felt an incessant urge whisper at the back of her skull.

"No," she replied with venom in her throat, "we need to find the ones who took us."

Before Reese could object, Casey reached inward, probing for the itch in her mind. She pulled at it, as if grasping a string. The stronger she pulled, the clearer her connection to the ship became. The men watched helplessly as walls morphed—changing, reconfiguring into a single straight line. At the end of the newly formed tunnel, an arched doorway awaited.

Exhausted from the strain, Casey stumbled, her breathing a dull rasp. Her stomach ached, hollow and ravaged. Still, she'd succeeded. After countless curved tunnels, time-lapsed staircases, and strange, horrible rooms, Casey had created a straight path to all the answers she sought. The whispered voice in the back of her mind grew louder. Closer.

Beside her, Arthur appeared speechless. Even Reese struggled to find the right words. "What the hell did you do?" he asked finally.

"I found our captors," Casey replied. "They're waiting beyond that door."

39

Blackwood, six months later

It had been half a year since the "Incident." Most surprising to Jacob was how easily folks slipped back into a normal routine. Few mentioned the events of the previous winter, and when they did, it was in hushed tones and with bated breath. Not even his sister or mother discussed it, no matter how often Jacob persisted. Unwilling to forget what had happened either to the town or to his father, his pain lingered. At night, lying in the dark, he heard the shotgun blast, felt the recoil slam into his shoulder, and saw the crimson explosion erupt from his dad's chest. At fourteen years old, Jacob was a murderer. Everyone knew it, but there'd been no repercussions, as if it had never happened. But it had, and the guilt gnawed at him like a cancer.

In late August, when summer was in its death throes, and fall threatened to turn Blackwood forest to crimson and ochre, Jacob hiked up the mountain. He preferred to be alone these days. After everything that had happened, he didn't look at the townspeople in the same way. They were forever changed, and so was he. Even the surrounding forest seemed altered in some way. The birds still hadn't returned, offering a hallowed silence. Perhaps that's why none of the townsfolk had gone hunting this season, he thought. Or maybe it was something else. No matter how many people populated the area, Blackwood seemed like a ghost town in all but name. Even the military had abandoned it. Scientists and doctors had lingered for a few months after the ship vanished, following up on strange stories of ghostly voices heard up in the mountains, though no one gave much credence to them. The townspeople had suffered a terrible fright, and the military scientists seemed to assume whatever voices people might be hearing were simply in their own heads. Jacob, however, wasn't so quick to discount anything anymore.

A sharp snap of breaking branches focused his attention behind him. Assuming it might be a deer, he hunched low, hoping to catch a glimpse. In a pink blur, Samantha exploded from behind some bushes, toppling him into a pile of dirt. Laughing.

Rolling over, he shoved her aside. "What are you doing up here?"

"Following you."

"I wanted to be alone."

"I know," she said, giggling as she stood up.

Jacob remained sitting, looking up at her wicked grin. "Then why come?"

"*I* didn't want to be alone."

It was a lie, he knew. Samantha worried about him. She never said it aloud, but for the last year she'd been a constant shadow.

Perched on his knees, as he pushed himself off the ground, something whisked past in his peripheral vision. *Scarlet mist.* Grabbing Samantha, he whipped around, searching the shadowy trees. Nothing moved. Samantha shot him a hard glare. "What's the matter?"

Jacob furrowed his brow, squinting, trying to pierce

the monolithic chunks of light and shadow surrounding them. The forest's overbearing silence felt like an omen. "Let's head back. Mom'll be worried about you."

"Why just me and not you?"

"I'm older."

"You mean uglier."

"Yeah, that's what I mean." He clasped his arm around her shoulders. "Come on."

Samantha danced beside him, heading back down the mountain. Overhead, the sun drifted behind the pines, dropping the temperature as they walked. Laughing and kicking up dirt along the way, neither noticed the sudden chill.

Then a distant voice trailed on the wind. Unsure if it was real or imagined, Jacob turned back. Not wanting to alarm his sister, he kept his ears open and his mouth shut.

"I found our captors," a feminine voice whispered. "They're waiting beyond that door."

As Samantha continued to dance her way back down the slope, Jacob realized she hadn't heard it. Instead, the sound seemed to come from inside his skull, reverberating like an incessant itch that he couldn't quite scratch.

A distant movement in the corner of his eye turned his attention to a point in the north, the ridge he'd climbed last year. Perched above the mountain through a haze of trees and mist, an enormous metallic hull shimmered into view. Floating directly above the mountain, its gray shadow blanketed him in wedges of darkness. Cold slithered around the back of Jacob's neck, threatening to crawl behind his eyes. Blinking back tears, his mind reeled.

It's still here.

Then, as quickly as it had appeared, the ship vanished, and the shadows retreated.

Catching his breath, Jacob stared at the empty ridge. *Major Reese*, he called inwardly, trying to reach the itch at the back of his mind. After a pregnant pause, no answer came, and he suddenly felt silly. With a shrug, he pushed the crazy notion aside. *Stop it*, he told himself. *It's over.* Some nightmares might not end, but maybe they could be ignored.

Ahead, Samantha noted his pause. "Now what?"

"Nothing." Jacob's face brightened and his step quickened. "Let's go home."

PART III

THE CRIMSON SPIRI

40

"What's the difference between Eve and Mitochondrial Eve?"

Arthur's marker stopped mid-sentence as he turned from the whiteboard, finding the source of the question three rows back amongst the high school students. A young girl wearing pink hair and far too few clothes for Arthur's taste sat erect, waiting for an answer. He tried to focus on the question instead of her thin black leotard outfit. It proved to be a losing battle.

Do their parents not see them before they walk out the door?

As DNA ancestry wasn't the subject of that day's class, he kept his answer short. "One is based on mythological belief. The other is rooted in science." Noting several sets of narrowed, young eyes clock his answer, Arthur decided to elaborate. "What I mean is, one can be proven while the other cannot."

"But what does Mitochondrial Eve actually mean?"

Arthur sat on the edge of his desk. "Mitochondrial

DNA is what we use to trace our lineage through the mother's bloodline. If you follow the line back far enough, you return to a single woman, which science has, for better or worse, dubbed Mitochondrial Eve."

"So," a boy jumped in, "was she the first woman?"

"No," Arthur answered. "Not even close. Mitochondrial Eve is simply the name we have assigned to the one who began the current bloodline that we all carry today." Hoping to put the subject aside, he grabbed his marker and went back to the board. "Now, if we could return to the matter at hand."

Even before his marker touched the board, another question sprang up: "What about aliens?"

This time Arthur didn't need to look to know the source of the question: Gregory, a blond football prodigy who could barely handle basic arithmetic. Glancing over, Arthur noticed the book gripped tightly in the boy's pudgy fingers. It was a familiar sight. Arthur tensed.

Here we go, he thought.

Arthur had given the boy a D on his last exam, resulting in the team's quarterback being benched for two weeks. Now, it seemed, Gregory had found his revenge. When Arthur didn't respond immediately, the boy continued. "Do you believe in little green men?"

I should have given him an F, Arthur decided with a huff. Irritation dried his throat. "Today's subject is ecology as pertaining to plant life and the atmosphere, *not* mitochondrial DNA, and certainly *not* little green men."

"But you believe in them." Gregory fingered Arthur's book. "It says so right here."

"As I, in fact, wrote the book, I feel confident in saying that it does not indicate anywhere inside that I have seen or believe in aliens. Now, may I *please* return to the subject at hand?"

"Then what do you believe?" the scantily clad girl asked.

I'm cornered.

Having been forced to give this speech a thousand

times to a thousand classes, Arthur kept calm and answered succinctly. "When I was young, not much older than you, I saw something I couldn't explain and wrote about it in the book Gregory is now excitedly waving about. However, I never said it was aliens or little green men or any such nonsense. It was a round shape in the sky, large enough to block out the moon. What the shape was or where it came from, I have never claimed to know." Sadness crept into his voice. "Nor will I likely ever know."

Arthur was reminded of those words as he stepped through an arched alien entrance. They'd crossed a straight, narrow pathway to arrive there, a path Casey had constructed *with her mind!* Now he wondered how deep her connection to the ship ran. *What else might she be capable of?*

Major Reese took the lead, rifle raised, his helmet's headlamp lighting the way. Casey and Bill stuck close behind, entering an oddly shaped domed room with thick beams pointing upwards, like a cathedral. Luminous shadows crawled over curved walls and ceilings while a damp scent of unknown chemicals snaked through the air filters in Arthur's armor. Reese stopped, tilting his lamp downward. The light shimmered on a moving surface. A tank of water no less than twenty yards square filled the center of the room. Light danced across the liquid, reflecting over Arthur's visor and causing shadows to swim about him in languid streams.

Reese's breath rasped behind his helmet. "I guess we found the alien spa."

Before Arthur could respond, Casey clutched his arm and gasped. "Look," she said. Moving forward in unison, they approached the enormous tank, finding two floating shapes lingering in the distant corner. Face down, their features were obscured, though Arthur noted they appeared to be roughly seven feet tall with two arms and two legs each. Their anatomical similarities to humans proved both surprising and concerning to him. His mind whirled at the implications.

"Wait." Arthur tugged at Reese's shoulder, halting his approach.

Reese's headlamp beam spun, momentarily blinding Arthur. "What's the matter?"

"We have no idea what sort of infections or contagions they might carry."

"That's why I'm wearing a suit," Reese replied, continuing toward the bodies. Bent low at the pool's edge, he used his rifle's muzzle to turn one over, revealing gray skin, an enlarged cranium, and blank black eyes that seemed to stare into nothing. While the others gasped in shocked intrigue, Arthur couldn't help feeling disappointment. His stomach turned.

"A cliché," Arthur spat under his breath. "Big head, big eyes, gray skin, their appearance is so familiar it's almost comical."

"I'm not laughing," Reese said, glancing at the surrounding shadows. A sound of shuffling feet yanked their attention toward the room's darkest, farthest edge. Temporarily abandoning the alien bodies, Arthur and the others trailed Reese as he moved through dancing liquid shadows, searching for the noise's source.

Behind the tank, three enormous chairs made of material that was similar to the walls and ceiling stood in a semicircle. Noting how closely their design resembled something manmade, the knot in Arthur's gut tightened while his thoughts raced toward a concrete conclusion, one he didn't much care for. Gritting his teeth, Arthur struggled to stay silent as the shuffling sound grew closer. Reese's flashlight fell on each of the chairs, one by one, from right to left. The beam stopped at the farthest seat, landing on a living, breathing alien. Its chest heaved in hard gulps, jagged ribs visible through blotchy gray flesh. Above, its oval black eyes creased into slits as it watched them approach.

"It's still alive," Casey whispered. Beside her, Bill leaned closer, a mixture of sadness and revulsion washing over his face.

Reese's expression couldn't be seen behind his helmet, but the implications of his weapon spoke volumes. He pressed it against the alien's heaving chest. "What the fuck are you?"

When the gray being didn't respond, Arthur answered for him.

"He's human."

41

Stunned silence surrounded the gurgled breathing emanating from the tall figure languishing before them. *Arthur's wrong*, Casey concluded, shivering. She stared open mouthed at the thing's pulsing cranium, at its insect-like black eyes. *There's nothing human about it.*

Reese seemed to agree, though his words sounded hollow and flat. "You can't be serious."

Seemingly too fascinated to peel his eyes away from the living specimen, Arthur spoke without turning. "Bipedal, carbon-based, two eyes, two arms, two legs . . . I would imagine their DNA has more in common with us than a chimpanzee."

"You're the biologist," Reese grumbled as if withdrawing from an internal argument.

So, Casey thought, *Arthur became a scientist after all.* Pain stabbed her stomach, imagining all he'd done in his life and all that she'd missed. She stepped back from the monster. "That doesn't make them human. Similar, maybe, but not human."

Arthur snapped his fingers in front of the creature. It didn't flinch. Sighing his frustration, he turned to Casey. "We are definitely related. Perhaps they created us, or maybe we were spawned from the same genetic source. Either way, the similarities are too exact not to suggest we share a *strong* connection with these creatures."

Reese shrugged. "Whatever they—"

The sound of shuffling feet stole his attention. Spinning around, his headlamp stopped on a hunched figure, crouching in the corner. Casey gasped, recognizing the shaking man, dressed in a blazer and tie. Reese raised his rifle into the light, as if the tiny, frightened figure might be a threat.

"No!" Casey shouted, jumping between them. "I know him." She knelt beside Donovan. His wide eyes were locked on Reese's weapon. Casey touched his arm. "Hey, Donovan, it's me. Casey. You don't look so good."

His eyes still on Reese, Donovan allowed Casey to help him stand.

"We were worried," Casey said. "Thought we lost you."

Donovan finally tore his eyes off Reese, finding Bill and Arthur. He returned to Casey with a questioning look, obviously wondering about Earl. When Casey shook her head, Donovan nodded silently in understanding.

Suddenly, the ship's bridge lurched again, knocking them off their feet. Sparks rained. Pressure built on Casey's chest, pinning her down. Her arms locked against her body, her ears burning, as if ready to explode. She didn't need to be a pilot to know the ship was taking off. A voice whispered in her mind, gentle and soothing, like a mother to a child. **You must help . . .**

The men beside her swooned, grabbing their heads as if suffering matching migraines. They'd heard it too, she realized. The ship's violent quakes slowed to a pulsing rhythm, as if the craft were leveling off. *He's controlling it with his mind,* she thought.

Yes. Help me.

The words sank in as she scrambled to her feet. "He needs *us* to fly this thing."

"Fuck that," Reese said. He shoved his rifle hard into the creature's heaving chest. "Put this thing down. Now!"

The creature stared blankly at Casey. **No. You.**

"Me?" Casey turned from the creature, toward Arthur and Reese. "Me what?"

Take control . . . or everyone . . . everyone on this ship . . . dies.

Stumbling, Casey felt her legs give out. Arthur's jaw fell open in surprise. Donovan glared suspiciously. Evasive, Bill dropped his eyes. Reese cocked his head as if not sure what to think. Trembling, Casey backed away from them. Stealing a peek at her left palm, she tried to rub the new gray flesh off her hand, but it wouldn't budge. Casey's voice came out in a choked whisper. "What's so special about me?"

Again, the ship lurched, tossing her across the creature's lap. Its black eyes bore down on her.

EVERYTHING! The voice thundered in her mind. Reeling, she dry heaved from the force of its tone. Arthur grabbed her shoulders, pulling her away. Reese and Donovan exchanged sideways glances. A veil of silence descended. No one moved. Breaking the unspoken stalemate, Bill crossed the bridge and knelt beside the shriveled creature's chair. They locked eyes. In suspended quiet, Casey felt the hairs on her neck prickle. *They're talking about me.*

"They're dying," Bill said, far more sadly than Casey would have expected. She also noticed that he called the creature *they* instead of he or she. Bill's brow furrowed, deep creases tightening about his eyes. He pivoted toward Casey. "Either you keep this ship in one piece, or we go down with it."

"How exactly is she supposed to do that?" Reese lowered his rifle, realizing the alien wasn't as much of a threat as the ship coming apart. Arthur glanced around for a control panel but found no machines or computers.

The pool, the voice said.

Donovan, who hadn't spoken a word since they entered, broke out laughing. "You want her to take a swim?" He leaned against the wall, grabbing his belly. "Oh, that's rich."

Arthur and Reese exchanged a worried glance. Bill and Casey ignored him. She turned back to the creature "Where are the controls?"

Weakly, the gray thing placed one of its three fingers against its temple. **Here.** Sensing their confusion, he elaborated. **No computers, no controls. *We are the machines.***

"What makes you think she's even *compatible* with," Reese waved his hand toward the tank, "whatever the hell is in there?"

The creature didn't respond. Casey huffed, knowing what she had to do. Raising her left hand, she revealed the gray flesh on her palm. "Something's been happening to me. I don't know what it is, but it's why he thinks I can fly this thing."

Arthur snatched her wrist. "How long has it been like this?"

"A couple of hours," she said. "There's another patch on my heel."

His face fell. Casey tried to smile, but it came out awkward. "Tell me you didn't become a physician, Arthur. You've got a terrible bedside manner."

"Whatever was done is on a genetic level," Arthur replied flatly.

She kept her grin and patted his wrinkled face. "Then it's a good thing I fell in love with a biologist." His eyes sparkled, and he matched her smile. The room shook again. She fixed her gaze on Reese. "Guess I'm going for a swim."

Bill and Reese pulled the gray bodies from the tank. Peeling away her jacket and pants, Casey slipped into

the tank as she'd arrived, in a T-shirt and underwear. The
room quaked as she took a deep breath and lay on her
back. Only a foot deep, the liquid splashed her face but
didn't cover her mouth or nose. Aware that her nipples
were standing cold and erect, the liquid leaving little to
the imagination of the looming men, she turned her face
away. Most seemed to be too preoccupied to care, except for Donovan, who leered. Suppressing a shudder,
due either to his stare or to the cold liquid lapping her
skin, she closed her eyes. The room rocked once again.
Casey grabbed the edge of the pool to stop from spilling
over. Between the chaos in the room and her inhibitions,
she couldn't focus on whatever she was supposed to be
doing. Nothing happened. Her body sloshed back and
forth, the liquid's turpentine-like aroma penetrating her
nose as the creature's voice hissed in her mind.

Then she gasped, thoughts whirling like a drunken
haze. Something indescribable consumed her, swallowing her mind and body as a whale might a guppy.
The sensation ran through every fiber of her being, every inch and every cell. She sensed her blood rushing
through veins, heard her heartbeat pumping in a steady
rhythm, and felt the liquid enter her pores at a molecular level. Big . . . small . . . These were concepts that
she now understood were a lie. Just as time and space
were a lie. Everything was connected and concurrent.
Our universe and the ones our cells inhabited were one
and the same in both size and purpose. *We are all cells of
a single organism*, she thought. The sensation filled her
completely. Casey writhed in the liquid. The feeling was
impossible to describe without a common reference,
though the human part of her still attached to the present orgasmed. Even that was a pale sensory experience
compared to the universe that opened before her. She
drank it in, and it drank her. Her mind stepped into an
unseen void that consumed her.

A void of time and space, the creature agreed. She
saw stars, countless points of light splattered against the

dark. And yet she sensed there was no life in it. None beyond the thin fragment she felt from Earth far behind. A vast emptiness greeted her.

In her mind, Casey was no longer inside a spaceship; she *was* the ship.

42

A new light came into view, blazing in the distance, brighter than any supernova or galaxy. Casey sensed another point of life: her destination. *How can there only be two points of life throughout the entire universe? Where is everyone?*

The universe didn't reply. Instead, she fell, tumbling weightlessly back into the ship, dropped unceremoniously into her fragile, mundane, flesh-and-blood body. Immediately, she sensed life standing above her. Without opening her eyes, she felt her companions watching her closely, both outwardly and inwardly, as if they'd merged in some way—interwoven within each other's minds and thoughts. They all felt it, and when it became apparent how close and intimate their connection was, they each mentally withdrew. But there was only so much they could hide from each other now. Their thoughts bubbled over, spilling out for all to see. Flashes of memory, times and places crumpled together, impossible to decipher one from the next. Voices mingled loudly, so she couldn't tell whose thoughts belonged to whom. Among the flashes of memory she saw a woman laughing. Brunette, beautiful. She was holding a child. Casey assumed it was Reese's memories. Then she saw a boy, maybe nineteen, named Todd, and she recognized his face. *Arthur has a son.* She saw another boy, now a man, graduating from college. *Two sons.* The image changed again. She saw a hand. It was Arthur's but also her own—signing divorce papers. Across a table, the once-beautiful, loving woman had lost her smile. Casey felt the sting of signing the document, a hollow pain, a wound she knew could never be healed. Her fingers trembled on the pen. *No*, she reminded herself, *not my fingers. His. This isn't my memory. This didn't happen to me.* Snapping out of it, she wondered what the others were seeing from her.

The world spun. Casey's gaze focused on something dull and round, made of brass. A bedpost. Lying on her stomach, her face crushed against a pillow, she felt something heavy press on her back.

No! Not this, don't let them see this!

Casey was twelve years old again. Her father smelled of booze and cigarettes. His beard bristled against her neck. "Shhh, baby girl. You just lie there nice and quiet," he said.

Knowing the men were experiencing this with her, Casey struggled to block the image, wanting to think about anything else while her father pulled her panties down. Cheeks flushed, bile rose in her throat, and her stomach turned. Biting her lip, she focused on the pain in her mouth as her father—

STOP! the men screamed inwardly with her, pushing the nightmare away.

With a shocked gasp, Casey's eyes fluttered, and she found herself back in the watery tank. Spitting the liquid from her mouth, she glanced nervously at the men. Thankfully, their eyes remained closed, as if pretending not to have seen. Noting tears behind Arthur's visor, she realized she'd never told him the truth about her father. Now he knew. They all did. No more secrets. She was laid bare before them both physically and emotionally.

While her thoughts languished, a new image rushed into view, crashing into her like a wave. Hot and red and full of rage. The sensations emanated from Reese, directed with laser precision toward Arthur. *Why?* She pushed, probing the fiery blaze in his mind. Fractured images glazed past: a naked woman in the snow, her body ripped apart by bullets. Lying beside her, an elderly man, similarly killed. The stench of the gore sickened Casey. Still, the carnage didn't reveal Arthur's part in it. Then a new emotion overtook the anger: guilt. Reese seemed to blame himself just as much as Arthur for the corpses in the snow. What was the connection?

Opening her eyes, she saw Reese standing motionless above her. No sign of outward fury or that he'd felt her invasion. Turning, she noticed Donovan's face turn pale. Eyes clenched shut, sweat poured from his forehead. *What's the matter with him?* As if to answer, Casey's mind flashed with horrible images. Her gut twisted, and she bit the inside of her cheek so hard she tasted blood. She wanted to turn away from Donovan, but it was too late. She saw inside him.

Casey watched, not as an outside observer but as if she were Donovan. She knelt around the corner, stopping on a dime. Earl came rushing into view. She took his weight into her shoulder like she'd learned in judo, twisting the big guy's weight away from her and sent him crashing to the ground. Springing upward, she ran before Casey and Bill came around the corner.

Casey was a murderer. She'd tripped Earl, so the creature would kill him instead of her. *Hey, survival of the fittest, motherfucker.*

No, she reminded herself, *that wasn't me.* Her eyes snapped open, and she glared at Donovan. Others turned as well, having seen the same images. Donovan's body quivered violently, as if struggling to run, but his legs refused. *Murderer!* they said with one mind, their voices in unison.

Pressure jolted them. **Stop**, the alien voice commanded. **Focus or die.** Catching Arthur's glance, she realized they'd all heard it. The ship quaked again. Sparks rained down, burning her arms and face. Donovan's glare seared her. Trying to ignore his looming figure, Casey refocused on the space around the ship. The void opened again like a lover's embrace, pressing her flesh, kissing her lips, and stroking her mind. Her body shook with a final orgasm, though this time she ignored it. Too entrenched within the glimpses of her life or the others' lives to worry about her physical form, she zeroed in on the time that linked each of them together. She saw time as an interwoven entity. *Past and future. Now and then, all the same. I am born now. I live now. I die now. I am in Blackwood forest, on Earth, in 1985. And I am on . . .* She gasped, seeing an alien world approaching in her mind's eye. A giant blue ball in the void of time and space. The alien voice returned. **Home.**

Instinctively, she and the others knew they didn't want to go there. They had to focus on Earth. On their own time and place. **No**, the voice said. **The ship will not survive.**

You **will not survive.**

The giant blue ball veered closer within the blackness of space. She sensed the alien's consciousness pushing them toward it. Using the last of his strength, she sensed his body heaving, his tiny slit for a mouth gasping to fill his blood-soaked lungs with fresh air. Casey struggled to fight the ship's course with her own mental focus, hoping to turn them back, but she was crushed against his singular will.

The ship lurched, rushing toward the planet. With a violent gurgle, she heard the creature die, spitting his last breath, and felt his presence blink from existence. Unleashed, she tried once again to divert their descent, but with the pilot gone, her tether to the ship seemed lost as well. She felt her consciousness detach from her body with a snap. Floating upwards, she recognized her flesh-and-bone body sloshing aimlessly about the pool. Around her, men huddled, trying to keep her body steady. She opened her mouth to speak but found she had no vocal cords. Continuing upwards, she moved through the metallic mesh of the ship's hull and into a rushing blue-green atmosphere. An alien surface greeted her behind a curtain of murky clouds. Violent, lurching waves spread out in every direction. A seemingly endless sea lay outstretched below.

At the horizon's edge, a single form rose into view: a red tower pointed upward from the ocean like a needle, stabbing the emerald sky. *So,* she decided, *they do live on land.* The thought offered little comfort as she drew closer, pulled by an invisible hand that yanked the wind from her nonexistent lungs. She knew the ship was following like a limb she could feel but not see, for she had no neck to turn. Through vaporish clouds, her disembodied consciousness rushed toward the needle's sharp tip.

Tumbling closer, she worried she might be impaled. Instead, the spire tore through Casey's astral body, and she felt nothing. Casey continued her descent through the hollow needle of colored glass and painted metal, past exterior red walls and interior beams, until her view opened to an unimaginable vista.

43

Through his mind's eye, Reese watched a liquid landscape roll beneath them. Like an electrical surge, he felt the others' mixed sense of horror and wonder, all except Casey, whose connection had suddenly blinked out. Forcing his physical eyes open, he turned to her, sloshing about in the tank. Her chest heaved silently, still breathing. Shutting heavy eyelids, Reese returned to his inner vision. Something appeared in the distance, growing larger. Over the horizon, a red spire pierced swirling clouds. The image reminded him of a blood-drenched sword.

Last stop, he mused.

The ship slid into an alcove on the side of the upper half of the spire, docking above and beneath seemingly thousands of identical ships. A tingle along his skin made him believe their ship felt comfort from the entrance, as if embraced by a mother. The notion that they might be standing in a ship that was in some way sentient enough to have emotions made his spine shiver and his arms crawl with goosebumps. For a moment, he thought of using their mental connection to reach out to the ship and see if he could contact it, but he heard a sharp *NO* from Arthur, and decided the old man might be right.

With a jolt, the ship locked into place on the side of the tower. Abruptly, their mental connection severed, causing them to collapse simultaneously to the floor, like marionettes whose strings had been cut. The metaphor didn't seem too far from reality. *Puppets on a string. Yeah, that sounds about right*, he thought. Beside him, Arthur lunged, splashing in the liquid ooze, pulling Casey from the tank. Her eyes remained shut.

"Casey!" Arthur shouted, shaking her. "CASEY!"

Reese knelt, grabbing her wrist and checking for a pulse. It appeared to be steady. To be certain, he leaned over, feeling her breath on his cheek. "She's asleep."

"You can be woken from sleep," Arthur snapped. Studying her left arm, they noticed thickened gray skin covered her flesh. It appeared almost reptilian. Reese flinched. Arthur ran his fingers over the gray scales. "We need to get her out of here."

Reese stood, watching Bill lean over the dead creature in the center chair. Then his eyes did a quick scan over the domed bridge, but he couldn't find Donovan. "We're missing one."

"He ran as soon as we woke," Bill said, wiping his eyes as if from a long sleep. "I guess we all know why."

Reese nodded. They'd seen what he'd done to the man named Earl, though right now Donovan was the least of his concerns. "We need to find a way off this ship before someone comes looking for us."

Arthur stayed at Casey's side. "What about her?"

"She stays. For now."

"We can't just leave her!"

Reese grabbed his rifle. "We're not."

"I don't follow."

"This ship got us here, so it can get us out," Reese

said, checking his rifle's fresh magazine and slapping it back in. "But first we're going to need a new pilot."

Reese, Arthur, and Bill made their way back through the cavernous hallway. "I'm telling you guys, we already searched," Bill said, his voice rising to a high octave. "There isn't an exit."

"We found a way in, so there has to be a way out," Arthur replied.

"We got lucky," Reese said.

"I wouldn't call that luck," Bill snorted. Reese nodded in agreement and continued down another tunnel. Arthur lingered, staring at the blank wall. He had an idea.

Reese noticed and stopped. "What?"

"I was just thinking," Arthur said, rubbing a gloved hand over the wall's surface. "If we were all in contact with that creature on the bridge, perhaps we can do what Casey did."

"You mean, manipulate our environment?"

Arthur shrugged. "It's worth a shot."

"Be my guest."

"The tunnel's already straight, Arthur." Reese turned back toward the tunnel, pressing on.

Arthur paused, closing his eyes. Breath fogged his visor, clouding his face from view. Softly, just above a whisper, Arthur said, "Open sesame."

The clang of sliding metal echoed through the passage. Reese stopped cold, jaw slackened. *You've got to be kidding me.* An iris formed in the middle of the wall. Reese crept over, peeking out the doorway, but it was too dark outside to see beyond the hatch. Arthur grinned, rocking back and forth on his heels, obviously proud of himself. "This ship let us *in* when we asked. It took us *across the universe* when we asked. So, I simply asked it to let us *out*."

"B-b-but the rest of us tried to escape for hours!" Bill stammered.

Grimacing, Reese led them out. "The difference is, now it's got us right where it wants us."

They stepped onto a catwalk created from an unknown substance. It appeared to be metallic, though Reese's footsteps made no sound. A whistling wind swept through the spire from an unseen opening far overhead. Even through his hazmat suit's air filters, the air reeked of sour milk and mildew. A few steps on the walkway, and he felt his stomach tighten. He wished he could clench his nose. Eyes watering, he wondered if their armor's ventilation system could stop a virus from an alien world. He doubted it.

"You should go back inside," Arthur said, noting Bill's lack of protection.

"Are you kidding? I just spent hours trying to get out."

Reese turned to Arthur. "What's the matter?"

Arthur waved at Reese's armor and his own, then gestured toward Bill, standing there in a button-down shirt and jeans. "We don't know what kind of bacteria is in the air."

Bill shrugged. "Probably the same shit that was in the ship, and I'm still standing. Hey, at least they breathe the same oxygen as we do, right?"

Arthur considered that before he replied. "That's because, like I said, I don't think they're alien, but this planet *is*. Our outfits may not help much either, but they're better than nothing. I think you coming is a mistake."

Reese considered the old man's words, then turned to Bill. "I agree. You should stay back."

Bill inhaled a deep breath of air, seemingly unaffected by the reeking stank, then offered a weak grin. "I'm fine. Let's go."

Reese led the way, Bill following and Arthur taking up the rear. The spire was a dark pit with seemingly no bottom. Red mist swirled about, and Reese had a distinct feeling that the mist didn't move randomly. It seemed to snake around him, coiling past his visor like a waiting serpent. The fog kept pace as they crossed the catwalk. Reese and Arthur switched on their suits' headlamps, revealing bits of alien architecture in piece-meal. Lost within a tour of investigation and discovery, Reese's eyes bounced every which way, studying tall red beams supporting the tower's structure. Its walls were iridescent, sparkling under the beam of his headlamp. He waited for someone or something to jump out and block their path, but nothing obstructed them. *Where are all the little gray men?* Reese wondered. They paused at an intersection that connected various catwalks to different ships. Perched beside Arthur and Bill on a round dais, Reese observed the hollow red spire. With its nearly silent breeze, lack of light, and putrid smell assaulting his nostrils, a thought crept into his mind: *This place is a tomb.*

His heart leapt in his chest as the dais suddenly gave out beneath them, drawing them into the abyss.

Reese steadied himself as the floor lowered. Stunned by the abruptness, it took him a moment to realize they were standing on some sort of elevator. It moved with lightning speed, though his stomach didn't turn as would be expected at such a velocity. He was certain they were hitting several Gs, but his body didn't protest, and his stomach remained still, as if the platform and his body were working at different speeds or with variable forces of gravity.

With a soft puff of air, the platform stopped at the bottom of the great tower. Reese's finger twitched on the trigger, prepared for an attack.

He led them through cavernous dark, headlamp beams glancing across jagged pieces of metal and debris scattered about the floor. The place was in ruins. Arthur excitedly darted toward something to their left. Reese swung his light around. "Hold up," he whispered. "Where are you going?"

Arthur didn't answer. Reese and Bill crept over to the old man as he knelt beside piles of broken metallic bits. Pulling an object out, his headlamp exposed a small toy with four wheels and a fiery strip along its side. "A

Hot Wheels car," Arthur said, "on the other side of the universe."

Reese's head swam, and he lost his footing, stumbling. "What the hell is this place?"

Picking through more debris scattered about the floor, Reese's flashlight stopped on a lamp sitting next to a crushed child's bed and a wooden dresser with cowboys painted along the side. "Earth stuff."

Arthur joined him, and they used their lights in conjunction to get a better look at the shadowy surroundings. They saw what appeared to be broken walls, one with a yellowed flowery pattern, another a plain blue slab. As Arthur ran his gloved fingers against the powder-blue surface, the wall crumbled beneath his touch. "Plaster."

"Pieces of a house." The knots in Reese's stomach tightened.

"Or a facsimile of one," Arthur said, tossing the plaster to the ground.

"Like a pretty cage?"

"Perhaps."

Reese caught a sideways glance of Bill, who remained quietly somber. His lack of reaction made Reese spin his headlamps into his eyes, as if checking for a red glow, but Bill only flinched. "Watch it, will ya?"

Satisfied that Bill hadn't been turned into one of those things from the forest, Reese led them across the large platform. Ducking and climbing over and under pieces of human furniture and decorations, they finally stopped at a large, round portal.

Reese turned to Arthur. "Go ahead."

"Open sesame." Nothing happened. Bill approached the circle, placing his hand against the dark-red metallic surface. Arthur protested, "You don't have gloves, you shouldn't be touching any—"

Arthur's words died in his throat as the door vanished.

Reese eyed Bill. "What'd you do?"

Bill shrugged. "I figured maybe it didn't understand the Arabian Nights joke, so I just asked it to open."

"Good job," Arthur said, his pitch rising with his growing excitement.

"Yeah, good job," Reese agreed, more suspicious than elated.

The three of them entered. The swirling shadows seemed to drink up Arthur's and Reese's light beams, barely visible ten feet ahead. The farther they walked, the darker the shadows grew. Something in the back of Reese's mind warned him that this was the place they'd been seeking, though now they were there, at the base of the tower, creeping among shadows, he doubted they'd find a pilot to fly their ship home. Trapped in the dark on an alien planet with no way home, he pushed rising bile back down in his throat. Years of combat missions, of facing possible death, and yet this was the first time his spine tingled, and his arms prickled with gooseflesh. With each step he cared less and less about aliens and spaceships or even military duty. His heart ached, knowing he would never see his daughter again.

Ahead, Arthur stumbled to a stop. Reese raised his rifle and flanked him. Their lights raked along a dangling sack, perhaps twelve feet long, clear with red filaments spiderwebbed across its surface. Within the sack a full-sized gray figure with a large cranium lay curled like a fetus yet to be born.

Their lights bounced left to right, revealing a seemingly endless number of similar sacks spread in every direction as far as their lamps would allow them to see. Despite the shortness of their lights' beams, Reese assumed there were vastly more of these things well beyond sight. Thousands. *Perhaps millions*, he thought with a shiver.

Arthur leaned closer to the nearest sack, running his gloved fingers across its surface. The thing inside twitched. Arthur stumbled backwards. "They're alive."

Reese peered past the veins and plastic-like sack,

seeing black oval eyes staring back blankly. No recognition or movement. "Alive maybe but not conscious. If we pull him out, maybe he could fly the ship."

"Y-you want to wake it?" Arthur stammered.

"No other choice," Reese hissed. "We're stuck here without a pilot."

With a huff that fogged his visor, Arthur nodded and reached toward the sack, looking for a way to pull it down. The sack dangled from a long red artery, thick and juicy, squishing under his touch as he pulled the sack down. It stretched like a rubber band. He sucked in his breath. "I don't know what will happen if I break the cord."

"Only one way to find out," Reese said, growing impatient.

Suddenly, hands were on Reese's helmet, twisting it off with a violent yank. The metal ring around his throat popped, and the visor slid from his face. Spinning, Reese raised his gun. Bill grabbed it and shattered the weapon with impossible strength. Shoving Reese to the ground he turned to Arthur. "Step away," he said calmly. "I don't wish to harm you."

Reeling on the floor, Reese pulled out his sidearm and rolled onto his back, firing three shots directly at Bill's chest. The bullets stopped a few inches from the gun before clattering to the floor between his legs.

Bill stepped forward, grabbed Reese's suit, and lifted him above his head with ease. "We are not your enemy." Twisting and contorting, Bill's face and body changed. His eyes grew large and black, his skin turned a pale gray, and his skull stretched to an enormous proportion.

Bill wasn't like the townspeople who had been controlled or possessed, Reese realized. The gray alien, now fully formed, turned. His voice whispered like an itch in the back of their minds. *Remove your helmet, Arthur.*

"Wh-why?"

"Don't do it!" Reese yelled.

It is the only way to save Casey, Bill silently urged.

Dangling in the alien's grip, Reese watched Arthur's shaky fingers unlatch his helmet. "No, don't!" Reese shouted.

Ignoring his warning, Arthur dropped his helmet to the floor. "Now what?" he asked.

Red mist swirled from the room's shadows. But unlike the mist Reese had seen pour from the townspeople's mouths earlier, this mist had a form. Two red streams with the distinct shape of large rounded heads, long necks, and compressed shoulders flew toward them like silent ghosts. One of them advanced, pouring through Reese's mouth and nose. Arthur gurgled beside him as a second crimson strand of smoke figure entered his gaping mouth.

Reese sensed his consciousness waning as the smoke worked its way through his lungs and bloodstream. Burning from the inside, he wondered if his fragile skin would contain the heat that built from his chest and flooded through his appendages and skull until, at last, Reese and Arthur's eyes blazed red, and they were no longer consciously human.

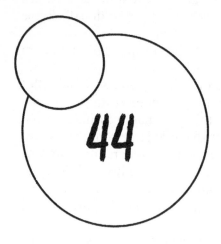

44

Discombobulated, Casey's consciousness drifted downward through the great spire, passing seemingly endless beams of angular architecture. Along the tower's interior, thousands of circular gray ships hung attached, connected by a spider's web of walkways descending level after level. An unknown force propelled her lower and lower into the tower's depths. The farther she fell, the more she sensed a tingling sensation. Distant and muffled, it reminded her of swarming bees. When she passed through the tower's bottom floor, the buzzing turned to voices, so many that she could not separate one from another. A cacophony of noise that pounded so loudly in her thoughts that she tried to cover her ears, only she had no arms to move and no ears to cover. Leveling off, she soared through the bottom floor, over chunks of debris, twisted metal, and broken objects drenched in shadow, passing like a ghost through a tomb.

Ahead was a round red door, sealed for what appeared to be centuries. Grime and dust caked it in layers of age, and yet even in the dark it shimmered, faintly iridescent. Projecting herself through the door, she hovered to a stop within a dark enclave. Although she couldn't see beyond the pitch darkness, she knew she was surrounded. The voices stopped abruptly, as if she'd just crashed someone's party. But someone had pulled her consciousness from the ship and brought her down there. She was definitely expected. Casey wanted to ask the sudden silence why she was there and how to get home, but she had no vocal cords to speak with, and when she reached out, probing with her consciousness, she received images instead of words. The images were a jumble, like figures blinking past in a rushing train. They were trying, she believed, to give her answers, but the images assaulting her came too fast and too frantically for her to discern more than a few fractured pieces. Tiny details bubbled above the din of chaos. She glimpsed fragments of information. She also knew—and her mind reeled at the thought—over a million years had passed by her calendar since she'd left Earth. Everyone she'd ever known and loved had died eons ago. She tried to ask if Earth remained and thought she saw an image of her planet covered in snow and ice. Though again, the image was jumbled, and she decided she might be interpreting it incorrectly. Casey pushed harder with her feelings, trying to communicate, asking them to slow down, to give her concrete images she could understand. After a momentary delay, the visions did indeed slow, and she began to understand where she was and why she was there.

They had no name for their race, though the ones who had abducted her were called "seekers." Hoping to decipher their purpose, she listened as the information continued in an unabated flood without stopping for questions. Their individual identities, she learned, were connected to a communal one, binding their consciousness together. The image used to convey the concept to her was a flash of water droplets splashing along the edge of a flowing river. There was no he or she and no genders or sexual orientations to differentiate them. Yet, they were not born from a distant star or alien—

NO! Her thoughts screamed loud enough for her emotions to reverberate through the apparitions surrounding her. She didn't want to see this. She didn't want to know or believe. She wanted to fly back to the ship and escape before they could reveal any more.

The slideshow continued. These beings were not aliens; they were humans. The very notion revolted her. Pushing away from the voices and surrounding consciousness, Casey snapped back to the present. She floated through a dark pit, noticing countless transparent sacks hanging on either side of her. Dangling from long umbilical cords, each sack contained a gray shape with black eyes, a large cranium, and clawed fingers. *Arthur was right*, she thought. These beings were not so dissimilar to humans after all. The concept disgusted her.

The voices returned, drawing closer, wanting to show her more. Trying to escape any further visions, Casey forced herself down through the floor, propelling her consciousness into the planet's depths. Fleeing.

She stopped at the next sublevel, drenched in blood-red light. The walls were catacombs with pink residue from a source she was sure she didn't want to know. Inching toward the light she recognized a twirling shape. A huge hypersphere, twenty times the size of the one on the ship. Another engine, she assumed, powering the great spire, feeding energy to the fetal sacks above. Still, if the bodies were asleep, whose voice was she hearing?

Upon that thought, vaporish smoke slithered about her, the wisps revealing themselves as spectral apparitions. *Ghosts?* she wondered.

No, the apparitions replied with a singular voice. **We are not dead. Not yet.**

Again, the voices were replaced by flashing images, though this time slower and easier for Casey to digest, as if they were spoon-feeding a child. Still, the implications horrified her.

Projected within her mind's eye, Casey witnessed the creation of the Great Singularity: men building machines smarter than themselves and the eventual conflict born from it. Amidst a deluge of atomic explosions, Casey reeled beneath a swell of dying screams until, at last, the horror ended as abruptly as it began.

A new image appeared. A human hand offered a flower to a machined claw. Not true history; rather, a symbol. These gray seekers, a name she now gave the entire species to make it clearer in her mind, evolved out of two dying races, trying to find a peace offering that might outlast them both. They were the flower, it seemed, though she found it an odd euphemism. The destruction of all computers and artificial intelligence, replaced by a race of new humans who developed their minds to think like machines, using their vast intellect to stretch out to the stars in hopes of finding a fresh start. And perhaps, they hoped, to discover a new species somewhere in the cosmos to learn from. Instead, they found a million years of loneliness. Searching countless galaxies and star systems, through all of space and time within the universe, they found nothing but supreme silence. Emptiness. Both outwardly, and eventually, inwardly. The image they projected was of a grand hotel with countless rooms yet no evidence of visitors or management. Each room, each hallway, meticulously crafted by an unseen hand, lay empty. In a million years they'd found no other intelligent species, no signs of life, and no signs of a god that they still hoped—prayed—might exist. The utter barrenness of it all grew unbearable, so they tried to find alternate universes to traverse, hoping others like themselves might be reached through black holes or at the edge of the known universe. The endeavor took countless centuries, but the efforts bore no fruit.

Eventually, what remained of humans was only a shadow of where they'd begun.

The images changed again, only this time she wasn't simply seeing the moments; she was inside them. Living them as one of the seekers. Seeing through their eyes. She assisted them in creating clones of themselves, to extend their lives and consciousness. Procreation ended, and new bodies were made sexless. New generations were no longer required. The same beings continued to exist for centuries, slipping from one newly cloned body to the next, as needed. The clones wore out and died, and newer bodies lasted no more than a few years.

Casey fell to the floor inside the alien body, writhing in agony. This was a living memory, and what it showed was not simply images now but sensations as well. Pain most of all. Unendurable pain. Her gray skin blotted with patches of black and red marks. She'd been infected with a plague of unknown origin. No, not her, she reminded herself. The seekers.

She pulled herself out of the vision. *You took us to save yourselves.*

We must correct the genetic mistakes of the past to ensure the future.

You mean kidnap countless people throughout history and play Doctor Frankenstein? That's not correcting a mistake; that's rape.

You should have been returned without any memory of being taken. A random atmospheric variable caused your vessel to phase out of time.

Atmospheric variable? A new image projected before her: the ship phasing into existence above the Blackwood tree line in the middle of a lightning storm. A single bolt of lightning electrocuted the hull. If she'd had vocal cords, Casey would have laughed. *Your big, fancy, time-traveling spaceship got brought down by bad weather?*

The bloodlines must be strengthened to ensure humanity continues.

I don't sense any humanity in you.

The sound of gunfire erupted from the room above. Startled, Casey stopped the conversation. Knowing it must be Major Reese firing, she soared upwards through the ceiling, the ghostly beings trailing close behind. Moving through metal beams and flickers of light and shadow, Casey emerged through the room's floor, taking in the scene before her with a feeling of slowed time. She saw everything at once: thousands, perhaps millions, of sacks with monstrous gray forms stretching into the darkness on either side of her. Arthur and Major Reese positioned in the center walkway, their eyes glowing with a red sheen. On the floor, a shattered automatic rifle and beside it a fallen handgun. She wanted to reach out and grab it but reminded herself she had no fingers. A gray figure stood before her, tilting his head as if aware of her presence but unsure of where to look. Most shocking of all to her was the gray figure's clothes.

A button-down and blue jeans. *Bill,* she realized. *The wolf in sheep's clothing.* All of this she saw and took in within slowed time. No more than a second passed.

Release them! she screamed in her mind.

"I'm afraid that's not possible, Casey." Bill's calm voice sounded strange coming from the grotesque figure, like a deranged puppet. "They can't return with you."

Why not?

"The short answer is," Bill replied, his face shifting with a blur to his human form, "once you return to your own time, they won't exist, at least not as you knew them."

Turning toward Arthur's blazing, inhuman glare, it took a moment to understand what Bill meant. Once she did, Casey recoiled. A domino effect, she realized. Arthur was on the ship searching for her, and Major Reese had joined him because of a crash that would no longer occur. Her mind turned to Earl. *What about all those who died?*

Bill smiled with an aw-shucks grin. "Time has a way

of sorting itself out. Earl will be fine. He'll be home in time to see his sister's baby born."

Casey wanted to believe him. Bill promised so much, everything she could hope, and yet she couldn't stop staring at Arthur's and Reese's burning eyes. She knew they'd been possessed by these apparitions. If Bill was the good cop, were they the bad? What wasn't he telling her?

What happens to me?

"Your body is undergoing a severe change due to the effectiveness of our procedure. It was a one in a million shot to find a new Mitochondrial Eve who could spread a cure through their bloodline. You are that Eve. We will correct the outward changes, and you'll be returned to the point you were taken with no memory of any of this. Like it never happened."

The outward changes. But I will be changed in some form?

"We're talking microscopic changes here, Casey. Nothing to worry about." Bill flashed that grin again; it made her uncomfortable. *He's lying*, she decided, *but about what?*

She decided to press further. *So, no more abductions? No more snatching people up and injecting them with God knows what?*

Bill lost his smile and sighed. "Don't you just want to go home, Casey?"

Sensing his hesitation, she reached out with her consciousness, touching the apparitions surrounding her. She didn't hear any of their voices, but their emotions swelled. Frustrated. Angry. A whirlwind of growing resentment. *Maybe*, she thought, *they don't like having to explain themselves to a talking monkey. Well, too fucking bad.*

No! This stops now. No more abductions. No more Doctor Frankenstein. No more mangled tests like that poor creature on the ship. NO. MORE.

"I hate to be the bearer of bad news, but you're not in

a position to make demands. Just be a good girl, Casey. Go home, get married, and have lots of babies." His eyes turned to black ovals. "Spread that new genetic material."

Casey hesitated, recalling the countless people locked in frozen containers within the ship. Her thoughts turned to Earl, torn to pieces. They had all been test subjects. And worse, Bill promised there would be more. Maybe not testing on herself but on others. When she awoke on the ship, all she'd cared about was surviving, getting home. But now, trapped so far from Earth, having seen humanity's destruction, felt their pain, and witnessed the grotesqueries of what awaited them, she felt an obligation to think about more than herself. They would continue these abductions over and over throughout centuries. Casey decided this had to stop. Now.

As if hearing her inner conflict, Bill reverted to his gray form. Glaring, he spoke without moving his lips. **We will do whatever is necessary to save our people.**

Me too.

She focused on locating the weakened tether to her physical body. Reaching out with her consciousness, she felt around her surroundings as if rummaging in the dark. First, she felt the entities surrounding her, then the tower's structure above, until finally she found the ship. It glowed softly in her mind's eyes. That was the tether. Casey pulled at the thread of light with all her focus and—

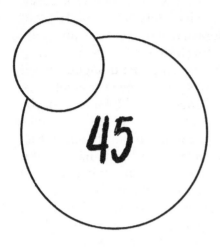

45

E yes bursting, Casey reeled, coughing water from her
lungs. An onslaught of sights and sounds accost-
ed her senses. Dimly lit bridge lights blinded her while
something putrid caused her nostrils to flare. Struggling
to find the source, her blurred gaze fell on the gray bodies. She glanced about, searching for any other signs of
life, but she appeared to be alone.

Casey worked her muscles to push herself up and
out of the water tank. Shivering, she found her clothes
on the floor beside the gray corpses. She reached for the
jacket and stopped, frozen. Her left arm was pale gray,
with scales running all the way to her shoulder. With a
quick scan, she noticed her left leg was patched with gray,
and one of her breasts had sunken to a flat, gray blob.
Staggering, she braced herself against the wall, panting
for breath. Again, she shivered, though not from the
cold. Ice crept up her neck, piercing her skull and stabbing behind her eyes. Panic set in. The full scope of the
grotesque transformation horrified her. She wondered if

she should take Bill's offer. She wouldn't remember any of this. She'd be home and normal and oblivious to all the horrible things she'd seen. *Let the next guy or gal stop them,* she decided. *I'm no hero. I just want to live my life and not look like a fucking monster. I need Bill. I need to go back and—*

A roar disengaged her musing. Scrambling, Casey snatched her shoes and clothes. She pulled the pants up over her wet hips, remembering the dead girl she'd yanked them off of. Zipping up the jacket, she flashed to an image of the black man's corpse she'd taken it from. He was young too, college age, she figured. There'd been other bodies as well. And of course, there'd been Earl. Bill had promised he could still be saved. All of them would be if she only returned to her own time. And yet, as if she could sense his thoughts, she knew that was a lie. His promises felt too perfect. Could she trust those who would snatch up thousands of people for their experiments? Another look at her deformed body and she knew that whatever Bill promised wasn't the whole truth. She and everyone still frozen in the chambers within the ship had been violated. No matter how much she wanted to go home and forget it all, she knew she couldn't let this happen to anyone else. Even if that meant Earl's death and the deaths of all those other people she couldn't save. What about Arthur? She knew she would have to go back down into the tower. First though she needed to find a way out of the ship.

The roar grew closer. The thing that tore Earl apart into bloody chunks of meat was coming for her. Eyes darting about, she searched for a second exit, but the arched doorway they'd come through seemed to be the only way out.

Casey made a run for it.

As she raced down the hall, time slowed. She glimpsed dust particles in the air, heard two sets of breaths in the approaching halls, one enraged, the other panicked. In mere seconds she traversed the entire length of the tunnel. Her body trembled from the enhanced velocity, moving much faster than she'd ever run before. Faster, she assumed, than any human had ever run. What the hell had they done to her?

Skidding to a halt, she realized her senses were more acute. She heard Donovan sobbing in the distance, trying to steady his breathing. She reached out with her mind and felt his presence. He was hiding. Not from the thing that killed Earl but from her. Closing her eyes, she saw him in her mind's eye, peeking around a corner less than a hundred yards away. Donovan had retrieved Earl's ax and was waiting for her to come down the tunnel. He was going to chop her up into tiny pieces. She sensed his panic and rage. Everyone knew what he'd done to Earl, and now the idiot planned to kill them all. How did he think he'd escape without them? The more she touched his consciousness, the less orderly it felt. He'd straight up lost his mind. Part of her wanted to shrink back and find another escape route. Another part of her wanted Donovan and the creature dead. Tired of hiding in terror, she felt her newfound abilities surging with untapped strength. Casey clenched her gray fist and approached the waiting shadows.

OK, boys. Come and get me.

Casey marked Donovan's location with her left (remaining) ear. He was wheezing like a wounded hyena. She didn't actually know what a wounded hyena sounded like, but the analogy seemed to fit.

Another sixty or so yards to her right, she clocked the creature's movements, thumping about, presumably looking for his next meal. *Ugh.* A vision of Earl's dying spasms stabbed her behind the eyes. Still, she reminded herself, the thing had once been human, like her. She wondered if that was what she would become, then doubted it. Bill had seemed too dependent on her. For whatever reason she was special to them while this sad creature was not. Either way, she knew she would have to keep her second vision locked on it as well as Donovan.

Swinging around the corner, she smelled Donovan's sweat as strongly as she heard his rapid breathing. She picked up an emotion in the air, as if snatching a blowing object with her fingers. Disgust, revulsion. He'd seen what she'd become, and now he thought killing her would be a mercy. Part of her wondered if he was right.

Taking three more steps into the light, she came around the hall's edge, inches from him. Casey offered him a prime target for the ax he was carrying. *Earl's ax, you bastard.* Pausing, she inhaled two quick breaths, then took a final step forward. She didn't need to look to know the ax was descending on her left. She could see, hear, and smell it all so clearly. *Like sonar,* she joked silently. It was funny to her. All of it. The descending ax seemed to take a lifetime in her mind's eye to swing toward her blond hair. She heard the creature's distant gurgles, noting that it had drawn closer. *Good. Two at once will make this go quicker.* Wind from the ax's descent bristled her hair. Casey decided it was time to react. Less than a second had gone by, but she felt as if she had all the time in the universe.

Spinning, she caught the ax's blade between her gray fingertips. Casey met Donovan's terrified, wide-eyed astonishment and was glad to see his reaction. She felt his anger turn to shock. Casey drank it in, enjoying the flavor of his fear. Twisting the ax blade about, she dug it into his shoulder with a heavy *chunk*. Blood splattered his screaming face, and she thought he sounded like a child. *Who's been a bad boy, Donny?*

Wait, that wasn't her thought. Where had it come from?

She heard the creature's loud stomps quickly approach. She wanted to smile at Donovan and say "Lunchtime," before tossing him to the creature, but she stopped herself. *This isn't me. This is murder. This . . . These abilities, this skin I'm wearing, does it come with mental alterations as well?*

Kill him, chop him up, and make him bleed in wet chunks, just like he did to Earl.

No, she replied. Someone was inside her mind with her, and it wasn't Bill. This was something different.

Donovan flailed in her arm while the creature congealed into view, its long yellow nails inches from her. Momentarily ignoring the others, Casey reached out with her second vision, probing the air particles around her for any sign of who or what was trying to manipulate her into murder. Then she felt the ship *breathe.*

With a long, extended sigh, the floor and walls swelled and contracted, like metallic lungs. The creature's nails were at her face now. She knew she would have to either toss Donovan into its waiting mouth or stop it. Time, though slowed, did not stop entirely. She had to make a choice. Again, she reached out and touched the presence surrounding her. It was the ship itself. And it was an angry, wild thing. If not properly controlled, it could turn one's fears into weapons. Of course, with no more machines or computers, the seekers would have to make living beings that could transport them. And to control them one would need strong emotions, the same as one would use to command a child or an animal. The concept knotted her stomach, and acidic bile revolted in her throat. *Monsters making monsters, making monsters . . . the future of humanity.* Monsters, all of them. Casey would not allow herself to become one as well.

She pulled herself out of second vision and returned to real time. Kicking with her newly reformed left leg, she struck out at the beast and sent it sprawling. The creature's screams made the hairs on her neck stand on end.

Donovan continued to flail. She looked at him with her one oval black eye and her other normal green one. Studying the sweat on his brow, the dilation of his pupils, the rasp in his breath, she wondered if Donovan had truly been to blame for Earl's death. *Maybe this ship did to you what it just tried to do to me.* Either way, she wasn't going to allow them to turn her into a cold-blood-ed killer. Not unless it became absolutely necessary.

Casey tossed Donovan into the other tunnel and then, with a wave of her arm, formed a metal barrier to seal him in, a makeshift jail cell. The last time Casey had summoned a steel barrier to stop the creature, she hadn't known how it was done. She thought she'd been helped by someone. Now she understood. This ship was one of her descendants. Not just hers, all the passengers', just as the gray beings were. She could talk to the ship, command it even, because it was created to be flown by humans. It was bred to be a good little doggie. All she needed to do was tell it to sit, play dead, or create a metal barrier.

Startled by her newfound power, the creature scram-bled to its feet and lunged again. Casey didn't bother to confront it. She turned her back on the beast as another barrier flew up, blocking it.

Strolling away, she heard Donovan's sobs and the creature's wails die out behind her in a violent cacoph-ony. With a final gesture, she opened a round portal in the ship and disembarked. *Time to find Arthur and Ma-jor Reese,* she decided. *And,* she added with a twisted, half-human visage, *God help whoever stands in my way.*

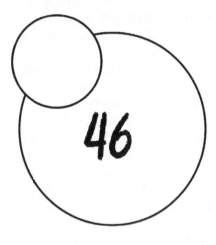

1985

Hours turned into a day, then a second day, and still the police asked the same questions, and Arthur provided the same answers. It was an infuriating round-robin for everyone involved. Arthur glanced at the wall clock, 9:30, and wondered if it was day or night. He decided not to ask, figuring that when the next meal came, either breakfast or dinner, he'd have his answer. A private game to keep his mind occupied as he blandly recounted the events of Casey's disappearance ad nauseam.

Arthur was at the part of his story when he saw a green light engulf her when one of the two officers sitting across the desk interrupted him. "See, this is where the rubber hits the road for us, Arthur." The plainclothes detective, Johnson, wasn't from Blackwood. He'd been brought up from Portland. Homicide division, Arthur had noted with a sense of dread as the case turned from a missing person to a murder investigation. They only had one suspect. While the town searched the woods, the police had brought Arthur back into that small room and asked the same things over and over. "Purgatory" was the word that came to mind. Johnson lit his fifth cigarette in an hour and offered another to Arthur. He took it, more out of frustration and boredom than a need to smoke. Leaning over, lighting the cigarette, Johnson continued. "Now, see, the problem here is, Arthur, I don't believe in little green men."

"I never said anything about aliens," Arthur replied, spitting smoke.

The second plainclothes detective, Stewart, a short man with a little mustache that Arthur thought made him look like Hitler, looked up from a transcript he had been reading. "But you saw a flying saucer."

"*No.*" Arthur's tone hardened. "I saw a large shadow in the sky that blocked out the moon and the stars. I saw a green light that blinded me. *No* little green men. *No* aliens."

"The ship was round though, right?" Johnson asked. "Like a saucer?"

"It was too big to make out any specific form. Like I've said many, many times, it was a dark shape with green lights, and it took up the entire sky."

"Sounds like a saucer to me," Stewart said, turning to his partner. "You?"

He nodded. "Yep. That there is definitely the description of a flying saucer. And where there's a saucer—"

"There are aliens," Stewart finished.

Arthur crushed his cigarette, letting smoke stream through his lips in an exasperated sigh. "You have my account. You've had it for two days. You can't hold me for more than forty-eight hours without charging me."

Stewart checked his watch. "We have time."

"I don't know what more I can tell you."

"We were hoping for the truth," Johnson responded. "Let's start again, shall we?"

Arthur's shoulders sagged, and he felt tears burn the back of his eyes. He was about to nod weakly when the door opened. An officer brought in breakfast from Burger King. *Morning*, Arthur thought, unwrapping an egg biscuit. The closest Burger King was twenty miles away. He knew the food would be cold even before taking his first bite. Johnson seemed to be thinking the same thing. "Local cafés are still closed," he said. "Everyone's out in the mountains looking for your girlfriend."

Nodding, Arthur wondered what would be for lunch. He knew she wasn't in the mountains.

Six hours later, they finally released him.

By the second month, things had returned to normal in Blackwood, at least for everyone except Arthur. No store or restaurant would serve him, not that it mattered much seeing as how the walk or drive to any store was accompanied by glares, groaned insults, and car horns blaring as he passed. Despite no evidence of wrongdoing on his part, the entire town had already convicted him of murder. The fact that a body hadn't been found didn't seem to sway anyone in the least. Arthur had been packing up the cabin, planning to live at school for the remainder of the semester, when a letter came saying he'd been expelled. It listed his number of recent absences as an excuse. Fingering the letter, he was thinking of how to respond, perhaps talk to his lawyer, when there was a knock at the door. The two detectives were back, and this time they had handcuffs. Even without a body, they'd decided to charge him.

Arthur's letter tumbled to the floor along with his aspirations.

The gray bars didn't close with a *clang* like he'd seen in the movies. He didn't hear them lock into place as the door slid closed, though he admitted the sound might have been drowned out by his heart thumping in his ears. Through the bars he watched the detectives walk away, leaving him alone in the only cell in Blackwood. He'd been told they would take him up to Portland in the morning. Arthur wondered if this would be his last night in his hometown and decided that no matter what happened, it would be. *Fuck the boxes and stuff. I'm not coming back here. Not ever.*

Arthur, a feminine voice called from behind him. Cold fingers slithered along the base of his neck as he turned. The jail cell was gone, replaced by an ink-black tunnel with not even a pinprick of light to focus on. He leaned against the bars for support, worrying that the shadows might swallow him whole. The female voice returned, and this time it sounded familiar. *Arthur! Wake up!*

Casey? A dream?

Utter silence lay in the dark like an endless void. With a stinging pinch to his left arm, he decided he was still awake, though the cell was gone, and only the dark remained. His body quivered, causing his feet to stumble as he edged into the shadow, searching for the feminine voice. "Casey?"

47

Behind closed eyes, Major Reese relived the grotesqueries of warfare in horrific detail. Dropping a whiskey bottle's remnants to the floor, he lurched from his Ford pickup and stepped onto gravel. Walking over to a freshly paved concrete road, Reese wondered why someone had spent time and resources to repave a street in the middle of nowhere. He groaned. *My tax dollars at work. Christ Almighty.*

Reese stopped. He'd had that thought before. Where or when eluded him, but something about this loomed familiarly in the back of his mind. Shoving the stray thought aside, he wavered drunkenly toward the street's double yellow line. Stopping in the center, he fixed his gaze down the road. Waiting.

Headlights appeared over the horizon, tall and bright. A semi-truck, he guessed. *That'll do.* Planting himself firmly in place, he watched the truck grow closer. Considering the vast emptiness surrounding him, with no city lights to give away his position, he figured the driver wouldn't see him until it was too late. The bigger the truck, the longer it would take to stop. The headlights grew closer. Again, a nagging sense of déjà vu set in, only this time it felt wrong somehow. Was something supposed to happen? The lights became blinding.

Absently, he brushed his pant leg, feeling his phone in his pocket. *Was I expecting a call?* The truck's horn blared, pulling his attention back to the quickly approaching headlights. Closing his eyes, Reese heard the screech of brakes, smelled burnt rubber.

Then the truck hit him.

The vision changed.

A scent of meat sizzling on a barbecue grill wafted into Reese's nose, waking him from a catnap. The sunlight seemed blinding as he heard distant laughs and clinking bottles. Focusing on a pink bag in his lap, he dug through colored tissue paper until he found something solid. A box.

"Hurry up, Daddy!" Noelle exclaimed, her bright blue eyes watching at his hip.

Popping open the box, Reese found a pink plastic heart with a candy-colored chain looped through its center. "Oh, wow, honey, I love it," Reese said, though his smile faltered as a chill swiped him. *Where have I seen this before?* Turning to his friends, crowded around the backyard, he saw Staff Sergeant Pidgeon holding up a Corona, a wide grin on his face.

"Put it on," Noelle urged. "I made it myself."

Reese kissed her warm cheek. She flushed. Placing the necklace around his civilian T-shirt, he felt the pink heart clink against something on his chest. Reese's gaze moved to the source, finding a second, identical pink heart already dangling from his neck. Had she given him one before? A sense of déjà vu set in, and the world swam.

Noelle's smile turned sour. "What's the matter?"

"This isn't right," Reese said, more to himself than to her. His friends and family watched in silence as he wrapped the second heart around his neck. He held up the matching pair. "I've been here before."

Noelle's smile returned, grotesquely wide, hinting at rows of sharp white teeth. "Happy birthday, Daddy!"

Reese balanced on wobbly legs, nudging her aside, and studied the backyard. He was home, in Texas. It was his thirty-fifth birthday, almost a year earlier. He remembered mowing the yard the night before because guests were coming. His nostrils flared, breathing in the scent of freshly cut grass mixed with smoky barbecue. It was the same as it was before, only something was missing . . .

Turning to the sky, he saw thick gray clouds swarming overhead. *That's not right either,* Reese thought. *It was sunny, and I didn't have any lotion. By the end of the day, Noelle said I looked like a tomato.* Yet, there was no sun this time. The gray clouds painted him in shadow. Stumbling about, his friends' laughter ceased, their faces creating a kaleidoscope. Pidgeon put his beer down and braced Reese's shoulder, steadying him. "Whoa, man, you need to sit down?"

"You should be in Blackwood," Reese mumbled. "I was on the ship . . . and . . ." His legs buckled. Pidgeon placed him in a wooden chair that creaked beneath his weight. *Keep forgetting, I've been meaning to get new furniture for the yard,* Reese thought. *No, that's not right. None of this is. I was on a ship and . . . and . . .*

"How'd I get here?"

Red veins slithered along Pidgeon's hand as he tightened his grip on Reese's shoulder. "Easy, man. You died."

Transfixed by the veins crawling up Pidgeon's bare arm, it took a moment for Reese to connect the words with what he saw. His eyes stopped on Pidgeon's face, which was morphing into a bulging gray skull with deep black eyes. This time he spoke without moving his lips. *Don't worry, we're all dead here.*

Reese's throat tightened, unable to speak as he fell backwards out of the chair. His skull hit damp grass, and dew stung his nostrils. Noelle bent over him, her visage a gray nightmare with dark, glaring ovals. "Daddy?"

The ground spun, tossing him. Reese's friends turned ashen gray, their elongated heads covered in twisting smiles that made his stomach turn with the still-moving ground.

Stumbling to his feet, he tried to keep his balance, shoving past Pidgeon, and grabbed Noelle. Her body shriveled beneath a pink dress with yellow flowers, and her hair fell out in clumps, revealing an enormous cranium. Noelle's smile stretched to the edges of her pale face. "Don't be scared, Daddy. We like it here. It's great to be dead!"

This isn't real, Casey's voice whispered over a gentle breeze. Reese spun, trying to find her, but couldn't see beyond the wall of looming figures.

"Stay, Daddy," Noelle said with unblinking black eyes. "Please don't leave me again."

Despite her appearance, he clutched her tightly in his arms. "I'm not going anywhere."

You can't stay, Casey said. *I need you.*

"So does she," Reese mumbled to the swirling clouds overhead.

That thing isn't your daughter.

The child's bulging cranium turned to the sky, her face pouting. "I'm not a thing!"

Casey's voice dripped down like falling rain. *Remember where you are, Major Reese.*

Standing, Reese released his inhuman daughter. The world pitched and turned. Reese tumbled through the dark until he landed with a soft bounce. Sheets curled around his legs, and a pillow cushioned his face. Flipping over, he discovered he was naked. Casey's voice returned. "There you are."

A wet, feminine form approached. Casey.

Her blond hair was swept back, and dribbles of water trickled down her face. Licking her lips, she crawled at his feet. Casey's shirt was soaked, as it had been in the tank, when she writhed in the water, and Reese pretended that he hadn't looked, but he had. And he remembered. He felt her breath running up his leg. Her damp shirt clung tightly to her rounded flesh, exposing hard nipples. She sighed. Reese did the same. Casey reached under the sheet, finding his member. It grew in her fingers.

Reese! Snap out of it! It was Casey's voice, though her lips didn't move. *That's NOT me.* The voice was sharp while the figure above him was warm, moist, and loving.

He grew hard in her hand. She offered a toothy grin until her eyes went black. Reese jumped, yanking himself out of her stroking hand and free from her waiting mouth. Fumbling off the bed, he landed flat on the wooden floor. Above, an engorged gray skull dipped into view, peering with inky oval eyes.

"Good enough to eat!" the thing that was not Casey said with a serpentine whisper. Her mouth gaped, revealing rows of pin-sharp teeth.

Reese screamed.

It's not real, Casey reminded him. The thing's mouth enlarged, big enough to bite his head off with a single chomp of those teeth. Its breath assaulted him with a scent he'd known in Iraq and Afghanistan, the smell of the dead and the dying. His mind reeled as he heard distant helicopter blades spin over an eruption of unseen gunfire. Those same real-world sounds that had invaded his nightmares for years were now the ones that awakened Reese to the realization that this couldn't be real. *Those things happened,* he told himself. *This never did.* Gathering himself, he struck at the monstrous form. Evaporating into black smoke, the thing vanished at his attack.

Reese's vision blurred in a red cloud as mist poured from his mouth and nose. Stumbling onto a metal floor, he found himself back in the tower's lower level, surrounded by hanging sacks. Arthur stood motionless beside him, eyes flaming red, his face and neck covered in veins. Reese grabbed the fallen 9 mm and his helmet. Placing the visor over his head, he inhaled deeply and clambered to his feet. Arthur loomed, unmoving. Remembering the naked woman's corpse lying bloody in the snow, Reese hesitated. *Not everyone deserves saving,* he thought. The motionless figure stared blankly at him as if awaiting Reese's decision. With a long huff, he made his choice and grabbed Arthur's shoulder, shaking him. "Arthur!"

Arthur sprang to life with newfound strength, swiping Reese to the ground with the back of his hand. More stunned than injured, Reese clutched his pistol and spun off his stomach. Lurching to his knees, he leveled the weapon. His finger twitched on the trigger, but he hesitated. In a blur of movement, Arthur raced forward. Reese met him, striking his head with the butt of his gun, and they tumbled to the floor in a heap.

Reese stumbled to his feet as red mist spewed from Arthur's mouth and nose in a gushing swirl. It curled around Reese's helmet, only to float harmlessly around his visor. He grabbed Arthur's helmet and placed it over his head with a secure snap. The old man's eyes fluttered, waking. While Reese helped him up, crimson mist encircled them.

"Stay behind me." Yanking Arthur's arm, Reese led him back the way they had come. He didn't bother to raise his weapon, which was seemingly useless against wisps of vapor. On the other hand, the vapor couldn't stop him either. Or so he hoped. Recognizing the stalemate, the sentient smoke split into countless strands and vanished among the surrounding sacks throughout the chamber. Arthur stopped, gazing into the closest sack as one of the gray creatures twitched with life. Its arms extended, eyes blinking. Wide-eyed with fascination, Arthur's helmet touched the membrane sack as he tried to see the body more clearly. Reese turned about while dozens of creatures stirred to life. A boney hand burst from the nearest sack, reaching out. Long fingers curled through empty air, inches from him.

"Move!" Reese snapped, dragging Arthur down the tunnel.

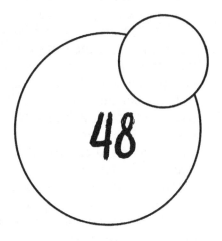

The elevation platform descended into the tunnel at hair-raising speed, but Casey ignored the rushing wind and strobing red walls flickering by. Deep in thought, her mind raced as quickly as the platform, calculating the level of resistance she would face once she reached the lower levels and tried to save Arthur and Major Reese. She'd been able to contact Reese, and what she'd seen didn't shock her any more than catching her big brother with a *Playboy* back in high school. The sexuality of Reese's preoccupations wasn't what disturbed her; rather, it was how insidiously the seekers were able to root themselves into the human subconscious, using fear and desire to control the physical forms they invaded. Casey couldn't help wondering if perhaps she might be able to do the same thing to the seekers, not that she had any desire to leave her body and take over one of theirs. Still, the idea lingered until she came to a stop at the base of the red tower. Darkness greeted her, and she knew Bill was close, sensing his probing mind like an insistent tapping at the back of her skull.

Knock, knock. Nobody's home.

Stepping off the platform and into shadow, she noticed the torn walls and makeshift bedrooms with broken plaster and shattered furniture. All the comforts of home surrounded her. A shattered façade created as some sort of lab. A human zoo. Even though the seekers considered themselves evolved human beings, she wasn't willing to concede the point. Not by a long shot. *These things may have evolved from us*, she thought, *but that doesn't make them human.*

"Casey," Bill said, approaching from behind the debris, "you look terrible." He stopped twenty feet in front of her, his human visage staring at her with a sour expression. "The cure we injected inside you was meant to remain dormant. The more you use the advanced part of yourself, the more it will eat away at you."

"I wouldn't call whatever you are *advanced*."

He extended his arm. "Please, let me help."

She eyed his outstretched hand and then stepped back, glancing over the broken furniture and plaster walls "Like you helped whoever was stuck in these?" When he didn't respond, she pressed the point. "How long have you been taking us?"

"Time is relative," he answered with a shrug. "For us, a generation. For you, much, much longer."

Casey flushed and clenched her fists. "And my friends? Where are they?"

"You alone must be returned."

"Why?"

"You have the cure within you. Once returned to your own time, your companions will not exist as they do now." His eyebrows drew up with a sympathetic sigh. "I've seen their thoughts, just as you have. Perhaps they'll be happier."

Casey hesitated, opening her mouth to speak, but she couldn't come up with an argument.

"Come with me, and this won't even be a bad dream," he said. "You'll wake up safe and sound in your home and go about the life you were supposed to live. You'll marry, have children." He moved closer. This time Casey didn't retreat. "You can be happy again."

Reaching out with her mind, she felt the truth in his words. Casey imagined Arthur growing old by her side as their children ran laughing across a large backyard. Two girls, both with blond hair and green eyes. Casey wondered what their names were. *My Little Pixies*, she thought, unsure of the title's origin yet knowing that was what she would call them. Little Pixies when they were cute and playful and Little Devils when they weren't. They were running closer to her. Casey reached out, inches from their flowing blond hair, only to stop herself at the last second. Their cute, round faces vanished into vapor as the waking dream slipped aside like a slide pulled from a projector. A pang in her heart told her how badly she needed this to be over. Why was she fighting? This was what she wanted. To go home. To forget everything and live her life. Her body trembled as she turned to Bill with outstretched fingers. He stepped forward to meet her.

Then a new thought flashed through her mind. Those same green-eyed daughters were now adults, bearing children of their own, only their skulls were deformed into twisted reflections of the gray beings. Seeing the truth, she ripped her hand aside. "It's not a *cure* inside me," she said, her voice choked with gravel. "I'm carrying a plague."

Bill's face and body shifted back to its alien form. Black oval eyes stared, unblinking. "For our species to survive, the change must occur before it originally happened. There must be no machine war. Instead, the evolution must happen through subtle genetic manipulation."

"You're reverse engineering the past," Casey said, surprised by the complexity of her own words and ideas. She'd opened herself to the cosmos, and in return, the universe had seemingly given something back. She understood their plan and what it would cost. "I return, and my grandchildren kill the human race."

"No more than Homo sapiens killed Homo erectus."

As he spoke, images of humanity's forebears played in a mental picture show: hunched, hairy creatures giving way to relatively hairless humans. The more she understood Bill's vision, the more horrified she became. "You're not describing nature; you're talking about genocide." She shook her head and stepped away. "I won't do it."

Bill's gray face twisted into a hideous snarl. "You have no choice!"

Casey felt her limbs tightening and her breath catch in her throat. He didn't reach out or grab for her. He didn't have to. Her mind swirled, and she felt his pent-up rage flowing through her like the ocean smashing against rocks. It flooded her every thought, freezing her in place, locked in an invisible embrace. She opened her mouth to breathe, but no air entered her lungs. The world grew hazy, and she knew she'd lose consciousness in a moment. Casey tried to fight the paralysis, but she felt as if she were a pebble being crushed under the weight of a boulder. The world dimmed. Casey crumbled.

A gunshot rang out. Putrid oxygen raced through her gagging lips, pouring into her lungs. She gulped the air as her vision returned. Looming over her, Bill's black eyes stared blankly. His enlarged cranium had exploded in a mess of black blood. His face contorted, flashing between his human visage and his true identity. She felt his surprise hit her like a wave and glimpsed a sad, final image in his thoughts: *monkeys escaping a zoo*. With the back of his skull missing, Bill collapsed beside her in a gory mess.

As Arthur and Reese's heavy footfalls rushed toward her from the shadows, she examined the black blood splattered along her hands and face. It didn't feel like her own blood. It wasn't simply the color but the texture.

Her mind whispered clues, revealing images of microscopic nanite machines interlaced within the organic
material. A synthesis of human and non-human. Upon
seeing the blood coating her gray left arm, revulsion
rose in her stomach, threatening to spill out of her in a
gush of vomit.

A hand pulled her from the ground, snapping her
focus back to Arthur. He blinked several times, and his
jaw slackened, disgust plainly visible on his face. Behind
him, Major Reese surveyed the corpse and then her. A
handgun wavered at his side, and for a moment she saw
a flash of his thoughts. He wondered if he should shoot
her as well. The image faded as quickly as it came. Reese
nodded with a relieved smile, better able to hide his reaction than Arthur.

She stood, following their gaze to the left side of her
body. Focusing on her flesh, she peered into her body
the same way she had Bill's blood and saw microscopic
nanites interlaced along her bloodstream. With a mental push she was able to separate the nanites from the
bloodstream. Receding, they dimmed from view, though
she knew they were still there. Fatigue from the strain
of her razor-sharp focus made her legs wobble. Arthur
caught her in his arms, and she noticed his expression
lighten. Casey's arms and chest had returned to normal,
and judging from the relief in Arthur's eyes, her face was
back as well. His words stumbled over themselves. "I—
you're alright . . ."

Unable to shake the memory of his first reaction,
she recoiled and stood on her own. "I'm fine. Right now
we—"

A cacophony of shrieks and painful wails echoed
through the tower. Casey's voice died in her throat as a
mass of gray figures rushed out of the dark, crawling over
broken plaster walls and peeling through hanging drap-
ery. Sensing Bill's death, the seekers' fury blazed inside
her mind like a flame. Whatever their plans for Casey,
she knew they would kill the others. Without empathic

powers, Reese seemed to come to the same conclusion. He fired three shots into the swarm. "Run!"

Casey led them toward the elevation platform until a second swarm of clustered bodies blocked their exit. Turning left, they raced down another tunnel, going deeper into the tower's lower bowels. The *click* from Reese's weapon told her he was out of bullets, not that it would have mattered against so many.

Arthur flanked her right. His breathing sounded like a sputtering engine as he inhaled large, wheezing gulps of air through his helmet. He wouldn't last long in this race. Casey reached out with her mind, trying to sense the inner workings of the tower in the hope of finding another exit. Sweeping through the architecture, she felt a blazing-hot rage touch her from far above. Walter. Hearing the seekers close behind, she decided the devil she knew was better than the devil she didn't. With her mind's eye, Casey touched the walls of the ship containing Walter, opening his cage. He dashed out of the ship, and she felt his surprise give way to hunger. Unable to communicate with the creature on any higher-functioning level, she kept her command short and to the point: *Revenge. Feed. Kill them all.*

Walter seemed to understand. She saw an image of him racing on hands and feet down the side of the tower, drawing closer. She only hoped he would arrive in time.

The seekers were at their heels, reduced to snarls of rage and snapping jaws. Up ahead the tunnel opened into a new chamber filled with crystalline equipment that she took to be biomechanical machines. The machines seemed to breathe through clusters of membrane-covered lungs, powering the devices. It revolted her the same way the infused blood and the thinking ship had before. This mixture of human interlaced with objects and shapes so inhuman made the hairs on her neck stand up and her stomach rise. She prayed this wasn't what she would become.

Arthur and Reese stumbled to a halt. Casey's focus

returned to the present. Spinning, she discovered they'd reached a dead end. Trapped. The seekers encircled them, inching closer.

Casey needed another plan. Quickly.

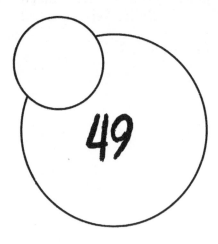

49

Arthur leaned against one of the pulsing machines
with globs of flesh attached to it, which seemed to
inhale and exhale, like exposed lungs. The combination
of organic material fused with metallic parts fascinated him, even as the gray beings surrounded them. He
stood beside Casey and Reese in the center of a round
computer room of sorts. Not quite a computer, he knew
instinctively, and yet not far removed either. Its architecture reminded him of the ship, though in a more compact form. His fingers swiped curiously across the clear
metal panel. Arthur felt a surge run up his arms, a jolt
not of electricity but of information. A flash of images
swarmed, and he reeled back into Casey, his legs buckling. It was too much for him to decipher, and yet within
the cacophony he sensed an intelligence attempting to
speak. Not with words but with images. The past and
the future interlaced. Within the vortex a single thought
pushed forward: *Casey.*

He flinched away from the machine, grabbing her.

Their eyes met, and somehow he knew she'd seen it too. Though he didn't understand what the machine tried to convey, Arthur felt certain that Casey did. For whatever reason, Arthur believed the gray beings closing in around them were not interested in him or Reese. They only wanted Casey. She was the key. But the key to what, he couldn't imagine.

Reese focused on the encircling beings, groaning under his breath. "I'm open to ideas."

Arthur felt Casey tense. The left side of her body turned gray again. He knew any attack would be fruitless, so he stepped forward in her place. The creatures eyed him, ready to pounce.

Mind racing, he attempted to piece together the fractured images he'd seen, connecting them to the alien figures before him. Like a puzzle clicking together, Arthur finally realized who they were. His voice quivered, more excited than frightened: "You are our children."

Reese shot him a sideways glance. "Wait, what?"

"Broadly speaking, at least. It's the only reasonable explanation," Arthur replied. "Oxygen-breathing, bipedal mammals who seem to have no concern about contagion or diseases from us. Not to mention, their overall physical similarity to humans means—"

"They evolved *from us*," Reese finished. Keeping his fists clenched, he turned to the gray beings. "I don't get it. Why abduct those who created you?"

We are dying, they said jointly, without speaking. **Deficiencies in our genetic material have grown over millennia.** The seekers' faces turned passive, eyes widening and mouths closing. **You can save us. Casey's tests worked. She contains a cure for our people.**

Arthur noticed that Casey's expression never wavered. Somehow, she already knew all of this.

"You ran out of time," she spat through clenched teeth. "That's how it goes."

Arthur stepped over. "Casey, please, wait—"

"No, Arthur, you don't get it," she said, yanking him

away from the circling figures. "Their so-called cure means the death of the human race."

You're already dead. Homo sapiens perished during a war with machines. But you live on through us. The seekers raised their hands in a submissive gesture. **Please help us.**

Despite everything he'd been through, Arthur's heart ached for the poor creatures. He couldn't contain his fascination at how far human evolution had taken them as a species. Where Casey and Reese saw monsters, he saw the next step for humankind. Still, looking around at the strange architecture, one question stuck in his mind: "Why travel all the way out here?"

You have not traveled anywhere. Black eyes bore down on Arthur. **Did you not see the ship's hypersphere?**

Arthur's mind leapt, and his stomach turned as the seekers' words sank in. His voice broke like glass. "Jesus . . ." he mumbled. "We never left."

"What are you going on about?" Reese grumbled behind him

Wide-eyed, Arthur turned to his companions. "We're still on Earth."

"That's not possible," Casey said. "I saw us travel across the universe."

"You saw us travel *around* it."

"You're losing me, Arthur," Reese snapped. "Get to the point!"

"There's a theory that the universe is not actually flat but rather that it appears so because it's wrapped around a continuous sphere. If you traveled straight across the cosmos, you would eventually end up back where you started."

Casey paced, fidgeting. "But if we never left, why travel at all?"

"Space and time are interconnected. You have to travel across one to traverse the other."

"This is pointless," Reese snorted. "I don't care *where* we are or *when* we are."

"He's right," Casey said, nodding. "Either way, they mean to destroy all human life."

"Not necessarily," Arthur protested, placing his body between them and the seekers. After all these years he finally had answers, and he wanted more. Aching for the knowledge this future species possessed, he extended his arms, hoping to placate all parties. "Surely, there must be a way to help you without harming us. If I could just see your data . . . I'm a biologist, perhaps—"

A wave of rage flooded Arthur's senses, sweeping through his mind and body. The blast sent him crumpling to the floor. Casey and Reese followed, hit by the same wave. The pain became unbearable, shooting from Arthur's brain to his bloodstream, burning his internal organs.

Arthur's last thought was regret at all he could have learned. Then the world went black.

Casey's eyes fluttered. Unlike Arthur and Reese, she hadn't lost consciousness, but the effects of the seekers' mental attack still made her woozy and her vision blurry. Wet, clammy hands picked her up. She allowed her body to go limp while attempting to locate Walter. Casey felt him like a hot spot amid her cool surroundings. He was climbing down the tower wall, several stories directly above them. The seekers were so focused on her, they hadn't seemed to note his presence. With Walter still a distance away, Casey needed to stall them for as long as possible. She could see Reese and Arthur lying prone on the floor behind her as the seekers carried her toward the breathing machine, covered in membrane lungs. Tentacles poured from the machine's fleshy parts, coiling around her, snatching her from the seekers, and slithering along her chest and torso. She felt a flood of emotions emanate from the device. It knew she was awake. **Yoooou wiiiill saaaave uuuus aaaaaallllll.**

The sickening voice at the back of her skull jolted

her into action. Casey's eyes flew open. Her body flailing and her legs kicking, she knocked over the two closest seekers. The tentacles tightened around her. Her lungs lost their air, and she saw stars. Consciousness waning, she began to lose her grip on the world. Unable to move farther or even gasp for breath, she focused inwardly, searching her body on a molecular level, probing her bloodstream until she found the sleeping nanites throughout her bloodstream.

As if sensing her mental touch, they activated in unison. It was a bodily horror. Pain erupted in every nerve ending and every fiber of her being. Casey would have screamed, but her lungs refused to work. Outwardly, her flesh turned ashen gray, her breasts receded, her eyes grew dark and enlarged, her hair melted into a domed cranium, her teeth extended in her gums, and her fingers became sharpened claws. Even her thoughts were no longer entirely human. She felt computations taking over, seeing into the future with a prescience that spoke of multiple avenues for escape or defeat. Among the visions, she saw herself returning to Earth and cradling a child as its eyes grew black. Around her, ghostly figures turned ashen gray and withered into lifeless husks. The prescience showed her a horror show of possibilities, but among the multiple avenues she also found *hope*. A narrow path for escape. The vision was dim, hazy, a glimpse of feelings more than images. In piecemeal, she heard Walter's roar and the distant, high-pitched screams of dying seekers. Wind rushed against Casey's skin as she ran back to the ship, the universe opening itself to her once again as she searched for a way home. She'd found her escape route. However, just as excitement raced her toward this future path, a new feeling entered the vision. She heard a gunshot and felt herself tumble. Anger burned her scalp, and her eyes watered, seeing the source of the gunshot. Arthur, his aged finger twitching on the trigger, fired point blank. "I won't let you erase my sons!" he shouted.

Unable to believe what she was half-glimpsing, half-feeling, Casey withdrew from the pathway and flung herself back to the real world, welcomed with pain from the tentacles' writhing grasp. Too drained to fight, she projected one final thought.

Walter!

50

The dark gave way to a bloodcurdling roar. Reese's eyes blinked open, his vision shifting into focus. Arthur lay sprawled beside him, still unconscious. Drumming footsteps rushed about them. The shriek of tearing metal was accompanied by hot sparks that splashed against their armor. Groggily lifting himself off the ground, Reese tried to stop his head from spinning long enough to take in the chaos around him.

It was the creature from the ship. Somehow, he'd gotten loose and was tearing through the gray beings, ripping them to shreds. Watching them clamber about the huge monster, the image reminded him of a Frank Frazetta painting. This was their chance, Reese decided. They still didn't have the pilot they'd come for, but anywhere seemed better than there. He grabbed Arthur, shaking him until his eyes opened behind the visor's glass. He was covered in sweat and panting through the helmet's speaker. Reese doubted the old man could make it out of there. Suddenly, Arthur's sleepy eyes widened, and his body jerked upwards, stiff as a board. Curious, Reese followed Arthur's gaze toward a grotesque sight: a dangling gray figure, suspended from a thick pink tentacle. Reese followed the tentacle to a machine that, for lack of a better word, appeared to *breathe*. The tentacle was attached to an oversized set of lungs contained in a large metallic frame. Nothing Reese had seen so far could have prepared him for that. His legs buckled, and his mind swam. The gray figure in the tentacle's grasp seemed like the other creatures, only it wore a T-shirt and jeans. Hearing Arthur's distant wails, Reese understood who he was looking at. Bile rose in his stomach, burning his throat. *Jesus*, he thought, gulping back revulsion. *What did they do to her?*

Casey's black eyes turned to Reese with a pitiful gaze. Below her, Arthur climbed the machine, trying to reach her, but he was too old and slow in his bulky armor. He slid, tumbling to the ground in a slumped heap. Studying his own suit, Reese wondered if he could make the climb. The suit's weight and bulk made him doubtful.

Stealing a glance at the chaos on the other side of the room, he knew he had only moments before either the gray beings or the half-human monster fixed their sights on them. Acting without thinking, Reese tore off his helmet, gulping the foul air, and continued peeling off the rest of his armor. Nudging past Arthur, he bounded up the side of the grotesque machinery. As he reached for the flailing tentacle, another appeared from behind, snaking around his neck. Gripping like a python, it squeezed the air from his throat. Steeling himself, Reese didn't panic or try to claw it away. Instead, he twisted inwards, moving closer to the machine's enlarged lungs, and dug his fingers into its pink flesh. The tighter the tentacle squeezed, the harder his fingers pushed through membranes and tissue. His nails punctured the soft flesh, exposing black, oily ooze and a stench so putrid his eyes watered. Shrieking from an unseen mouth, the machine's tentacles whipped and flapped madly, releasing

Reese and Casey. They crashed to the floor as the tentacles tried in vain to flop over the lung's wound. Arthur cradled Casey's deformed head as Reese noticed only fragments of her blond hair left on her inhuman scalp. Her eyes stared blankly, as if unaware of them. Again, he wondered what the hell those things had done to her.

Thunderous squeals from across the room stirred him from his thoughts. Reese snatched Casey's limp, deformed body and raced down the tunnel. Arthur followed, his panting breath escaping his helmet as a series of metallic wheezes.

Behind them, the creature tore through the crowd of grays, making its way toward a series of hanging sacks with more fetal forms inside. Reese's last glimpse of the once-human creature was of its wide jaws biting through a gray figure's elongated neck.

He didn't feel any pity for the last remnants of humanity. Better dead, he supposed, than to end up like them. Dropping his gaze to the rasping, heavily breathing gray figure in his arms, he wondered if there was any way to save Casey. Staring into her unblinking black eyes, Reese decided he'd do whatever was required to rescue her from such a fate.

Even if that meant putting a bullet in her head.

PART IV

A LIBRARY OF STARS

51

Weightless, Casey felt herself carried by Reese onto the elevation platform. Her stomach lurched as they sped up through the tower. Probing inwardly for the nanites within her bloodstream in hopes of altering her body back to normal, her thoughts were interrupted by an alien consciousness. With a painful, commanding tone, it urged Casey to stop. Pushing the eerie pleas aside, she turned her attention to the swirling emotions that hung close to her. Arthur's anxiety and fatigue rushed like an invisible wave, crashing into her, fretting over how they might escape. *He needn't worry*, Casey thought. She had a plan.

The platform stopped at a catwalk connected to the ship they had arrived in. Reese's arms tensed around her as his feet faltered.

"What's wrong?" she asked, her voice sounding weak and distant through her malformed mouth.

"We're not out of this yet," Reese groaned.

Her oversized head flopped to the side, enabling her black eyes to follow his gaze. In the center of the catwalk, blocking their path, stood a single seeker. His anger pulsed like a mental beacon, blazing orangish red. She struggled to speak, but her throat was too weak. Instead, she reached out to Reese with her mind. *Wait here.*

She sensed Reese's confusion, before, with a popping sensation, she projected herself out of her physical form, soaring toward the gray figure. Its eyes went wide, surprised by her plan of attack. Casey flew into his mind, entangling him with her projected arms. In an instant they were joined, and she found herself swimming in an ocean of calculations, prescience, and equations that consumed his every action. Focusing on his emotions, she pushed further into his mind, forcing her consciousness into his deepest, most intimate thoughts. His fear and anger lay just beneath the surface of equations and calculations, swirling about in a tumultuous kaleidoscope of colors, one for every emotion. The seeker stumbled, feeling her probe. It was a violation. *Get out!* he roared, sickened by her internal fingers.

His thoughts became form, revealing a chamber filled with humans trapped inside crystal cages. They pounded against their chambers, desperate for breath. Dying. In that instant, she realized all the other abductees asleep in the ship were now dead. Every single one of the poor souls she'd left behind, killed by the monster staring back at her. *Earl was right*, Casey raged inwardly. She should have awakened them when they had the chance. Her anger flooded the seeker, twisting within him like a whirlwind. His body convulsed under the assault. Legs quaking, he lost his balance, teetering on the catwalk's edge. Casey's voice screamed in his mind, echoing like a sonic blast. *You murdered them!*

The seeker pushed back. **They were already dead. They died a million of your years ago. All that matters now is the cure. We must survive.**

Casey tore at his mind as if she possessed physical fingers, ripping his flesh from the inside. Screaming in agony, his legs buckled, and his back reeled over the walkway railing. An explosion below rocked the tower, inching him farther over the edge. His focus turned away from Casey's internal attack, peering down at the creature that was destroying everything the seekers had built. His rage turned to pleading. **Stop! We are the last of humanity.**

There's nothing human about you. With a final shove, she pushed his body over the edge, tossing him down the shaft, toward the distant explosions far below. The seeker didn't scream. Instead, it pulled its consciousness out of the gray form, reverting to a red mist that spit out from its nose and mouth with a deathly gurgle. Casey yanked out of its body just before it hit the flames, seeing the chaos Walter had initiated. The tower creaked over sprawling corpses. Black blood lined the floor and the walls. Feeling her body's tether tighten like a string being pulled, she snapped back up the tower, soaring into her deformed body.

Eyes popping awake, she found herself rocking back and forth in Reese's arms. He was staring ahead, running across the rocking catwalk. Mere feet from the ship's entrance, the seeker's red mist returned, streaking into Reese's nose and mouth. He coughed, stumbling. His arms went limp, and Casey crashed onto the shaky catwalk. Above, the tower's walls leaned and creaked. Several ships along the side slid away, falling off the tower as if it were shedding dead weight.

Arthur grabbed Casey, steadying her while Reese stumbled and swayed. Red veins slithered across the major's face and arms. Screaming, he fought the burgeoning consciousness from taking control. His eyes flamed red. Casey reached out, pulling him closer to the ship's doorway. But he wouldn't budge. His face contorted in pain, fighting the seeker's control. His voice grew hoarse, as if every word caused pain. "Go! You . . . have to . . . go!"

"We're not leaving you!" Casey screamed. She fought against Arthur's grip as he yanked her into the ship. Her body had grown too weak from the metamorphosis to stop Arthur's urging pull. With a last, desperate attempt, she clutched Reese's shoulder, but her fingers slipped down his chest, resting on one of the chains about his neck. Reese shared a solemn last look, meeting her black eyes with his own burning gaze, and then flung himself off the catwalk's ledge, falling out of view. Casey screamed.

As Arthur pushed her into the ship's portal, a candy-colored string dangled from her gray fingertips. At the end of the string, a pink heart gleamed. She clutched it in her hand.

"Come on, get inside, now!" Arthur shouted over the sound of explosions. The tower shook, and beams crumpled. Behind them, the catwalk dissolved into tumbling pieces. Without another look back, Casey entered the ship.

With more reflex than conscious thought, she ordered the ship to seal the hatch. Thick, hot smoke filtering through the tower vanished from view as the ship's wall sealed behind them with a loud *snap*. Catching her breath, she felt a gust of cool ventilation touch her altered flesh. Fresh air poured into her lungs as she tried not to think about Reese's sad, blazing red eyes. Pushing the vision aside, she turned back down the hall, searching for another presence. When she couldn't sense Donovan anywhere on board, Casey turned back toward the hatch, wondering if she should try to find him. But if he was alive, she told herself, he was most certainly out of reach. Another casualty on a long list: Earl, Donovan, Reese, the thousands she'd promised to save in the crystalized chambers . . . all murdered by monsters who called themselves human. Limping to the bridge, Casey hoped the tower's flames burned the seekers' souls along with their bodies.

The ship shook in violent protest, lurching against the tower's exterior. Casey heard metal grinding against metal and could picture the ship dangling from its support beams, leaning toward a vast abyss. Arthur helped her to the bridge, stumbling as they went. Still weak, Casey leaned against his armored shell for support. Lungs ablaze, her legs trembled from bodily trauma. Like ants crawling beneath her flesh, she felt the nanites running rampant within, trying to keep her from collapsing. She knew they wouldn't last much longer, and she wasn't sure what would happen when the invasive so-called *cure* ran its course. Casey needed to subdue the nanites before it was too late to change back. But for now, escape required her to stay the way she was for a bit longer. If she survived this, Casey hoped she would still recognize herself. She doubted it. Meeting Arthur's pained glance through his visor, she saw her reflection in the glass. Casey turned away from the oval face and black eyes, not wanting to see the monster she'd become.

Returning to the liquid tank, Casey didn't bother to strip off her clothes, sliding in without delay. The room tilted, and Arthur fell.

"Get in the chair," she ordered, then forced her consciousness outward, searching for the ship's presence. The familiar tickle at the back of her skull reported their connection. While Arthur pushed a gray corpse out of the chair behind her and sat, Casey closed her misshapen eyes and focused on the ship. As if urging her to action, the vessel lurched to its side, sending bodies sliding along the floor and pushing Casey to the tank's edge. Clear liquid splashed what remained of her nose. Smelling the fluid, she realized it wasn't water but rather saline solution. The splashing liquid also felt different against her new flesh, less a separate liquid and more an extension of herself, as if her body was as voluminous and fluid as the saline she lay within. The liquid's embrace ran up and over and through the creases of her body, penetrating Casey's senses. Her mind reeled, her lips offering a welcoming gasp as the universe opened its arms and pulled her close.

Casey dove into the void.

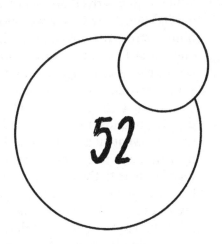

52

Stomach lurching, Arthur's fingers dug into the chair, bracing himself. The ship plummeted from its height, twisting, turning. Within the silent bridge, Arthur's heartbeat pounded in his eardrums. Fearing he might vomit from the pressure crushing his chest, Arthur yanked the helmet off, sucking in deep gulps of air. More concerned for the impending crash, he ignored any other danger. The ship flipped end over end. Then, with a soft shudder, Arthur realized their descent had slowed. *We're underwater*, he assumed, *sinking like a wayward pebble*. Arthur spun from the chair, slamming into the curved ceiling and then fell to the floor as the ship righted itself. Despite the armor's protection, his chest ached from cracked ribs. Still, as the pressure subsided, he breathed a pained sigh of relief. Another slight shudder, and Arthur felt the ship rise. Climbing back into the chair, he noticed Casey's misshapen form lying serenely in the tank. He knew she had stopped their fall, and he wondered what else her new body might be capable of.

When they'd arrived on that planet, one of the pilots had guided her. Now Casey was alone. Could she get them home, across the universe, a million years into the past? Staring at her gray, hairless body with its domed cranium, elongated fingers, and ashen, nearly transparent skin, he wondered how much of Casey remained.

Perched on his chair in the deafening quiet, Arthur decided he'd lost more than he'd gained from the knowledge of what he'd seen. As a biologist, he understood how humans might have evolved over centuries into a form similar to the one sloshing in the tank before him, but how one could so rapidly transform eluded him. It broke every rule of molecular science. She should not have changed so quickly, unless . . .

Leaping from one idea to another, his thoughts rested on the organic machine in the tower, with tentacles for arms and external lungs. Casey's transformation had been nearly instantaneous. A machine-type organism multiplying faster than the body could fight might create the form he was now watching. Part of him could no longer bring himself to call the thing lying in the pool at his feet "Casey." Maybe she was still in there though. Arthur studied her with a clinical eye, wondering what was going through that enlarged cranium. What secrets were being revealed? Matching revulsion with a pang of jealousy, Arthur stared at the figure lying in the pool. Concrete evidence of the next evolution of humankind. He couldn't help but want to study it. If, by some miracle, they found a way back to their own time and place, Arthur would be the lead scientist on the greatest biological discovery of all time.

Stifling tears, Arthur mused about everything he'd lost . . . and all he might still gain.

Suddenly, a backwash of images swept through him from Casey's connection to the ship, an echo of her thoughts. He assumed the effect had something to do with the domed architecture, focusing her mind to the ship and reverberating those same feelings to anyone on the bridge. Closing his eyes, he tried to focus further, seeing what she saw. The images made no sense. Casey didn't appear to be looking at space or time. Rather, rows of books without end. Millions, perhaps billions of volumes. Arthur assumed this was her imagination, not an actual place. She stood wholly human, beautiful, and naked inside a library. Trailing behind her, he followed her supple form down a long aisle, towers of books on either side.

Stopping abruptly, she turned left, focusing on a green volume, six shelves from the bottom. Her feminine fingers danced along the book's leather spine, lifting it off the shelf, creasing the back of the cover, and offering a horrific spectacle . . .

Arthur screamed and clutched his head, dazed by nightmarish visions burned into his mind. Below, he felt the floor vibrate. The ship was gaining speed, heading back to Earth. An idea that would have given him immense satisfaction only seconds before now made him shudder in horror. He'd glimpsed what would happen if Casey returned home.

Reeling, Arthur didn't notice a shadowy figure creep closer until an ax swung for his head.

53

The ship tumbled into the violent sea. Casey felt the metallic hull break apart, felt the pain of the injury. She was both a part of the ship and yet separate from it, as if it were a ghostly limb that had been amputated, though the pain remained. Crashing through the water's surface, she found herself immersed in thick liquid, trying to see through the blackness of the ocean's depths. Below, vague shapes appeared within the murk, outstretched beams of metal covered in spider-webbed coral and thick, bubbly layers of greenish moss. A sunken city, stretching beyond view. A *human* city. Precisely which one, she couldn't determine, though the implication was horribly clear: Earth had become a deep-sea graveyard.

Arthur was right, she thought. *We never left.*

Jagged buildings drew closer as the ship descended into the city's bowels. Sinking deeper, swirls of bubbles obscured her view, and her thoughts turned to another realization: nothing was moving down there. No fish, no

sea life of any sort. The world, for all intents and purpos-
es, was dead. The emptiness of it all sent a chill along her
proverbial spine, far colder and darker than the ocean's
depths. *This is what became of us*, she realized. *All we'd
accomplished, gone.* Science, music, art, everything that
made humanity what it was had been drowned in a
seemingly endless ocean. And all that remained were
those creatures lurking above. She cursed inwardly. Desperate to escape, Casey attempted to communicate with
the ship, screaming without lips, using the simplest term
she could conceive: *Up!*

With a lurch, the ship paused, suspended hundreds
of feet below the ocean's surface. A canopy of ruined
structures below. Amongst the wreckage, dozens of
broken ships lay in pieces. More spilled from the tilting
tower overhead as she watched it teeter in flames above
the ocean's surface. Her mind swirling, she thought of
Walter and wondered if she might still save him. But
when she reached out, there was no reply. He was already dead, and he'd taken those things with him. Casey
offered a silent thank-you, then returned her attention
to the ship.

She sensed Arthur inside, his ribs aching from the
sudden stop, felt his anxiety brush her skin like a cold
breeze emanating from the ship's bridge. Then she realized it wasn't Arthur she was feeling; it was the ship. It
hated the human sitting in its chair. He was not its master, and he didn't belong. It was an emotional response.
And that, she decided, was how she would communicate
with it.

Thinking of Earl and Reese and even Donovan, she
poured her sadness, desperation, and anger into a single
emotional image: *home.* Concerned it might not fully
understand her meaning, she added, *Blackwood.*

The ship rose, breaking from the ocean's depths,
floating past the collapsing tower, higher and higher
through thick clouds, pushing out of the atmosphere.
Peeling back the sky's curtain, the ship burst into the

waiting darkness beyond. Casey floated alongside the ship, through the vast cosmos, released from her body and the ship beneath her. As before, she could feel it connected to her by a tight string pulling on her consciousness, but her focus remained fixed on the endless abyss. Countless colors dimpled the darkness. Space out there was neither empty nor dark. Moving far beyond the glow of the planet they'd left behind, she swam through oceans of gaseous clouds of every color imaginable and gazed at shimmering stars that blazed brighter than her own sun at high noon. Within the vastness, she felt lost. Again, she reached back to the ship and pushed forward a single emotion: *fear.*

Hearing her command, the ship touched her with a warm, green light, and the endless void vanished. Casey's bare footsteps slapped against a marble floor. She was in her own human body again, stark naked, standing in a well-lit aisle with endless bookshelves on either side. Behind her the aisle stretched out of sight. Choosing to continue forward, she hoped there might be some rhyme or reason to whatever the place was. Casey touched her arm, felt cool human skin, and yet she knew it was only a facsimile, as, she assumed, was the library.

The books were marked on their spines with a series of digits and decimal points. Reaching for a blue volume, she pulled it off the shelf. The leathery cover was embossed with a painting of a white, ice-covered planet. Flipping through pages, she had the sensation of standing on the planet's frozen waste. She witnessed its birth, forming from a craterous rock. Then atmosphere and rain and finally ice peppered the landscape about her. Until, in a burst of red fire, the sun above exploded, and the world turned to ash. Her fingers stopped on the last page. She'd seemingly read it cover to cover, seeing the planet's entire lifespan.

Putting the book back, she studied the aisle more closely. It was a library of stars and planets, the universe represented in the construct of marble walls and floor,

with vast, seemingly endless rows of books filling its voluminous space. The physical sensations, from the cold
air on her chest to the smooth marble beneath her toes,
told her this was all somehow real, and yet the soft tug
from an invisible string connected to her actual body
reminded her that it wasn't. The ship, she decided, had
found a way to show her the universe in a way that was
not so frightening. Now all she needed to do was find
the book of Earth and hope she flipped to the right page.

Casey walked for what seemed like hours, though
she doubted time was quite the same in that astral-pro-
jected world. She hoped not. Finding the end of the aisle,
the library abruptly opened before her. Row upon row
of enormous bookshelves extended in every direction.
Each shelf was seemingly stacked with an incalculable
number of books. How did she hope to find a single
planet amongst all of these?

Pausing, Casey wondered if there might be a cat-
aloguing system somewhere. She figured if the ship
wanted to make it easy, it could put up a billboard with
"EARTH, CIRCA 21ST CENTURY" written in big, bold,
blinking lights. But so far, no such luck.

Making her way down the center of the library, she
approached a distant glow. The closer she drew to it,
the brighter the light became. Blinding, its heat blazed
her naked flesh. Throwing up her hand, she squinted
through tapered fingers, hoping to find the source. In
the library's central crossway, a swirling cloud of light
burst out and then retracted over and over again. In
mere seconds she watched countless stars leap forward
and spread out from the source, only to be pulled back in
and the action repeated. The closest analogy that came
to mind was of a rubber band snapping back and forth.

Transfixed, she stepped closer, trying to see the apparition more clearly, but as she peered into the light, her
body wobbled. Her mind swirling with a strong sense
of vertigo, it was as if she was peering down through a

floor with no bottom. Over and over the gaseous cloud erupted, expanded, and then retracted. It went from a pinprick of blinking light to a wide burst and then back again to a pinprick. Finally, she realized what she was watching. The beginning and ending of time. The Big Bang, it seemed, was not a singular event but rather one that repeated, each time creating the universe, over and over again. Most surprising was the universe's actual shape: a *hypersphere*, much like the one she'd seen on the ship earlier. As if the red ball hidden away in the ship's belly was a mock representation of the real thing. *Or a map*, she thought. Then another question bubbled to the surface: was she standing within the ship's hypersphere?

A feeling of warmth at her shoulder drew her attention to an aisle on the right. Following the new heat source, she heard soft whispers dancing on the air, drawing her closer. A green book amidst a stack of spines glowed. Casey knew what it was before her fingers touched it. Earth. The ship had guided her home.

Opening the volume, a flood of images cascaded from the pages, swirling about her like snaking monitors. Each screen an event in human history. Each page a moment in time. However, instead of starting from the beginning, the book began at the end: mutated forms created in a lab, their craniums enlarged, with black ovals for eyes. The culmination of man and machine.

The next image took place earlier, a war with no winners. Destroyed buildings, mechanical beasts tearing through soldiers, a plague, corpses lining city streets.

Next, a great anomaly, the creation of artificial intelligence. The scientists laughed and cheered and high-fived. Humanity had sealed its doom with smiles and laughter.

The book's pages flipped faster. Future history became a blur. Then the flipping stopped. From the page a new image spun before her. A green light engulfing a cabin in the woods circa 1985. The night she was taken. Casey felt her imaginary stomach tighten as she relived the moment the emerald light had trapped her, pulling her toward a black shadow in the sky. She tried to turn the page, either forward or back, but her fingers couldn't loosen the leaf to turn. The book was locked in time.

"You have to go back," a male voice said behind Casey. Recognizing the voice's guttural tone, created from years of booze and cigarettes, she knew what she'd find even before she turned.

Her father stood inches away. He was smiling with the smug *I'm gonna get you girl* look in his eyes that he always wore. In his hand he held a swath of loose pages. He opened his fingers, and the pages flew from his grasp and slid into the book. Casey saw a jumble of new images. Amongst them was a child whose green eyes had turned black. Her granddaughter.

"Cute little thing, isn't she?"

"No!" Casey tossed the book aside. The pages slipped into the cover without aid.

Her father leered. "I'm afraid you don't have a choice." Picking the book up, he dusted off its cover like a careful caretaker. "You wish to save a people who cannot be saved. I *must* save the ones who can be."

"You're not my father," she said, her voice hardening. "He's dead."

"Alive, dead, here, there, now, then . . ." His voice trailed off.

Sucking in breath through gritted teeth, she understood. "You're the ship."

Nodding, her father's image placed the book back on the shelf. Its cover glowed brightly, and Casey felt the marble floor humming beneath her toes. They were moving. Flushed, she reached for the book, trying to pull it back off the shelf, leaning all her weight against it. It was useless. Her body, like the book and the library, wasn't real. Her father's face creased, observing her with a sad expression. Casey glared. "I won't give you what you want."

"Funny, that's what you used to say to Daddy." He smiled; it wasn't a warm smile. "But you always *did* give him what he wanted, didn't you?"

He approached, his eyes turning red with a crimson glow. "My Honey Bunny . . ."

54

Catching blurred movement in his peripheral vision, Arthur turned just before the ax's blade swooshed past his right ear, missing his skull and striking his collarbone. Thwarted by armor plating, the blade didn't cut his skin. Still, the force of the attack was enough to send Arthur to his knees. Two more strikes to his back forced the wind from his lungs and sent him sprawling. His assailant tried to wrest the ax from Arthur's back, but it seemed stuck between the armored plates. Sparks sizzled from his suit, his armor locking up and grabbing Arthur in a vise. He couldn't move, paralyzed within a metallic coffin. His attacker left the ax stuck in his back and lumbered into view. He was tall and gangly, wearing a torn blazer and a rumpled tie. Arthur fought through waves of pain to recall the attacker's name: Donovan.

Noting Arthur's incapacitation, Donavan approached the water tank. His gaze locked on Casey. "She's one of them," he spat.

"No," Arthur gasped through ragged breath, struggling to move. "She's a victim, like you."

Donovan glanced over his shoulder. "I'm not *anything* like them, and I'm sure as hell nobody's victim."

"What are you doing?"

"What needs to be done," Donovan said, hoisting himself to the pool's edge.

Arthur attempted to roll over, but even that simple movement proved impossible. A flash of memory from their earlier connection reminded him of just how far this crazed man would go. "Like . . . like you did with Earl?"

"Survival of the fittest," Donovan replied with a shrug. "You know what I mean, don't you?" Arthur's insides twisted, but he didn't answer. Donovan snickered. "Yeah, your girlfriend didn't see it, but I did. You gunned down two people. In cold blood."

"The ship made—"

"I doubt it works that way. Oh, this ship might *heighten* our primal instincts, but don't go fooling yourself, doc. You were a killer all along." His pale expression transformed into a grim grin. "Guess you just never had a reason before. Same for me."

Disgusted by the implication that they were alike and the nagging truth of his words, Arthur tried a different tack: appealing to Donovan's self-interest. "Casey's the only one steering this ship. If you kill her, the ship will crash, and you'll die."

Donovan plunged into the pool with a violent splash, wading toward Casey. Revulsion washed over his features as he glared down at her enlarged cranium and gray skin. "Better dead than to become like that."

Arthur fought through the pain, urging himself to move, to leap up and crush that pasty smear stain of a man, but even his fingers were locked in place within the armored shell. His protection had become a prison.

Donovan snickered at Arthur's silence. "Yeah, you know I'm right."

Arthur watched helplessly as Donovan thrust his hands around Casey's neck, shoving her mouth and nose underwater. Killing her.

All Arthur could do was scream.

Casey ran through narrow corridors of bookshelves, seemingly without end, turning one corner, then the next, only to find a similar endless path in each direction. Her father's laugh echoed behind her:

"Where do you think you're going?" The voice grew closer; her bare feet ran faster. "Seriously," her father said, "if you want to leave, all you gotta do is ask."

The world pitched beneath her while the library shuttered from view.

Casey felt something soft against her cheek and bare stomach: pink sheets with yellow flowers caressed naked flesh. Her head rested on a wrinkled pillow while a bronze globe shone inches from her eyes, revealing a familiar bedframe. She was lying in her childhood bedroom, naked, writhing in the dark.

A choked whimper escaped her lips as something pressed her back. The smell of cheap whiskey and Marlboro Lights flared her nostrils. Her father pressed himself on top, licking her buttocks with his sickly tongue.

"Stop!" Casey struggled beneath her father's enormous weight. Pinned face down, she felt powerless. "Please . . . no! Not this . . . not this . . ."

His bearded lips bristled against her ear. "You can stop it. Just focus on home. Imagine the cabin. Smell the pine trees. Think about that sweet, *young*, desperately in love boyfriend of yours studying in the kitchen. Details are important."

"This isn't real!" Her words were defiant, but her tone was meek. Tears soaked the pillowcase, and her flesh crawled at his touch. *I can't go through this again. Dear God, not again.*

"This can all be a bad dream," he said, reaching

beneath and caressing her breasts. "It's time to go home, Casey. But which home will you choose?" His hand inched downward, toward her crotch. "Back to the cabin with no memory of any of this. Or remain here with me. *Forever.*"

"No!"

Fury overtook fear as Casey spun, elbowing her father with a blow that sent him reeling. Blood dripped from his nose, snaking over his beard. *I can hurt it*, she realized. Renewed strength poured through her imaginary body as her muscles coiled and tensed. She punched his eyes, kneed his groin, and kicked and beat his face and stomach in a flurry too frantic and haphazard to discern. Years of fear and torment came gushing out in a flood of blows. Her father tumbled off the bed, crashing to the carpeted floor. Casey lunged, continuing her attack.

Her knuckles ached but still she pressed on, knocking out teeth. Grabbing his hair, she slammed his skull repeatedly onto the floor. A pool of blood covered the carpet in a deep black ooze. Finally, his cranium caved in, and brain matter splattered her bare chest.

Still, she didn't stop. Though it was long dead, she continued pounding her father's bloody corpse until, at last, it vanished beneath her, and her fists crashed against the floor.

Wake up, a distant voice urged, snapping her from a sullen daze.

Gulping air, Casey hunched, crying into her gore-drenched hands. No amount of violence would take back what she'd lost, what her father had *stolen*. Consumed with rage, she'd momentarily forgotten where she was or why she was there.

As her sobs subsided into a shaking silence, reason crawled slowly back into her mind. Wiping away blood and tears, she tilted her head, looking about, only to find herself once again staring down endless bookshelves. Casey was back in the library, her momentary victory snatched away as she realized the futility of fighting within an imagined world.

Casey, wake up! Louder, more insistent.

More games? she wondered. Pushing the thought aside, she found the green Earth book lying beside her, still open. Closing the cover, she stood on wobbly legs and returned it to the shelf. As if in response, the library lurched, twisting upon itself. Books flew, cascading about in a violent storm. This time, however, Casey didn't flee the danger. Feet planted, she shut her imaginary eyes and focused on locating her physical form. Amidst the darkness of her inward view, a taut, invisible string pulled at her insides like a lifeline.

Wake up! The voice became clear. It was Arthur, screaming.

She yanked the string with all her might.

Casey was flung back into her physical form and awoke without breath. Her eyes fluttered into focus as Donovan's face materialized above her. Choking her. Casey flailed in the liquid solution, thrashing from side to side as she gripped his hands, trying to push him off. The shock of his attack accentuated the fire in her lungs from lack of oxygen. Struggling to open her mouth, she tried to speak. Her weak gurgle caught his attention, and their eyes met. She noted his frightened madness. Reaching out with her thoughts, she projected her surprise, pleading, *Donovan, release me!*

If he heard her silent command, Donovan ignored it. Instead, it was Arthur's distant, strangled voice that caught their attention: "Casey, use the ship!"

Entangled within a desperate fight for her life, it took Casey a moment to understand Arthur's meaning. Water sloshed up her nose and gurgled down her throat as Donovan's steel grip tore into her vocal cords. Her vision became blotchy as the world slipped away.

Only she wasn't alone in the darkness.

A familiar scent of cheap whiskey and cigarettes crept through her drowned senses. Whether imagined or real, this time her father's presence felt different, no longer threatening. The bristling whisper had a soft tinge, more like a concerned parent than a monstrous predator. She realized the ship needed her to survive. It spoke not through words but through rushing images. Casey had trapped Walter, created fiberglass axes, re-shaped the ship's tunnel, and, finally, destroyed her own father. The ship had reminded her of just how power-ful she'd become and that now was the time to use that power.

Opening her eyes, liquid blurred Donovan's mad-dened visage as he raged incoherently above her. She focused inward. Time slowed, and his grip loosened. Casey's mouth inched above the water, finding fresh air. Gasping desperate breaths, she drank the oxygen in, clearing her vision, and felt her muscles burn with re-newed energy.

In the blink of an eye, Casey took in her surround-ings. Arthur lay helpless on the floor, an ax shoved through the back of his armor. Above, cables snaked and coiled about the ceiling. Within Donovan's mind, a whirlwind of rage burned. Reaching into his thoughts, she plucked memories, like picking weeds from a rotten flower bed. Amongst the weeds, Casey found what she needed. As her mouth sank back underwater, time re-turned to normal.

Donovan's fingers tightened, crushing her larynx. Suddenly, whispered laughter swirled about, growing with intensity. Shrill and high-pitched, voices chanted a childish taunt: "Dipshit Donny! Dipshit Donny! Dipshit Donny!"

Turning toward the noise, his grip slipped. "Shut up . . . shut up!"

Using the distraction to her advantage, Casey flipped onto her side, breaking free from his loosened fingers. She bolted to the other end of the pool, trying to catch her breath. Her sight gradually cleared, but stars still blotted her vision. A blurred streak in her peripheral view announced Donovan's lunge, too fast to dodge. He grabbed her about the waist.

Casey spun out of his reach and reeled over the pool's edge, slamming onto the metallic floor. As she left the water, the ship lurched, and lights flickered. Without a navigator, the ship would soon shut down.

Donovan crawled from the tank, trailing liquid in lumbering footsteps. Instead of running, Casey stood her ground, mentally retracing the steps she'd taken to get to the spot where she now waited. Projecting each physical movement she'd made, Casey imagined a series of copies of herself, like a time-lapse image. Before her eyes, a dozen versions of her in various poses stretched from the pool to her. She took a few more steps, creating more copies. It was a variation on the tumbler tunnel they'd gone through before, only now she controlled the effect. Donovan paused, spitting liquid from his frothy mouth, his eyes darting from one figure to the next.

"Stupid fucking games," he muttered, barely coherent. Choosing the figure closest to him, he leapt, slamming through the image. When the copy vanished, he laughed, thinking he'd found a solution, but it was merely another diversion. While Donovan busied himself with illusions, Casey focused on the cables lining the domed ceiling overhead. They slithered behind him, coiled, ready to strike.

"Donovan, we don't have to do this," Casey said, trying one last time to get through to him. "I might still get us home."

Balling his fists, he charged. "Fuck you, bi—"

Ceiling cables sprang around his neck and arms, yanking him off his feet. Casey felt his desperate struggle, as if the cables were appendages of her own body. It was her fingers wrapped around his neck now. Her will was squeezing the life from him, crushing his throat . . .

No, she chastised herself. *I won't do this.*

With an exhausted gasp, she flung him against the wall. Even from across the room, she heard his faint heartbeat, unconscious but alive. No matter the ship's intentions, Casey was not a killer or a monster. As if to prove it to herself, she focused on the nanites within her bloodstream, slowing their frantic work, and her flesh returned to normal.

From where he lay on the floor, Arthur's brightened smile told her she'd been successful. He was on his stomach, the ax still buried deep within his sparkling, shattered armor. Part of her couldn't help but smile at the ridiculousness of his pose. Kneeling beside him, she tore the back plate off, then the arms, and finally the legs. At last, he was able to sit up, leaning against the wall with pained effort. While the ax had not cut his flesh, the attack had obviously damaged his aged body. She worried he might not survive.

"That bad, huh?" he asked, noting the sadness of her expression.

She shrugged. "I've seen worse."

"Liar."

No longer concerned with his age, she wanted one final, tender moment with the man she loved. She wished for more but knew that was impossible. Her lips found his, kissing him passionately. After a moment, Casey pulled away, confident in what she had to do next. She propped him against the wall and then stood. "Stay here."

"If you return us to nineteen eighty-four, this ship will erase our memories."

"I'm not," she replied. Sadness trembled in her voice. "There's no going back, Arthur."

"Then what are you doing?"

"I'm going to make sure this never happens to anyone else."

Arthur caught her meaning and nodded weakly as Casey turned and walked out the door.

She was going to bring the ship down.

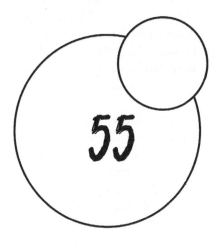

55

Leaving the bridge, Casey focused her mind on the engine room and stepped into a hallway. Dull gray walls crunched and bent, repurposing the curved tunnel into a straight shot. A red glow emanated through a distant arched entrance. Capable of manipulating the ship's structure, Casey no longer needed to search for doorways; they appeared on command. She stepped into the engine room, its domed space swallowing her tiny figure in a red glow. Ahead, the pulsing, rotating hypersphere flickered transparently. Pulsing with energy, it waited. A familiar tickle in her skull whispered, **Stop**. Casey ignored it.

She approached the twisting sphere, its image constantly rearranging itself in a spectrum of multiple dimensions and lines. Casey stopped a few feet from the sphere, standing in the warm, crimson glow, its light reflecting on her green eyes.

"I guess this is it," she said to the watching ship. "All roads lead here."

Casey's fingers hesitated inches from the sphere's moving surface. She had an idea about how to destroy it but wasn't sure if it would work. When the voice returned, she noticed a slight tremor. The ship was afraid. **If you destroy the cure, you condemn an entire species.**

"You condemned yourselves. I'm only finishing the job."

Her father's visage appeared. "I've found myself ruminating on why your tests were successful when so many others were not." Pausing, as if waiting for a response from her, he continued. "It was the sphere. Something happened when you touched it. Something that went beyond our blood work and tests. Perhaps if we were to try again with a fresh start, we might find a cure without inflicting further damage on your own people."

She glared, spitting her words. "You wanna hit the *reset button*?"

Her father walked around the sphere. Keeping her distance, Casey matched his movements. His voice remained calm, his tone light. "Time and space can always be rewritten."

"Like you rewrote my life?" Choking back tears, her throat quivered.

"All of this was the result of an accident. But the next time we—"

"Next time?" She leapt to his side, grabbing his flannel shirt. "What gives you the right to decide our fate? You stole us from our homes. Killed countless people. And for what? *Who are you to play God?*"

"I am Ship. I do what my navigators command."

"Good," Casey said, stepping to the sphere. "I've got new orders for you."

He sprang at her. "Don't!"

"Crash."

Before he could reach her, Casey's hands shoved through the transparent sphere. Drawing herself inward, she focused on the nanites dormant in her bloodstream, activating them all at once with a burst. The world sparkled with a blinding white light. Fire burned through her veins. Fueled by the new energy source, the sphere emanated a shock wave that burst forth and consuming everything in its wake. The wave knocked her clear across the room. Beside her the man vanished with a flicker. Domed architecture sparked with wild currents as the sphere's ruby color turned ashen brown, like an autumn leaf. Casey rolled limply as the room lurched. With a pained whine, the ship went dark.

Lights flickered as Arthur limped off the bridge, hoping to find Casey. The tunnel flipped on its head and sent him scrambling for purchase. His ribs ached, and his back burned, his legs bending awkwardly beneath him. His heart racing, he wiped sweat from his dripping face and crawled along the ship's ceiling. Pressure kept him low, unable to rise, as the ship descended in a vertical dive. Desperate to find Casey before the end, he continued on his hands and knees. Another pang of fire ran up his right arm, and he winced. Knees giving out, he fell face first onto the shimmering gray surface. Too weak to move, he lay spread-eagle, trying to catch his breath. Hands reached down and helped him stand. Arthur wiped tears from his eyes and saw a bearded man in a flannel shirt. He looked familiar, though Arthur couldn't place the image. A thought came to his mind: **She must be saved.**

Then the figure was gone.

With a burst of renewed strength, Arthur heaved himself through an arched doorway. A domed structure stretched into the darkness. Spiderwebs of flashing electricity combed the curved walls. Arthur was careful to avoid them as he searched. On the floor a body lay still. Casey.

Rushing to her, he turned her over, relieved to find her still in human form. Leaning over her face and pressing his ear to her lips, he felt air escape her mouth. She was still alive. He shook her shoulders, and her eyes fluttered. She tried to speak, but no words escaped her lips. Arthur held her tenderly in his arms as the pressure of the ship's descent pressed down on them with invisible force. *This is my coffin*, he thought, looking around the sparkling domed structure. *Not bad,* he admitted, half smiling to himself. *Could've been worse.*

Her eyes opening, Casey's gaze turned upwards, focusing on Arthur. All around them, metal groaned, and sparks flew. Part of him hoped she wouldn't fully awaken to the horror of their inevitable deaths. Casey smiled at him, a pained grimace.

"You'll be alright," he said.

"Liar."

Chunks of metal plating smashed down on either side of them. Arthur thought about trying to help her stand, but the pressure from the ship's free fall was too great. His arms tightened around her, hoping the end would be quick and painless. Her eyes closed, and he kissed her forehead. *That's right. Go to sleep. I've got you.* He wished he'd had another chance to see his sons.

The world tore apart around them, and the ship's whine turned to an asthenic gurgle as a thick blast of wind rushed through the ship. He smelled fire and silently hoped they died before they burned.

A few more violent shakes, and a piece of the dome ripped clean off, revealing dark clouds beyond flickering flames. *An atmosphere*, he realized. He knew they had only seconds left and kissed her again. She didn't react, and he was glad for it. No need for her to suffer. Then a warm glow touched his face, and Arthur turned to the source. A faint red sphere appeared, twisting slowly before them. Gasping, he realized what it was. A hypersphere.

Inside the sphere, a faint image appeared. Deafening wind and layers of smoke blocked his hearing and vision, but through the sphere he saw a piece of brown rock. Ground, dirt, earth: a planet. His jaw slackened as he peered through the hypersphere's portal. It was a way out.

Hope rose in his chest as he looked closer, still cradling Casey. Gathering his last remaining strength, he pushed himself off the floor. Staggering toward the portal, he rushed against the wind and smoke, shoving her through the hypersphere's gaping hole. Once he saw her land on solid ground, dust and stones kicking up beneath her limp form, Arthur jumped to follow. Inches from safety, a domed panel crashed down, severing his shoulder and blocking his path. Screaming through the whirlwind, the air left his lungs before the world went black.

He never heard the ship crash.

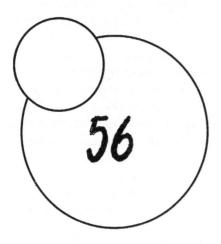

56

Casey opened her eyes, raising herself up on her knees. Her nostrils flared as she smelled a mixture of burning grass and another, stronger odor that made her want to retch. *Manure?*

She glanced around, looking for Arthur. He wasn't beside her. Feeling a blazing heat at her back, she turned. The giant ship lay in a heap along the night horizon, engulfed in flames. Somehow, she was outside the ship. Scanning the smoky, dark ground, she realized Arthur hadn't followed. Fixating on the burning hulk, she knew he'd died in the crash.

Arthur, she called inwardly. *You saved me.*

Standing, she wiped dust and rocks off her clothes and stumbled on wobbly legs toward the ship's blazing remains. Looking around, she tried to figure out where she was. The air was too warm and dry to be Blackwood. *God*, she thought, *please don't let this be Tatooine.* Casey laughed with inflamed lungs, relieved to be alive. She decided Arthur—her Arthur, the young man she'd loved in the cabin— would have liked the *Star Wars* reference. Choking back tears she dug in her pocket, finding a child's necklace with a pink heart. Earl, Donovan, Reese, Arthur . . . everyone but her was dead.

Shoving the necklace back in her pocket, she turned away from the burning metal skeleton and headed along a dirt trail. Cactuses and dry brush dotted the brown landscape. *Where the fuck am I?*

As if in answer, a row of headlights appeared over the horizon, bright in the utter darkness of the desert. She waved at their approach, and three army trucks encircled her, throwing up dust in billowing clouds. Covering her eyes, she coughed as men stormed out of the trucks, rifles raised. Staring down the barrels of a dozen weapons, she noted an older soldier heave himself tiredly out of the passenger seat and approach. His face was strong, weathered, with a drooping mustache that Casey thought would make him look like he was frowning even when he smiled. He certainly wasn't smiling now. His eyes danced to the burning debris that stretched far behind her and then back to Casey. His right hand rested on a holstered sidearm.

"Who are you?"

Too tired to stand, Casey plunked down in the dirt. "Casey Stevens, sir. Mind telling me where I am?"

"New Mexico," he replied, eyeing the ship's burning skeleton.

Casey sighed with relief. "Thank God."

The more he examined the ship's structure, the more his jaw slackened. Finally, he spun toward her. "Is that . . . what *is* that?"

"Exactly what you think it is."

His grip tightened on his sidearm. "And you?"

"Just a girl from Oregon, sir." The soldiers fidgeted around her, growing uneasy. She tried to calm them with a warm smile. It didn't seem to work. Noting their trucks and olive-green uniforms, something struck her as off, but she couldn't place it. "Mind telling me the date, sir?"

"Monday, July seventh," he answered absently, still fixated on the crash site. He shot a look at the truck driver beside him. "Call in a crash. Tell 'em we need fire trucks. *Lots* of fire trucks."

Casey's stomach rebelled, clenching. "And . . . the year, sir?"

The man in charge, who would probably have laughed the question off under different circumstances, answered without pausing. "Forty-seven."

Casey's shoulders slumped, her heart sinking. Permanently trapped in the past. Bile rose in her stomach, burning its way up her throat. *New Mexico, 1947.* She'd heard that time and place somewhere before. When it dawned on her, Casey's voice was barely audible over the crackling flames. "Roswell . . . I'm in Roswell, aren't I?"

Without another word, the man waved for his soldiers to take her. Casey turned limp in their arms, stumbling along. Nighttime breezes sliced across her back, causing a tremble to ripple down her spine. She'd heard the stories, urban legends about an alien ship that crashed in a field outside Roswell, New Mexico, back in the 1940s. Countless conspiracy theories, none of which Casey had ever paid much mind to. Now, while soldiers placed her in the back of a truck, she grasped the truth. The conspiracy wasn't to hide aliens. It was to hide what she'd discovered. To hide the future.

To hide me.

EPILOGUE

Area 51, nine years later

Casey awoke in a soft bed with white sheets that smelled of bleach staring up at a spinning ceiling fan. The sun warmed her skin through an open window beside the bed. Focusing on her surroundings, she saw a series of beds beside and across from her. She recognized the infirmary but couldn't recall why she was there.

Clicking heels announced a nurse's approach. She leaned over, checking Casey's pulse. "You had us pretty worried there for a minute, Miss Stevens."

"It's Doctor Stevens," Casey replied, sharper than she'd meant too. No one on that base, including the female staff, ever seemed to get used to a woman with a doctorate. It was another in a large pile of grievances she'd acquired over the last decade, though a lack of good music still topped the list. She warmed her tone, offering a weak smile. "What happened?"

"We were hoping you could tell us, *Doctor*." Seemingly satisfied with Casey's pulse, the nurse put her wrist back on the bed. "You've been in here for two days. But outside of seeming dead tired, we couldn't find anything wrong with you."

Casey sat up, taking an inward account of her vitals. She searched her body, finding the comatose nanites still deactivated in her bloodstream. Pushing her consciousness further inward, she steadied her heartbeat and lowered her adrenaline levels. It was one of her hidden abilities. She'd given the military plenty of information over the years, making her one of the government's most prized assets, but Casey still had some secrets. If they knew everything she could do, they'd throw her in an examination room and lose the key. Once she was sure her body was undamaged and that her nanites were not going to activate, she climbed out of bed.

"We need to run some more tests, ma'am—Doctor," the nurse protested.

Springing to her bare feet, Casey eyed her revealing gown. "Where are my clothes?"

Within a cavernous underground hangar, the ship hung seemingly impotent and confined, its weakened structure no more than a broken shell formed by jagged lines of torn hull and scraps of unearthly metal. Casey remained outside the ship, not eager to approach the hypersphere again. Recalling what had happened the last time, she decided one glimpse at her past was enough. Lingering about the hazmat armor still in development, she hoped that with a few more modifications they might give Arthur and Reese a better chance at coming out alive next time.

It won't work, a familiar itch at the back of her skull whispered.

"Why not?"

Her father appeared. After all these years, his visage no longer frightened her; he was now simply one of many monsters who had tried to harm her. Like the others, he'd died while she survived. Still, that thought didn't offer any consolation. Her father looked down at the armor, his ghostly hands passing across its metallic surface.

"This timeline is a closed loop, locked in a series of events that cannot be altered." He turned to the ship, regarding its fractured hull. "My being here proves the hypothesis."

"You've been wrong before," Casey reminded the ship's presence.

"Have I?"

"You told me I *had* to return to 1985, yet here I am. Both history and me, safe and sound."

Her father smiled grimly and then vanished. "We'll see."

Considering the ship's words, she absently stroked the pink heart around her neck. A reminder of the sacrifices others had made, so she could be there. She'd decided long ago to help the military use the ship to stop others from coming and taking any more people. But she knew some abductions couldn't be stopped. History had to repeat itself for her to aid them. Heading back to her office, she decided it was as good a time as any to write to President Eisenhower about what needed to be done to prepare for the future.

Digging through her desk, she found an envelope and a stack of paper. She typed up a report, labeling it "The Blackwood Event," and put it in an envelope. Sighing heavily, she took off Reese's necklace and placed it inside as well. Something told her it might prove useful someday.

Ever since she had touched the hypersphere and glimpsed her past, Arthur, Major Reese, and Earl stood out fresh in her mind. Part of her wanted to write separate letters, warning each of their future selves what was to come, but she knew she couldn't. The ship was right about that much. Time was a closed loop. If she warned them, she wouldn't be there, and their sacrifice would be in vain.

Strolling out of her office, she watched the last rays of sunlight die behind the vast military base. With only a sprinkling of hangars and a single airstrip, she assumed most people who came to Area 51 would be damned disappointed. There wasn't much to admire from the outside unless one knew where to look. Her eyes focused on the mountain with the ship lying hidden below.

Her father bubbled above in her thoughts—not the ship's poor copy but the real flesh-and-blood man who had tormented her for so long. Casey would have liked to further erase his sins by bearing a child of her own, but she knew that was impossible. Her blood was tainted, not through family but through a science even she couldn't fix. Some things couldn't be undone, she reminded herself. Like the loss of her friends. They'd made their sacrifice, and she could do no less. Tearing her eyes from the blazing sunset, Casey solemnly swore never to bear any children.

Perhaps she might adopt though. Someday.

Making her way across the empty parking lot late at night, Casey found a splash of color amongst the bland darkness: her cherry-red Chevy convertible. *So,* she decided inwardly, *not everything in the olden days sucked.*

Before she could climb in, however, a young soldier ran up. "Doctor Stevens!" he shouted, out of breath. "The colonel needs you."

She checked her watch; it was almost eleven. "What's the matter?"

"A bomber group's gone missing," the officer stammered, wiping sweat from his brow. "Twelve planes just up and vanished from radar."

"Where?"

"Three hundred miles east of Miami."

Casey's mind conjured a mental image of an east coast map, offering up projected latitudes and longitudes. Realizing the planes' last known location, her lips curled into a Cheshire grin.

"You mean in the Bermuda Triangle."

THE END

WANT TO KNOW WHAT HAPPENS NEXT?

Go to ALIENSKYPUBLISHING.COM to be among the first to find out!

AND –

If you enjoyed THE SHIP please leave a review on AMAZON!

DOUG BRODE is the creator of HBO/Cinemax's sexy sci-fi series *Forbidden Science*, currently streaming on Amazon Prime. He has also been a storyboard/concept artist on such popular films as *Star Trek*, *Iron Man*, *Thor*, *Looper*, *Van Helsing*, *Planet of the Apes*, and *MIB: International*, among many others. He lives in California with his wife, Pamela, and their two little monsters, Leia and Hayden.

Made in the USA
Monee, IL
11 January 2024

51571570R00194